PRAISE FOR

SADNESS IS A WHITE BIRD

"Rarely does one come across a debut novel as artistically accomplished, politically unsettling, and emotionally unflinching as Moriel Rothman-Zecher's *Sadness Is a White Bird*. . . . At once a celebration of youth and love, and a lamentation for the daunting odds of sustaining either in the tragic circumstances of the Middle East, this novel of inconvenient truths is a triumph of the aesthetic and moral imagination, one that will likely leave its readers (one can only hope that many Israelis and Palestinians will be among them) feeling unsettled and perhaps utterly transformed."

—Ranen Omer-Sherman, *Jewish Book Council*

"Nuanced, sharp, and beautifully written, *Sadness Is a White Bird* manages, with seeming effortlessness, to find something fresh and surprising and poignant in the classic coming-of-age, love-triangle narrative, something starker, more heartbreaking: something new."

—Michael Chabon, author of the Pulitzer Prize–winning novel *The Amazing Adventures of Kavalier & Clay*

"A passionate, poetic coming-of-age story set in a mine field, brilliantly capturing the intensity of feeling on both sides of the conflict."

—*Kirkus Reviews* (starred review)

"Searing in its beauty, devastating in its emotional power, and dazzling in its insights, Moriel Rothman-Zecher's debut novel, *Sadness Is a White Bird*, is, I promise you, like nothing you've ever read."

—Philip K. Jason, *Washington Independent Review of Books*

"I loved *Sadness Is a White Bird* for its profound meditation on how we each strive to hold ourselves morally and politically to account, an individual resistance to a world of walls and violence, in defiance of the belief that 'Each man has limited space in his heart, for sadness and for sorrow and for regret.'"

—Madeleine Thien, author of the Man Booker Prize finalist *Do Not Say We Have Nothing*

"While offering an unusually political coming-of-age novel, Rothman-Zecher frames the conflict in human terms. Passionate, topical, and thoughtful, this heartbreaking tale is vital reading for anyone who cares about the future of this part of the world."

—*Library Journal* (starred review)

"Conveys the complexities of Israeli and Palestinian life with passion, nuance and tenderness. . . . Rothman-Zecher is an incredibly talented young writer. . . . He has shown a fearlessness and vulnerability on these pages that speak to his ability to explore difficult terrain without feeling the need to draw any neat or concise conclusions. That is the gray matter of great fiction. It shuns certainty and is open, nuanced, inconclusive, and often contradictory. Just like Israeli reality."

—Elaine Margolin, *The Jerusalem Post*

"Rothman-Zecher's brilliant debut eschews political polemic in favor of nuanced narrative, giving us a love triangle to rival Bertolucci's *The Dreamers*, set against the backdrop of the most heartbreaking conflict of our time. Intelligent, sexy, dazzlingly beautiful—no less for being utterly heart-wrenching."

—Taiye Selasi, author of *Ghana Must Go*

"Rothman-Zecher digs deep into his country's past and present, through difficult truths and beautiful stories, illustrating one boy's journey of finding himself and his history, finding peace in a state of war, finding love in a world of hate."

—Rebecca Gerny, *The Daily Californian*

"A lyrical debut by a rising literary star. . . . *Sadness Is a White Bird* is part coming-of-age tale and part unblinking observation of a political situation that continues to defy solutions, treaties, or agreements."

—*BookPage*

"Rich and complicated . . . *Sadness Is a White Bird* is a bold debut."

—Laura Farmer, *The Gazette*

"Unflinching in its honesty, unyielding in its moral complexity, *Sadness Is a White Bird* offers thoroughly original insights into the holy and the broken place that is modern Israel."

—Geraldine Brooks, author of the Pulitzer Prize–winning novel *March*

"Rothman-Zecher . . . addresses complex, urgent issues through his vital and memorable characters."

—*Booklist*

"*Sadness Is a White Bird* is an exquisite love story, with teeth; a war story with a beating heart. Moriel Rothman-Zecher has written a timeless story, exactly for our times."

—Kirstin Allio, author of *Garner* and *Clothed, Female Figure*

"[An] outstanding debut. . . . Rothman-Zecher has an unusual way with words, giving lovely, fresh descriptions of desire, violence, and injustice."

—*Publishers Weekly*

SADNESS IS A WHITE BIRD

MORIEL ROTHMAN-ZECHER

WASHINGTON SQUARE PRESS

ATRIA

New York   London   Toronto   Sydney   New Delhi

ATRIA

An Imprint of Simon & Schuster, Inc.
1230 Avenue of the Americas
New York, NY 10020

A portion of "A Soldier Dreams of White Tulips" from *Unfortunately, It Was Paradise*, by Mahmoud Darwish, edited by Sinan Antoon and Amira El-Zein, translated by Munir Akash and Carolyn Forché, © 2013 by the Regents of the University of California, is reprinted by permission of the University of California Press.
A portion of "The Earth Is Closing on Us" from *Victims of a Map: A Bilingual Anthology of Arabic Poetry. Mahmud Darwish, Adonis and Samih al-Qasim*, translated by Abdullah al-Udhari, © 1984 & 2005 by Abdullah al-Udhari is reprinted by permission of Saqi Books.
A transliterated portion of "Bitaqat Hawiyya" ("Identity Card") from *al-'Asafir tamut fi al-Jalil* (*The Birds Die in Galilee*), by Mahmoud Darwish, © 2013 by the Mahmoud Darwish Foundation, Al Ahlia and Dar Al Nasher is reprinted by permission of the Mahmoud Darwish Foundation in Ramallah.

First Washington Square Press / Atria Paperback edition February 2019

WASHINGTON SQUARE PRESS/**ATRIA** PAPERBACK and colophon are trademarks of Simon & Schuster, Inc.

For information about special discounts for bulk purchases, please contact Simon & Schuster Special Sales at 1-866-506-1949 or business@simonandschuster.com.

The Simon & Schuster Speakers Bureau can bring authors to your live event. For more information or to book an event, contact the Simon & Schuster Speakers Bureau at 1-866-248-3049 or visit our website at www.simonspeakers.com.

Interior design by Amy Trombat

Manufactured in the United States of America

10 9 8 7 6 5 4 3 2 1

The Library of Congress has cataloged the hardcover edition as follows:
Names: Rothman-Zecher, Moriel, author.
Title: Sadness is a white bird : a novel / Moriel Rothman-Zecher.
Description: First Atria Books hardcover edition. | New York City : Atria Books, 2018. |
Identifiers: LCCN 2017024243 (print) | LCCN 2017031832 (ebook) | ISBN 9781501176289 (eBook) | ISBN 9781501176265 (hardcover : acid-free paper)
Subjects: LCSH: Jewish-Arab relations—Fiction. | Jewish fiction. | BISAC: FICTION / Literary. | FICTION / War & Military. | FICTION / Jewish.
Classification: LCC PR9510.9.R69 (ebook) | LCC PR9510.9.R69 S23 2018 (print) | DDC 823/.92—dc23
LC record available at https://lccn.loc.gov/2017024243

ISBN 978-1-5011-7626-5
ISBN 978-1-5011-7627-2 (pbk)
ISBN 978-1-5011-7628-9 (ebook)

For Kayla.

And for Jesse.

OH, LAITH.

I don't know shit about flowers. I was a soldier who dreamed of her breasts in evening blossom, though. We left our pants on and for hours our torsos touched like two jean-handled torches. The truth, Laith. The truth is that Nimreen and I could have named our kids Amir and Sara. You could have taught them names for raisin stars.

But when I last saw Nimreen, my hair was cut. And when I last saw you, your wink was blotted out. And I could only hallucinate white lilies and the smoke of your breath on my eyelids, the stroke of her tongue in my ear. The truth is that I chose to forget Nimreen's eyes, which were exactly the same sidewalk color as yours. I miss your eyes so much I can't breathe right, habibi. Can I still call you that, "habibi," my darling?

Laith!

Maybe we'll meet again, like Yossi and Mahmoud, in a city far away from here.

I

Muskeljuden

ONE

EVERYTHING WAS SALT AND SWEAT, summertime and sharpened swords. It was Friday, July 25th. The date of our catastrophe, Laith.

Or mine, at least.

Two days after my 19th birthday. Two days before I was sent here. One lifetime ago. Now, in the fluorescent glow of this jail cell, I can still feel echoes of the South Hebron heat on my skin. Mostly, the desert painted in shades of red on the canvas of my face, but when I looked in the mirror that morning, on July 25th, I thought I saw a faint hum of brown glimmering beneath the sunburnt crust, threading between the black and ochre tapestry of my almost-full beard. A twinge of Saba Yehuda's complexion, maybe. A twinge of my grandfather's Salonican toughness. You might not have recognized me. My scalp was a hedgehog. My eyes glinted strangely in the glass of the base's bathroom, yellow-green and nearly fearless.

We'd been in the Territories for almost a month by this point. One night, on guard duty outside the settlement of Kerem El, I pulled hair after hair out of my beard, just to stay awake. Afterward, back in my bunk, I wondered blearily if the Commander would notice patches and revoke my beard permit, make me shave it all off. He didn't. I kept the tiny, coiled hairs in my pocket for three days, until I came to my senses and realized how weird that was.

Patrolling the Palestinian villages in the area was more interesting. No one else called them "Palestinian," of course: everyone said "Arab villages" or "enemy villages" or "Arab outposts." They were wobbly shanty-clusters that seemed like something you'd expect to find on the outskirts of Mumbai or Sao Paulo, only here there was no major metropolis in sight, just desert and the sprawling town of Yatta, whose economy was reportedly based on stolen cars and whose yellowish houses huddled together along the horizon's hills.

None of the South Hebron villages had running water or electricity. Eviad claimed that was how they chose to live—"It's their Bedouin culture, and shit"—but I was skeptical. I was usually skeptical when other Israelis spoke about Arabs. I was a discerning soldier, a different kind of soldier: ears always perked, eyebrows always raised. Almost always, at least. I remembered Kufr Qanut. I'd promised myself to sever my right hand, Laith, to suture my tongue to the roof of my mouth before I let myself forget: I was here to protect the Seven Other Villages, just like I told your sister I would be.

Some of the dusty children scampering between the tin-sided structures would ask us for candy during our patrols, and I'd give it to them when I had it. American candy too, that my dad brought back from a visit to our old home in Everbrook, Pennsylvania. I could feel through the wrappers how the heat turned the sweets gooey and soft, just like I liked them, but I didn't allow myself to open even a single package. They weren't for me. They were for the saucer eyes and twinkle laughs I'd get as I told the kids, in Arabic, not to eat all the candies at once, making a silly face to go along with my silly suggestion.

And then there were the dogs: chained to various desert shrubs, their rib cages bulging like broken accordions, raspy gurgles in their throats as they barked halfheartedly. They didn't seem threatening, the dogs or the villages, but still, in the back of all our minds (yes, even mine) were the stories: the shepherd Yaron Ben Yisrael, stabbed in the throat. The ambulance filled with explosives. The old farmer in the suicide vest. The ambush at the Sheep Junction in '03, where three guys from the Lavi unit were taken out in less than a minute. One moment: three boys laughing, pulling jackets tight, thinking about warm blowjobs and hot chocolate. Next moment: three corpses draped in torn olive green, blood coagulating in their chests alongside foreign lead and misplaced bone shards and half-baked hopes for the coming weekend and the one after that.

On a shelf inside my head, alongside the piles of my good intentions, I'd placed a little sign that read "No Illusions." These were the Territories, after all. This wasn't Beit al-Asal.

There was one village, Suswan, which seemed to have more going on than the other villages. Structurally, it was the same: dilapidated houses, tragic mutts, graffiti sprayed on the rocks reading "Freedom Falestine" in English and "No to the Zionist Colonization" in Arabic. The difference in Suswan was the number of people who seemed to be constantly coming and going. On the day of my birthday, July 23rd, our patrol passed by Suswan and I noticed a big group seated in a semicircle by the village's olive grove. We were packed into the belly of an armored vehicle called a Ze'ev—a Wolf—whose shell was built around the skeleton of a Ford F-550, and was designed to protect against light weapons' fire, as well as Molotov cocktails and rocks. The driver was a sullen, chain-smoking professional soldier named Evgeny. He was at least five years older than us, and Russian, and it wasn't clear how well he actually spoke Hebrew, so he sort of faded into the background of the Wolf: dashboard, windshield, Evgeny. I'd been appointed patrol commander for the afternoon, and I told Evgeny to stop at the outskirts of the village. At first, it didn't seem like he'd heard me or, if he had, like he gave a shit about what I was telling him to do.

"Evgeny, man," I repeated, in louder, slower Hebrew, "Atzor kan. Stop here."

The Wolf veered left and rolled to an off-road stop, earth clods and small plants crushed under its tires, and from the way Evgeny looked over at me, I wondered whether he might murder me in my sleep. This was a running joke I had with Gadi and Tal and Eviad: "Good night, dudes," we'd say. "See you in the morning, unless Evgeny gets you first." I looked at him now, at the bluish bags under his gray eyes, and felt a little bad that we'd decided he might be a serial killer, just because he was pale and brooding. Maybe he wasn't even brooding. Maybe he was just shy.

"You don't have to come," I said. "You can wait here and smoke or something."

Evgeny blinked.

I looked back at Gadi, Eviad, and Tal, at their lopsided smiles as they stretched their arms and cracked their knuckles and tumbled out of the Wolf into the sweltering sunlight.

"I'm going over there, guys," I said, closing my door gently. "Any of you want to join?"

"Is this Arabian booty call, America?" Gadi said, in English, and Tal and Eviad laughed.

"Go fuck yourself," I said, in Hebrew, running a hand over the side of my beard to obscure some of the blood vessels glowing below the skin of my cheeks.

"The Commander said we should make sure they notice us, right? And anyway, aren't you curious to see who all those people are?"

I gestured toward the semicircle: eight or ten fleshy pink faces sheltering from the sun in the sparse shade supplied by Suswan's silver-leaved olive trees. They were wearing beige vests, and some had crucifixes dangling from their necks. In the silence that followed my question, I could hear that they were speaking what sounded like German. There was one Palestinian guy sitting there with them.

"Not so curious, to be honest," Eviad said, and Gadi made a thrusting motion with his pelvis and I flicked both of them off and Tal laughed. I took a deep breath, tasting the smoke from the three cigarettes lit, almost in unison, around me. Evgeny had gone to smoke on the other side of the

Wolf. I was the only guy in my platoon who didn't smoke, as well as the only one who spoke Arabic. A few others could speak a bit, and everyone knew "Waqaf, waqaf walla ana batukhak" and "Iftah al-bab." We'd all learned those phrases—"Stop, stop or I'll shoot you" and "Open the door"—from postdraft friends or older siblings, back when we were still in high school. And "Jib al-hawiya," of course. "Give me your ID card."

As I walked toward the group, leaving Gadi, Eviad, and Tal leaning against the Wolf's boxy frame, I felt the hot air grow brittle. The Germans began babbling anxiously and a few reached into their fanny packs and withdrew digital cameras, which they pointed at me. I froze. I was tempted, for a split second, to raise my hands, just to clarify that I meant no harm. But then I reminded myself that I didn't owe anyone an explanation, definitely not a group of Germans. I decided to try talking to the Palestinian guy, who I saw as my likeliest ally, alone.

"Ta'al hoon," I said, gesturing to him like he was an old friend. "Come here."

He was wearing a purple polo shirt with a tiny silhouette of a porcupine emblazoned on the left breast. His hair was cropped close on the sides and was longer and heavily gelled on the top. He had dark skin, and hazel eyes whose color I found comfortingly pretty. He looked up at me and then looked around.

"Ana?" He asked, touching a finger to the center of his chest.

Who else would I be talking to in Arabic, I thought, Rolf and Hildegard? Then I felt bad for feeling impatient. This guy was probably a decade older than me, and I was holding an M-16—and one that was fixed with a grenade launcher, at that. Although "holding" might not be the right word: too separate, too distant. My weapon had come to feel like a fifth limb. We'd only been out of Advanced Training for a few weeks, and this was the first time I'd ever actually spoken to a Palestinian adult while in uniform, not including the occasional text messages I sent to you, Laith, or to Nimreen, but that was different.

"Min fadlak," I said, making my voice softer, taking my sunglasses off. "Please."

The man stood up slowly and walked over to where I'd stopped, about ten paces away from the group.

"Ma saweitish ishi," the man said, as he neared me, his hands tilted upward, palms out. Not totally unlike how I'd thought to position my own hands a moment earlier, but I didn't think about that then. My mind was focused on the sandpaper *h*s and guttural *a*s and rumbling *r*s. I wanted my accent to sound good, for him to know how well I spoke his language.

"Aarif, ya zalameh," I said. "I know, man. I didn't say you did anything. I just want to talk."

It did. My accent did sound good. Languages are mostly about confidence. At that moment, my private tutor was shaped like an M-16.

His shoulders relaxed a bit, but his eyes were still narrowed, and his hands floated for a moment like two confused birds, wondering whether to flit into the safety of their nests or not. He eventually pretzeled his arms across his chest, burying his hands in his armpits. I get, in retrospect, as I retell this story, that he was probably afraid. That his pockets were not comfort nests for the birds of his hands but rather the opposite: his pockets were filled with danger. The danger that I, the armed soldier, might suspect danger: knife, screwdriver, grenade, box cutter, et cetera. But I didn't yet know myself as someone to be feared.

I cleared my throat. I could hear the guys laughing back by the Wolf.

"Salam aleikum," I said. "May peace be upon you."

"Wa-aleikum," he said. "And upon you."

"Ana ismi Jonathan," I said, introducing myself, taking my right hand off the handle of my gun and extending it toward him.

The man hesitated, and I felt a burst of sour fear in the back edges of my mouth. That he might not shake my hand at all. That he might leave me standing in humiliating limbo, vulnerable and exposed to the flashes of the German Canons and Nikons and to the knowing smirks of Gadi and Eviad and Tal. I wondered if they would see this rejection and turn their laughter on me: "Bleeding Heart Yonatan can't even get a handshake from the Arabs he loves so much."

After a moment, though, the man did shake my hand, limply, but no one else around could know that, not the Germans, not the Israelis. He did not introduce himself in return.

"Tell me about your village," I said.

"What?"

"About Suswan. For example, how many people live here? What's life like? Who are they?" I gestured toward the group.

"Our guests," the man said.

"Guests from where?"

"Austria," he said. "International solidarity visitors."

"What kind of solidarity?" I said, my Arabic sharpening as I glanced at the dangle of crucifixes, at the shiny cameras cradled in veiny hands. "Against the Jews?"

I wasn't thinking about my accent, then. I was thinking then about my grandfather, about Salonica, about the Germans.

"No, no," the man said, "just against the demolition orders given to us by the Jews."

"What demolition orders?"

The man snorted and mimicked my question in a nasally voice, "Ei awamr hadim?"

I bit down on the soft flesh of the inside of my cheek.

"Demolition orders for our entire village," he said.

"Why?" I said.

"B'tisalni ana?" he said, with a woodchip laugh. "You're asking me?"

I took a moment to try to pluck the splinters of his laughter from my mouth before speaking again. "Did you get permits to build here?"

"You don't give us permits, here or anywhere. Do you really not know this, or are you playing games with me?"

"I'm—I'm new here," I said, my accent faltering. I wondered if I should switch to Hebrew.

He snorted again.

I thought about my grandfather, about his voice when he said he was proud of me. I straightened my back and spoke in what I hoped was a crisp tone, still in Arabic: "What I mean to say is, I'm sorry to hear that. I don't know all the details. It seems complicated."

The man was quiet.

I thought about you and Nimreen, about how I told you I'd be decent, told you I'd still be me.

"But if there's anything I can do to help," I continued, "just tell me, okay?"

The man looked up at me, his eyes wide, a little smile playing on his lips. I thought he looked grateful. I felt hairs rising on my nape. This was why I'd started learning Arabic in the first place: to communicate with the Other. Even before I met you and Nimreen, that was something I wanted.

———

Do you remember that night on the beach in Haifa, when you and Nimreen tried to list for me all twenty-six Arabic synonyms for "love"? I only remember two of them now, aside from the basic one, "al-Hub," which is the root of the word "habibi."

"Al-Kalf," Nimreen said, passing the joint to me, our fingers brushing. She blew two pillars of smoke out of her nostrils. I told her later that night that she'd looked like the most elegant walrus ever to grace the coast of Palestine, and she'd laughed, wild and loud, and punched me in the shoulder, "It's like . . . exaggerated love. Overstated."

I looked down at the sand, where Nimreen's bare feet were buried up to her ankles. On her left leg, there were two tiny black hairs that she'd missed while shaving, right above the shell anklet she always wore. I thought these two hairs might be the most beautiful thing in the entire land.

"Al-Jouah," you said, the bass of your voice blurred by the rush of the water, "love that leaves you with a feeling of, like, deep sadness."

You looked beautiful too, Laith, your lanky frame origamied into compactness, knees pressed to your chest, arms wrapped around your shins. The dark threads of your scraggly beard were glistening, catching shards of hidden sunlight reflected off the moon, nearly identical to the hairs on your twin sister's ankle.

I held the joint between my fingers, testing the give of the melted hash and wisps of tobacco rolled tightly into the little white paper.

"Puff puff pass, J," you said, laughing, and I was blown away by the fact that you knew that phrase.

Al-Kalf and al-Jouah.

Of course those are the two I remember now, habibi.

———

I know it sounds silly, Laith, but I was thinking about that night on the beach and how the Arabic blended with the sizzle of the sea and the crackle of the slow-burning joint, and so I was caught off guard when the man in Suswan spit, a heavy, viscous glob that stayed intact as it landed on the toasted earth, not far from my red-leather Paratrooper boots. He looked back up at me, and only then did I understand that the smile growing bigger on his lips was not one of gratitude.

"You want to help me?" he said. "Here's how you can help me: Get out of Palestine. All of you. Go back to Europe."

I was frightened by how quickly the tingle on my nape turned to raised hackles; by how ugly his eyes seemed; by how much I wanted to drive my fist or the butt of my M-16 into one of them. If I'd been Gadi or Eviad, I might have done it. Instead, I just spoke: "It didn't exactly go that well for us, back in Europe."

He was silent.

I thought about telling him that Tal's whole family was from Iraq and that Eviad was part Moroccan, but decided that would sound defensive. Anyway, I thought, what did it matter, Baghdad or Fez or Warsaw or Salonica? Jews deserved a home here too.

"This is our home too," I said.

He didn't say anything.

His silence pushed me over the edge.

"No, you know what? You're right. Maybe the Holocaust was just a mu'amira sahioniya," I said, repeating the Arabic phrase I'd heard a handful of times over the past year and a half, mostly from your sister. Usually Nimreen would grin when she'd say it, but I wasn't grinning now: "Maybe everything is a Zionist conspiracy. All your problems are because of a Zionist conspiracy. Is that right?"

The man spit again. He no longer looked at all afraid of me.

"Do you want anything else?" he said. "To search me? To arrest me?"

I pressed my tongue against the back of my teeth. It's hard for me to admit how badly I wanted his fear to return. I glanced over at the group under the olive trees, whose members had seemingly lost interest in the two of us and were gabbing to each other, comparing pictures on the small screens of their cameras. I thought about Jacko and about my grandfather and about refuge and about hopeless yellow-eyed revolts. About how history never seems to manage to wipe its tracks clean as it slumps into the present.

"No," I said, "go ahead. Go make up some more stories for your German friends."

Anger flashed unmistakable onto his face. He didn't say anything.

"Sorry," I said, "Austrian solidarity visitors."

I shifted my grip on my M-16 and glanced over my shoulder performatively, reminding him of my brothers standing by the Wolf. I didn't think about you then, Laith, or your sister, or what you would have thought if you saw me like that, chest swelling, nostrils flared, palms resting heavy on my pygmy angel of death, twisted into four kilograms of black metal warmth. He remained in place and swallowed. A current shot through my teeth. I felt invincible.

"What sort of critical intelligence did you gather, Yonatan?" Eviad asked as I rejoined the group. Tal rested his hand on the back of my neck, stroked his thumb over the nub at the top of my spine. You once told me it was called the axis vertebra, Laith, but I clucked my tongue and said that I was pretty sure that "topmost spinal nub is the more technically accurate scientific term," and you conceded. I took off my helmet and Gadi patted my head, bursting the sweat droplets balanced on the spikes of my hair like dew, and we all climbed into the Wolf, where Evgeny was already waiting in the driver's seat. I sat shotgun.

"Nothing," I said, trying to steady my voice as I shifted from Arabic to Hebrew, and from Jonathan the Curious to Yonatan the Patrol Commander, "I just wanted to know who the internationals were."

"Nu? And?"

"Nazis," I said.

Gadi leaned forward, smiling impishly. "Listen to America here. Forty seconds in the desert and Yonatan's already getting hard."

Evgeny may or may not have let out a small laugh. He could have just been clearing the postsmoke mucus from his throat.

"You know what else?" I said. "That guy I was talking to said some shit about how the Jews want to destroy his village, and when I offered to help, he told me to 'go back to Europe.'"

"Wait, what?" Tal said. "You offered to help? What exactly were you planning on doing?"

I shrugged.

"Exactly," Eviad said. "They live in this dirt pile, and we try to help them, and what do they do in return? Jihad. They blow up our buses and cafés in order to get their fucking seventy-six virgins. It's not about land or freedom. It's a holy war for them, and they're mostly just starved for pussy. Ha!"

Eviad's laughter then was a hyena's, and everyone in the Wolf went quiet. Eviad's little sister, Maya, had been on a bus that exploded in Haifa in 2004. She was thirteen and had lost most of the right half of her face. The doctors managed to keep her alive for almost a week.

"Seventy-two," Tal said.

"What?" Eviad said.

"It's seventy-two virgins."

I turned around in time to see Eviad's dark-blue eyes widen first, and then crinkle as he started to laugh, a pretty, clear laugh, like a cool spring bursting forward from the earth's belly. The tension inside the Wolf evaporated.

"Wait," Eviad said, "don't tell me that if an Iraqi Jewish guy gets killed in battle, he gets seventy-two virgins also?"

All of us laughed, except for Evgeny, who wasn't really one of us anyway.

Tal was bespectacled and as scrawny as Eviad was muscular. His dad's parents were Communists from Baghdad, who fled to Ramat Gan in 1950. Despite his familial history of flight—and from Muslims, at that—Tal was the other bleeding heart in our company.

We drove in silence for a few minutes until we arrived back at our base. We climbed out of the Wolf, and Evgeny shuffled slowly inside, his hands stuffed deep into his uniform's pockets. When Evgeny was out of earshot, Tal spoke in a hushed tone, and Eviad and Gadi and I crowded around him, leaning close, inhaling each other's familiar scents and recycling each other's familiar breaths.

"I heard there's going to be a demonstration there on Friday," Tal said.

"Really?" I said. "In Suswan? Where'd you hear that?"

We'd finished Advanced Training ready to be sent into battle, but we hadn't seen any action to speak of so far, just patrols like this one, and a false alarm outside Kerem El, when a fox had tripped the security wire. Eviad shot at it and actually hit the stupid critter, which lay there whimpering for a good three minutes until we finally got radio permission from the Commander to leave our posts and put an end to its suffering. Eviad executed it with another bullet to the head, and I covered it in rocks, trying to stay somber but gagging as the weight of the stones pressed into the creature's soft body and a bit of its organs bulged from the hole in its side, blood surging out onto the ground around it, stench filling the air. We left the animal half covered, and Eviad and I ran back to our post in silence.

"I just heard it," Tal said.

I pictured then what I wanted to picture: men wearing purple polo shirts and keffiyehs wrapped around their faces, brandishing weapons and burning tires, chanting "Go back to Europe," a row of Germans standing there, clucking their tubby tongues and clicking pictures with their fancy cameras, proving to the world that the Jews were just as bad as they'd always said we were. I had mixed feelings about guarding the settlement that I didn't think should be in the West Bank in the first place, and I felt a little uneasy about waltzing into tin villages like we just had, but I was ready to fight the actual enemy. I was ready to feel like I was there for a reason.

"If you're wrong, Saddam," said Gadi, "I'm having you transferred into one of those shacks."

Eviad laughed. I did too. Tal raised his hands.

"Hey, I'm just repeating what I heard. As they say, 'Don't force the messenger to go live in a Bedouin shack.'"

I laughed again. "I hope you're right, man."

"Inshallah," Tal said. "God willing."

And of course, Tal was right.

TWO

IT WAS A WINDY, DELICIOUS DAY when we went to al-Birwa, Laith.

Remember?

The spring breeze was swishing through the grasses, the sun splashing golden onto the green. Pine trees swayed and beckoned outside the bus's window. We took the 262 from Haifa to Ahihud. We missed our stop. Nimreen and I were talking breathlessly, interrupting each other and ourselves. What were you doing? You were probably lost in thought, gazing out the window at the trees. You noticed a moment too late, just as the door was sighing shut.

"Fuck, guys," you said, laughing and tapping the glass as the Ahihud Junction grew smaller behind us. Nimreen crumpled up her bus ticket and threw it at you, hitting you in the face. You fell over in your seat, wounded, and then jumped up and skipped toward the front of the bus. You tried valiantly to convince the driver to stop there, in the middle of the road, to please let us off, my dear sir, but he just glared and mumbled something about it being too late. A collection of stuffed animals—

camels and pandas—and two glossy Israeli flags were pinned up around his seat; they wobbled and fluttered as he accelerated.

We got off at the next stop and looked around, blinking like moles in the afternoon glare. A few meters from the bus stop, by the entrance to an industrial zone, there was a parked ice cream truck. A dark-skinned man sat next to it, under a bright blue umbrella, smoking. He had a diamond earring in his left ear, and silver stubble flecking his narrow chin.

"Slikha," I said, in Hebrew. "Excuse me. How do we get to Ahihud from here?"

"What are you looking for there?" He looked at me. Then he looked over at you.

You were wearing a loose, well-worn Red Hot Chili Peppers T-shirt and a small cloth backpack. Your puffy headphones were wrapped around your neck, sort of like the ridiculous travel pillow my dad always brought with him on the plane, only you didn't look ridiculous. The man's eyes flicked over to Nimreen, who was wearing a short-sleeved white button-down, and I followed his gaze as it settled on her chest, where a hint of her dark bra was just barely visible beneath the fabric. I didn't like the way he was looking at her, even though, ultimately, who was I to speak, given that I'd looked hard enough to see the bra's faint silhouette myself. Still.

You lit a cigarette. I felt a jolt of nervousness stiffen my tongue as I wondered if he might somehow know what we were up to in Ahihud. Not that I totally knew what we were up to myself, but I did know that two of the three of us were not Jews, and that that already made us at least a little suspect.

"We're not looking for anything in particular," I said, "just traveling around."

"Mm," Nimreen said, "just a plain old afternoon trek."

Nimreen's Hebrew *r*s were sharp, tongue vibrating against the roof of her mouth.

The man's eyes narrowed. "Where are you from?"

"Haifa," I said, "more or less."

My Hebrew *r*s came from the back of my throat, tongue resting flat and passive.

"Huh," the man said. He looked at me again, then at you, then at Nimreen. Her eyes dared him to continue with the line of questioning all four of us understood him to have begun.

There was a long pause.

"Ice cream?" The man said.

"No, thanks," I said, my mouth watering as I thought about the milky wash of vanilla on my lips, the crunch of a sugar cone between my teeth.

"Take a left down that dirt path," he said.

I thanked him and we set off.

"'Haifa, more or less,'" Nimreen said, in Hebrew, as we walked the green gauntlet between slender olive trees on one side and tumbling piles of cactus on the other. I was walking sandwiched between the two of you, as usual.

"Are you embarrassed that your friends are Arabs?" Nimreen said, in English, rolling her *r*s exaggeratedly: *Embarrrassed—Arrrabs.*

"No," I said, "it's not that. I was just—"

"You were nervous, J. It's cool. I get it," you said, in English. "I was actually sort of nervous too."

Nimreen peered around me to look at you. She arched one of her dark eyebrows, the one without the silver ring threaded through the soft pinch of flesh and hairs. Over the month and a half since we'd met, I found myself constantly imagining kissing her piercing, the crisp coolness of the metal on my lips, the taste of sweat beads dissolving on the tip of my tongue. I imagined other things too, dark whorls, wetnesses, the glide of skin on skin.

"Pussies," Nimreen said.

"Come on, ya habla," you said, in Arabic. "We're not exactly here to support the local economy."

My chest swelled as I replayed your sentence in my head and realized that there was only one word that I didn't recognize. (It helped that you said "support the local economy" in Hebrew.)

"Shu ya'ani 'habla,'" I asked in Arabic. "What does 'habla' mean?"

You and Nimreen both laughed. Nimreen's laugh was like a fast, narrow river. Yours was slower, wider.

"It means 'idiot,' for a girl," you said, in English.

"Ironic, right, that my idiot of a brother calls me that?" Nimreen said, and made a clicking sound in the side of her mouth, tilting her head toward you.

I laughed. I laughed so much with you and Nimreen. That was part of why I'd grown so addicted to our Fridays, skipping family events gladly and even occasionally ditching my other friends—my Israeli friends—as our weekends began, in order to be with the two of you.

We arrived at a yellow gate, the kind that most Jewish towns in the North have at their entrances, only here the guard booth was empty. Nimreen and I squeezed around the gate's edge, trying to avoid the scratch of a small twisted tree bowing toward the paint-chipped metal.

"Ahlan wa-sahlan, dude," you said, vaulting over the barrier like a gangly gymnast. "Welcome to al-Birwa."

Nimreen was surprised a week earlier, sitting on an amber wooden bench in a small café in Haifa, surrounded by dark coffee-scented air, when I told her I'd never heard of Darwish.

"Not even the name?" she asked, ripping open the tops of two sugar packets at once and emptying the contents of both into her steaming mug.

"I don't know much about poetry," I said, feeling self-conscious about the hot chocolate I'd ordered. The only poem I'd ever read outside the framework of school had been the one written by my grandfather's brother, Jacko. "Tell me about Mohammad Darwish?"

"Mahmoud Darwish." Nimreen laughed, not too meanly. "No big deal. He's just, like, the most famous Palestinian poet ever."

"My sister, she is very, very, very much liking him," you said, putting on a strong accent. In general, your accent in English was mild but present. Nimreen, on the other hand, sounded basically American. Which was strange, the difference: you'd both spent the exact same years, ages ten to thirteen, in "a little ex-hippy town in the middle of corn-wobble Ohio," as you put it, where your mom taught as a visiting professor at the local college.

"My brother, he is very, very, very much dumb," Nimreen said.

You stuck out your tongue at your sister.

"Darwish was from a village not far from here, called al-Birwa," Nimreen said.

I nodded, taking a sip of my hot chocolate. It tasted very good.

You called me a few days later, telling me that you and Nimreen wanted to take me to al-Birwa on Friday.

"My sister's idea," you said. "I'm just coming along for the ride."

"Sounds great," I said, elated that you and Nimreen wanted to spend yet another Friday with me. I didn't think much about Mohammad Darwish or al-Birwa then.

———

Now, in Ahihud, I looked around. There was no trace of an Arab village anywhere. I thought about Beit al-Asal, your family's village, where I'd first met you and Nimreen, with its winding, narrow alleyways, its full olive groves, the carcass of a whole cow hanging in the entrance to the butcher's shop, and the halwayyat store where your parents had insisted on taking me and my mom before we left, for the "best baklawa in the Galilee." Ahihud, on the other hand, just looked like a sleepy, sparse version of Pardes Ya'akov, where my grandfather lived, and where my family had moved to from the States the summer before: red-roofed houses, Hebrew street signs, cacti growing in jumbled piles, pretty blue and white flags fluttering in the wind, the Star of David planted proudly in their centers. A quiet, northern Jewish Israeli town.

"Slikha," you said, in Hebrew, to a thin man, probably in his midforties, who was walking down the almost-empty streets toward us, slowly, with a limp. "Excuse me. How's it going, brother? Do you happen to know where we can find old ruins, buildings, that sort of thing?"

He looked at you. Your accent was more obvious in Hebrew than in English. I tensed. I felt like I should be the one interacting with "my side," the way you and Nimreen spoke to the Arabs we met in Haifa or Beit al-Asal. The parallel wasn't precise, of course: not only did you speak better Arabic than me, obviously, but your Hebrew was arguably better than mine too. Still, this man was one of my people, and there was the issue with the *r* sound, the Hebrew letter reish.

———

Later, toward the end of Training, they'd teach us this trick, a sort of shortcut toward knowing who to stop and question at a checkpoint:

"Just have them say a sentence with a reish in it."

Arabs rolled their *r*s, Jews didn't.

The system wasn't perfect, they went on to say, what with the older Mizrahi Jews, who still spoke Hebrew with Arabic inflections. But most of the Yemenites and Moroccans out in the Territories wore kippahs, which helped to preemptively clarify which side they were on.

———

This man, standing in front of us in the quiet streets of Ahihud, looked to be Yemenite himself. I felt a wave of guilt swish through my stomach. Why were we snooping around his village anyway? I'd started to gather that Ahihud had probably been built around or over al-Birwa, but this guy definitely wasn't even born back in 1948. And anyway, who knows what sort of terrors his family fled when they came to Israel? What would he think if he knew why we were here? That we wanted to take his home away from him? I certainly didn't want to take his home away from him. I didn't think you did either. I wasn't sure about Nimreen.

"Kilu, m'lifnei Milhemet Ha'atzmaut?" you said, in Hebrew. "Like, from before the War of Independence?"

The man's shoulders seemed to relax.

"Ah, no," he said, "those are all gone. They covered them up a few years ago. There was a building or two, before that, but nothing serious."

"Which way?" I cut in. You turned to me, but I didn't look at you long enough to see if your expression was one of irritation or mirth or something else entirely.

"Just up the hill, that way," the man said, and limped off down the road.

"*The War of Independence?*" Nimreen said, when the man was out of earshot. "First it's Jonathan with 'Haifa more or less,' and then it's you with 'the War of Independence'? Jonathan, just in case it wasn't clear, my brother is what we call an Ashkenazi Palestinian."

"Got it." I laughed, savoring Nimreen's strange adaptation of Israeli slang, in which Ashkenazi was synonymous with milquetoast.

"Me? No!" you said, leaping up onto a small boulder just off the side of the road and flexing your scrawny biceps. "I am a real man! A frrreedom fighter!"

"Uskut," Nimreen said. "Shut up, Laith."

"I will not be silent!" you cried, jumping back down off the rock. "Anyway, do you want to find the buildings, Nunu, or to end up in a police station as suspected mehablim?"

Nimreen laughed. I was quiet. I'd never heard anyone use the word "mehablim," Hebrew for "terrorists," in a jokey way before, which is not to say that my Israeli friends were oversensitive: at my school in Pardes Ya'akov, people would make Holocaust jokes all the time—i.e., "Don't make jokes about the Holocaust. Hundreds of Jews were killed." Ha. Ha.— which was hard for me, at first, because of my grandfather Saba Yehuda, and Jacko and Salonica, but I got used to it and even started to appreciate some of the jokes, especially because so many of my classmates had Saba Yehudas of their own. In fact, it was during my class trip to Auschwitz that past fall that I'd been annexed into my group of Israeli friends.

Back then, as our class walked into the entrance of the camp, I'd been startled, Laith, by how green and lush everything looked. I'd never imagined grass and little white flowers growing in the death camps.

"If there were times in which there was grass here during the Shoah," our guide began, as if reading my mind, "they were brief. The prisoners would have eaten it."

Inside the first chamber, I thought about people who walked in alive and then, soon after, became dead. In between, maybe they tried to tear down the walls with their fingernails. Maybe their fingernails came off. Or maybe they just sat down and wept and choked. Or maybe, hopefully, they died quickly. Could you suck in the gas to make it go quicker?

In a small room, somewhere in the camp, we listened to a recording of "El Maleh Rahamim," a Jewish prayer for the soul of the departed, or in this case the six million souls of the departed, and then our guide asked if any of us had names we wanted to say, in remembrance. Names floated into the cold air, one after another after another, and when it was my turn, I recited the only three names of Saba Yehuda's family members that I knew. I said his parents' names, "Moises Sadicario, Rosa Sadicario," in a steady-somber voice, but when I said his brother's name, "Jacko Sadicario," I thought about a part of Jacko's poem to his lover in Salonica:

> Your voice, my love, is minor key mist
> All mourning, moistness and right
> How many times can your eyes I kiss
> Before they melt into puddles of light

And before I could finish his name—I got stuck somewhere around the third syllable of my grandfather's former family name, Sadicario, a name that is no longer alive in our family—my voice cracked, and a high-pitched wail scrambled from my chest, like a bleating animal made aware of its impending slaughter, ugly and piteous, and I was, for a moment, ashamed, and then Avichai—who had dark hair, big brown eyes, crooked bottom teeth, and bulging biceps, and who had lived in America for two years as a kid—put his strong arm around my shoulder. And then, Rinat—who had golden hair, cut short, and a quick smile, and had said seven names, just before, when it was her turn—stood up and moved across the room, toward me. We'd barely spoken before then, but I'd noticed, as soon as I'd arrived at school, her large, pillowy breasts. As she wrapped her arms around me there, in that small room in Auschwitz, and I felt her breasts pushing against my stomach, I was afraid for a moment that I'd get an erection, but I didn't, and the wave of lust passed from my loins, and soon more arms were around me, more hands on my shoulders, and my tears evaporated on my face, and I didn't feel alone or sad anymore.

That night Rinat invited me to come hang out in the room she was sharing with another girl, named Maayan, who had long eyelashes and a slight lisp. Avichai was there too, and so was another friend of Avichai's, a narrow-faced guy named Meron, whose grandparents were from Libya, and who had a golden-tan complexion even in the late fall. We all talked for a bit about the day, in serious tones, and then Meron pulled out an iPod player, scrolled until he found what he was looking for, and clicked play.

It took me a moment to recognize the Queen song, so familiar but so strange to hear playing here, in Poland, not so far from the death camps where a third of our people had been exterminated. I wasn't sure if Meron meant to play this as a sad song, and I sat there, my hands stuffed under my thighs, blinking, confused, embarrassed for him and for all of us, until Rinat stood up and began swaying and mouthing the words: "Mamaaaa, just killed a man." We all watched as Rinat rotated her hips back and forth, her eyes squeezed shut. Then Avichai, next to me on the bed, chimed in with the "ooh-ooh-ooh-ooh"s, and Maayan leapt up onto the other bed to take the solo on air guitar, her face scrunched up and focused, and by the time we were halfway through the song, we were all jumping on Rinat's and Maayan's beds, laughing and singing at the top of our lungs, screaming "Bohemian Rhapsody" in a dingy hotel in the middle of Poland, belting out nonsense about silhouettos and scaramouches that amounted, I understood, to a graceful sort of fuck you to the ghosts of our people's tormentors: because we were here, pulsating, alive, filled with sex and meaning, boys and girls with fast-approaching draft dates, preparing ourselves to take up arms to continue the defense of our people, to become men and women standing proud under the blue and white banner of never again.

After we got back from Poland, Avichai and I started hanging out more and focused our friendship around long biweekly runs together after school, to get ready for tryouts: he wanted to make it into the elite Navy Special Ops unit, while I'd set my sights on the Paratroopers. Rinat wanted to go into Intelligence, and Meron was gunning for the Golani Brigade all the way, following in the footsteps of his dad and both his older brothers. Maayan wanted to be a soldier-teacher. They all started inviting me out with them, more and more: restaurants, paintball, weekend parties, barbecues on the beach, hikes in the woods. Sometimes on those hikes, Laith, we'd pass over some old ruins. None of us would stop then to comment.

Now, with you and Nimreen, I walked up the hill in silence, each of us glancing under olive trees, to see if we could see anything more than dust and weeds and pebbles.

"Have you been here before?" I asked, after a few minutes.

"Never ever," Nimreen said. "Special for you."

"The Education of Little Jonny Apple Tree," you said.

I giggled, even though the joke didn't entirely make sense.

"Laith," I said, "how do you know so much about American culture, man? You were in the States for like a millisecond."

"Habibi," you said, "when I get a chance, I'm moving to Brooklyn or Seattle or North Carolina."

"Yeah?" I said. "North Carolina? That's where I went to summer camp, you know. Maybe you could be a counselor at Camp Samaria."

"Salam aleikum, kids," you said, tamping down your grin into a mock-serious face. "Today, we're going to talk about Zionism."

"You're hired," I said.

You danced a few exaggerated steps of the hora, and hummed a few off-key bars of "Hevenu Shalom Aleichem," the Hebrew folk song whose lyrics declare, "We have brought peace upon you."

"Seriously, though, J," you said, stopping your dance and brushing your hair to the side, off your forehead. "I don't care. I'll go to North Carolina, South Carolina. Guam. Anywhere far away from here. This place is suffocating. Everything here is too black and white, you know? Either you're this or you're that. You're a Jew or you're an Arab. You're a man or a girl. A hero or a traitor. There's no slippery here."

"Slipperiness," Nimreen said.

"Whatever," you said.

"Slipperihood," I said.

"Really?" Nimreen looked at me.

"No," I said, and she laughed and I felt like I had won something. Her laughter faded as we reached a small, fenced-off area. Hanging from the barbed wire was a sign, in Hebrew. All three of us read, in silence:

Private grazing area. Entrance is forbidden. The violator will be punished.

"Come on, guys, let's cross," I said, feeling a wave of adrenaline and indignation. On the other side of the fence, there were a few flattened areas of earth, stones peeking up shyly from the dirt. They might have been—but also might not have been—part of al-Birwa.

You shook your head.

"It doesn't work like that here, J. Not for us, at least. You know the whole thing with Shai Dromi?"

I nodded. A few months earlier, a Jewish farmer, Shai Dromi, had shot four Bedouins who'd broken into his property to steal his animals. He killed one of them.

"Not a total coincidence that it was a bunch of Arabs who got shot," you said.

"He'll get off, for sure," Nimreen said.

"No way," I said, "He won't get off. He killed someone."

"Mm-mm." Nimreen shook her head. "He didn't kill someone. He killed an Arab."

I looked at you, waiting for you to contradict your sister, but you only nodded, and I remembered that over the past few weeks I had seen a few cars with bumper stickers: "We are all Shai Dromi." Still, though. He'd killed someone.

We stood silently for a moment, and then Nimreen began to speak, in a deeper, more melodic voice than usual, in rhythmic, formal Arabic.

"Sajil, ana Arabi, wa-raqamu bitaqati khamsun alf."

She looked over at you and told you to translate for me.

You complied, reciting: "Write it down, I am an Arab and my identity . . . Identity card number is fifty thousand."

"Wa-atfaali thamaniyatun, wa-tasa'ahum, sa-yati ba'ada sayf," Nimreen said.

"And my children are eight," you said, your eyes focused downward, "and the ninth of them will come after the summer."

"Fa-hal taghdab?" As Nimreen said this, she looked at me. The late-afternoon sun was glinting off her irises. I understood the question but wasn't sure if it was part of the poem. Then you spoke, softly, still translating, your own identically glinting eyes still fixed on the dirt.

"So will you get angry?"

Nimreen continued. It seemed like she knew the whole poem by heart, and although you kept translating, I soon slipped out of focus, losing track of the metaphors, floating into a cozy, thoughtless space. No one else was around us. Nimreen's voice was soft and yours was softer. The wind was warm and sedative. Then Nimreen's voice grew louder, and I focused back on her words, and yours.

"Wa-lakinnee, itha ma ja'atu," Nimreen said.

"But if I become hungry . . ."

"Aakul lahma mughtasibi."

You turned to Nimreen and said something in fast Arabic that I couldn't understand. She said something back, and I picked out the word "tarjim" again: Translate.

You looked down and spoke quietly, "I will eat the flesh of my . . ."

"Usurper," Nimreen said.

"Khalas," you said. "Enough, Nunu."

My stomach clenched. It's just a poem, I told myself. The barbed wire fence was strung tightly before us. It did not sway in the wind that whistled around us. Why did Nimreen think I needed to hear this? Wasn't I standing there, with you and her, trying to find the ruins of a Palestinian village buried beneath an Israeli town that I would probably love if I had the chance to get to know it? Sniffing around people's homes, scrounging for some shred of a long-gone past? How much more was I expected to do, to give? You'll eat my flesh? Or my people's flesh, at least?

"That's one of my favorite poems by Darwish," Nimreen said, her voice suddenly quiet, shy almost. "It's called 'Identity Card.'"

I nodded brusquely. We were all silent.

"There's one that I really love," you said, after a while. "It's called, 'Jundi Yahlam b'Zanabiq al-Bayda'a.' 'A Soldier Dreams of White . . .' uh, keef minqool 'zanabiq' in English, Nunu?"

"Lilies," Nimreen said.

"How does it go?" I asked, trying to sound nonchalant, but my voice got stuck on some ridge in my throat and came out sounding narrow.

"I don't remember." You laughed.

"Oh," I said.

"It's a conversation, though, between Mahmoud Darwish and his friend Yossi, after the war in 1967."

"Yossi?" I asked. "Darwish had Jewish friends?"

"He was part of the Israeli Communist Party in Haifa, back then," Nimreen said. "Not everything is black and white here."

"It's a great one, J," you said. "I'll find it for you sometime."

Was that really your favorite poem, Laith? We hadn't yet talked about my draft notice, the tryouts, the Paratroopers, but you must have known, or at least assumed, that I was thinking of staying, that I didn't want to leave this land, that my soldier dream was the fourth member of our group, following the three of us wherever we went, waiting silently around corners, grinning under piles of cactus, its eye sockets filled with gleaming light as it crawled between the words of the poems. I looked for your eyes, Laith, trying to read something there, but you were busy digging around in your small backpack.

Your hand emerged, cradling your cigarettes, and from amidst the rows of identical white chemical sticks you pulled a shorter, fatter hand-rolled one. You licked your lips and lit it. "This one's for the homies of al-Birwa."

I laughed, unable to not, and accepted the joint when you passed it to me, inhaling the smoke deep into my lungs and holding my breath for as long as I could, willing the high to latch on to the back of my face quickly. I exhaled hard and passed the joint to Nimreen. Emboldened by the familiar tingle of tetrahydrocannabinol in my bloodstream, I asked, "Does Darwish have any poems that aren't so political?"

Nimreen took a deep drag, and when she spoke, her voice was wrapped in a cloud: "There is nothing 'not political' in Palestine, habibi."

She blew out a beam of smoke.

On another day, I might have taken issue with the fact that she'd called this place, all of it, "Palestine," but on that day, as the wind darted through the shimmering fields around us and kissed its secrets into the pores of our teenage skin, I only cared that your sister, Nimreen, had called me "habibi."

We smoked in silence, each of us thinking our own thoughts.

"Yalla, let's go home," you said, as the joint neared its end.

Nimreen took the remainder of the joint from you and then held up her right hand, telling us to wait. In her left hand, the embers crept toward the skin of her fingertips. A thin thread of smoke floated upward into the sky.

The two of us stood, frozen, obedient.

"The earth is closing on us!" she said, in English.

"Give me that roach back, Nunu," you said to her, laughing. "I think she's lost it, J," you said to me, winking.

"Shh," Nimreen said, and motioned to us to step closer. We obeyed, again, and then stood still as she hummed to herself, almost frantically, her eyes closed. I was standing near enough to her to see her eyeballs moving back and forth underneath her eyelids. A tiny strip of eyeliner had blended with a film of sweat, and swirling patterns of blackness were etched along the creases.

Then her eyes popped open and met mine, for a brief second. I cast my eyes to the ground, flustered, but she didn't seem to notice that I'd been staring. She was elsewhere.

"Ila ayna nathhabu ba'ad al-hududi al-akheerati?"

"To where will we go after the last borders," you translated, unprompted, your voice soft like your sister's, loamy like the ground.

"Ayna tateeru al-'asafeeru ba'ad a-sama'a-i al-akheera?"

"Where will the birds fly after the last sky?"

Nimreen looked at me and smiled a smile that I couldn't translate. She flicked the still-lit roach over to the other side of the barbed wire fence.

We all went quiet again, and then you laughed and pointed up.

Nimreen smiled also when she saw them, and I did too, Laith. Two birds, white with black wings. They were trying to move forward, but the wind was too strong. Despite their flapping, they were borne backward, through the air over al-Birwa, until eventually, first one and then the other, they turned around, giving up their struggle to get wherever it was they'd originally hoped to go, and instead gliding easily with the breeze, back toward where they'd come from.

Later, on the bus, seated across the aisle from you and Nimreen, I asked, "What was that line again?" I was desperate to taste Nimreen's voice in my ear once more, before the day ended and the sun dipped away into the Galilean hills, and I mixed up the words as I spoke: "Where will we go after the last sky?"

"Something like that," Nimreen said, looking out the window, her voice curved around what was almost definitely a smile.

"Something like that," you repeated.

IN HERE, LAITH, THE AIR HAS NOTHING IN COMMON with the THC-soaked breezes we once sipped to the rhythm of your sister's recitations. Here, a bird could only flutter in frantic circles until its wings grew tired, until it collapsed into a pile of sharp feathers and fragile bones.

When they first brought me in, I was put in a cell along with seven others. There were metal bars on the windows, fluorescent lights murmuring anxiously overhead 24/7. Bulbous security cameras were posted in each corner of the room, watching everything. We didn't look each other in the eyes. All our eyes were filled with poison. But at least in their voices I could latch on to something human. In the rush of their minor belligerencies I could find, momentarily, something external to despise. In the glow of their small kindnesses I could almost convince myself that I still deserved to fill my lungs.

And at night, when everyone else was sleeping, floppy hats pulled down over sparsely whiskered faces, shielding them from the brightness of one hundred thousand daylight suns, I could creep between the bunk beds stuffed with the sweating bodies of atrophying Hebrew warriors and I could place my tongue against the wall and almost taste the salty winds that I knew were pressing against the outside. I could tell myself that it was you urging the winds forward, toward me, your friend Jonathan.

Laith. What have I done? Down here, the walls don't press against the wind. There are no human voices, just shrieks and crashing metal and the memories of birds, crumpled bodies splayed out on the ground. Above, I can hear the ceiling sagging under the weight of so much sand and loneliness.

I am waiting for this starving land to open up and swallow me.

THREE

"ARE YOU A JEW-LOVER, OR WHAT?"

I was standing with a mixed cluster of seventh and eighth graders. I was a scrawny twelve year old, Laith, not yet the nearly beautiful almost-man I felt myself to be when you first met me, or the fully beautiful person I felt that I became when I was around you and Nimreen. Back then, I hated my face, hated my body. I stood toward the edge of the cluster with my thumbs hooked through the belt loops of my jeans but quickly worried that that would look like false bravado, so I shoved my hands into my pockets instead. Then I took them out again, not wanting to seem nervous in front of the eighth graders.

I was so busy agonizing over what to do with my hands, Laith, that I barely registered what I heard. Joey, an eighth grader, was addressing Sprout, who was in seventh grade and whose real name was Owen, but whose status at the bottom of the school's food chain was made clear by his vegetative nickname.

"Hey, Sprout," Joey said.

Sprout turned to look at Joey, an expression of surprised gratitude plastered across his strange face. I think he was happy then just to be spoken to directly.

"Are you a Jew-lover, or what?" Joey said.

Sprout couldn't have been expecting the content of Joey's question, but it was clear from the way his expression seamlessly morphed into one of resignation that he wasn't shocked by the cruelty.

A thick, foamy feeling rushed into my throat from the depths of my hairless belly.

I was the only Jewish kid in Everbrook Middle School, and one of the only Jews in Everbrook, Pennsylvania, period. Laughter puffed from the rest of the group, fluffy and light like cotton candy.

"Sprout is such a Jew-lover," Joey repeated, a grin pulled over his hideous face.

His upturned snout.

His rodent hair.

In my memory of that moment, Joey was not a person but a beast or a ghoul.

I think he was actually plain-looking, Laith, actually fine-looking, but it can be hard to differentiate between actual memories and the shape-shifting wraiths that pose as memories but are really just the run-off of my hopes for a better, cleaner, simpler past.

"Nah," Sprout said, looking down at the ground, his mouth pursing and then unpursing, "I'm definitely not."

Can I blame him, Laith? Can we blame anyone for the ways in which fear opens up their lips? I don't know. I do know that I hated Sprout then.

Joey swung back toward Sprout. "So loan me a dollar."

Sprout fumbled for his wallet and pulled a bill from the folds of dark leather. Joey snatched the money from Sprout's bony hand. In my memory, Laith, Joey might as well have goose-stepped over to the vending machine. The conversation moved onward—homework and gossip and approximated cup sizes and the football game against Hercules, PA, on

Friday—but Joey's words bounced around my head like an echo off the walls of a crater.

> *Hey Sprout.*
> *Sprout sprout sprout.*
> *Are you a Jew-lover, or what?*
> *Jew-lover. Jew-lover. Jew-lover.*
> *How could anyone love a Jew?*
> *Even a Sprout?*
> *They can't even stand up for themselves, never could.*
> *Never could. Never could.*
> *They don't even love themselves.*

Then Joey returned to the center of the cluster, sipping a Mountain Dew: Code Red. This is not what happened next, Laith, but my memory wraiths have enacted this scene so many times, in the minutes and months and years that followed, on the main stage of my mind, that the details feel as though they might as well have been real:

I pushed my way to the center of the cluster, so that I was face-to-face with Joey. Without saying anything, I grabbed the soda can from Joey's hand, a glob of sugary red liquid splashing out onto his left sneaker, fizzling as it struck. I threw the can aside. "This doesn't belong to you."

Joey's face twisted into a mask of rage, nostrils flaring, cheeks flushing beet-red. Joey was a solid four inches taller than I was and at least twenty pounds heavier, but I wasn't afraid.

"Clean it up," Joey snarled, pointing to his shoe. "Lick it up."

"Be quiet, Joey," I said, my arm muscles vibrating. I'd been doing push-up sets every day since the summer before middle school.

"Who is going to make me? Some skinny, weak Jew like you?" Joey laughed an ugly laugh and then lunged toward me.

"Ever heard of Krav Maga?" I said, ducking as Joey's fist swung over my head.

Before coming up from my crouch, I rammed my left fist into Joey's gut, and as Joey doubled over, I straightened up and sent my right fist—a messenger on a holy mission—in an arced uppercut that collided with Joey's nose.

Joey cried out in pain as blood rushed down onto his shirt. I stood silently, breathing hard, my eyes narrowed. Everyone was watching. Joey bellowed, a wordless pod of sound, and charged once more, but I was ready for this too. I sidestepped his lowered shoulder and stuck out a foot, sending him sprawling onto the hard hallway floor.

I strode toward where he lay, facedown, and said in a voice loud enough for everyone to hear, "No more jokes about Jews. We'll fight back this time."

Then the bell rang, Laith, signaling the end of the ten-minute break, and of my fantasy.

What actually happened was, of course, nothing. Joey returned from the vending machine, sipping his Mountain Dew: Code Red and I didn't say anything, not then and not throughout the rest of the school year, even as Joey—whom I decided to refer to as Joey von Ribbentrop, my middle school historiographer's wits seeking a sliver of the revenge that my fists failed to exact—and a few others continued to joke, here and there, now and then, ha ha, about cheap Jews, weak Jews, ha ha ha, stingy Jews, small-dick Jews, Holocausty Jews.

Ultimately, Laith, he probably wasn't a bad guy, Joey. I understand now that he was barely holding on, with the tips of his fingers, to the edge of social acceptance, not much higher on the ladder than Sprout. Once, years later—after I'd torn a six-pack into my stomach from nightly sit-up sets, after I'd grown pretty, grown a few inches, grown the beginnings of a good beard by virtue of dumb genetic luck—I was driving home with two friends, and it was raining hard. I saw Joey walking, alone, his shoulders scrunched against the downpour, his light-brown hair slicked to his forehead. I had two extra spaces in my parents' car, and I thought about offering him a ride but didn't. I didn't drive into a puddle and splash him either. I just drove on.

Still, Laith, "Jew-lover" had crawled into my chest, etched its syllables into my memory, alongside the feeling of standing there, speechless and motionless, tears scratching at the edges of my eyes, wishing I were stronger, braver, more powerful, less alone. Calling Joey by the last name of a Nazi minister didn't feel like enough. I was sick of being People of the Word. I wanted to be People of the Sword. I wanted tanned arms and campfires, braided folk songs and righteous rifles. I wanted to be like Saba Yehuda, teeth bared like tiny shields against the stabbing world.

It was in another room filled with young men and bunk beds, a few months later, that I began in earnest to map out the path that would harden my teeth.

On my first night at Camp Samaria, all the boys gathered, shirtless, in the center of the cabin, the wood floor creaking beneath our preteen weights. It was a humid night. It was an important night. It was the first round of "hit-for-hit," in which we punched one another as hard as we could, in the shoulder, and thereby determined the cabin's hierarchy for the next twenty-nine days. I was paired off with Benji, a chubby kid from Mahwah, New Jersey, with black mustache fuzz on his upper lip. He was new at camp but within hours had already been dubbed Manboobs. I thought, of course, that this was mean and vowed, privately, not to say it out loud. But facing off against him, I had no intention of holding back. The stakes were too high. I heard Manboobs whimper as my fist connected with his fleshy upper arm.

"Ouch," he said, looking at me like a puppy, misty eyes, saggy jowls. I knew that he knew that I was his greatest hope for redemption in the cabin, but at that moment, I had no room inside myself for anyone but myself. He tried to meet my eyes. I looked away.

"I guess I'm out," Benji said. Gleeful yipping filled the bunk: a pack of famished jackals.

"Good try, Manboobs!" Micah crowed from across the room.

Micah was blond-haired and smooth-skinned and had been coming to Camp Samaria since he was seven. According to legend, and to Micah himself, Micah had French-kissed almost every girl in our age group. Micah had already defeated his first opponent. In the other corner, Sy Sudfeld was preparing for his second victory. Sy was almost six feet tall, and his Miami tan glowed in the cabin light. His hair was chestnut-brown, and his bulbous nose was the only thing that distinguished him from my twelve-year-old imagination of what Ari Ben Canaan— the Israeli warrior-hero from Leon Uris's *Exodus*, which my dad had me read in preparation for my bar mitzvah—looked like. Sy gazed down at his opponent, a beatific boy named Davie who stood just over five feet tall. Davie let out a mighty war whoop and then embraced Sy's torso in a bear hug, his smiling mouth just next to Sy's nipple. Sy patted Davie on his back and everyone laughed.

"I'm out before I'm in," Davie said.

"That's what she said!" Micah yelled.

I didn't think that made sense, but I kept quiet. Micah and I were paired off next.

"Good luck, Jonathan," Micah said.

"In Israel," I said, "we don't believe in luck."

From the moment I arrived at Camp Samaria, I took pains to ensure that I was recognized as the Israeliest kid at camp, not including the three actual IDF soldiers, Gabi, Dotan, and Shirli, sent to train us in archery, Zionist thought, and sing-alongs, respectively. Over the course of my time there, I invented memories from my childhood in Israel (withholding the fact that my American-immigrant father and Israeli-born mother had heartlessly whisked me away from the Holy Land before I could even speak), confidently referenced the nuances of Israeli history (gleaned mostly from my copy of *Exodus*), and mused about how "we Israelis don't show emotion in the same way Americans do" (based mostly on how weird my mom sometimes was). I did show my emotions at camp, but strategically: during the prayer for the State of Israel each Shabbat, Gabi or Dotan would read out the names of all the Israelis killed in terror attacks since Rosh Hashana of that past year. Lots of the kids cried, but I made sure I cried the loudest.

Micah went first. His punch was solid and punishing, but I didn't make a sound. As I prepared for my turn, I let my gaze settle on Micah's blond hair and blue eyes. Micah, I knew, was Jewish—this was Camp Samaria—but I still thought Micah looked a little like a Hitler Youth. And I knew that this thought would be helpful, so I kept thinking it as I hit him, hard.

The look on his face told me that my blow had hurt, his icy eyes registering fear beneath a wavering layer of confidence. Micah's second punch was wobbly, while mine was nearly as hard as my first one had been. Micah moaned and clenched his jaw. His third punch was so hard that I nearly cried out, but I bit my tongue and then grinned wolfishly as a coppery wetness seeped into my mouth. Better to bleed on the inside than to show weakness on the outside. Micah was desperate. I didn't fear pain. The flush of testosterone is a wild thing, Laith. My next punch drove into Micah's arm like a miniature mortar.

Micah's face crumpled, and his right hand shot up to his left shoulder. Everyone was watching. Our counselors had not yet returned from sneaking out to make out with the female counselors and perhaps even touch their boobs. It was just us boys. No one would step in to stop this.

"I'm out," Micah said. "Fucking Israel-boy here hits hard."

A cheer went up around the room.

Fucking Israel-boy is right, I thought to myself. I was close to becoming the Camp Samarian hit-for-hit champion. But I wasn't there yet. I didn't even allow myself a smile.

I turned to face Sy, who grinned and stuck out his hand. Confused, I stared at Sy's palm until Sy said, "Mercy rules, Jonathan, remember?"

The rules of hit-for-hit at Camp Samaria were that if either of the finalists had gone more than two rounds in the semifinals, then mercy rules applied and there were two winners. The game was over. I had won. Sy had won. I looked over at the Jewish man who was my equal, at Sy Sudfeld, his sweat-slicked torso glowing strong and beautiful in the humid night.

"I prefer to go by Yonatan," I said, and clasped Sy's hand in mine.

The next night in the cabin, Sy had a question for the group:

"How long are your dicks?"

We all laughed and then dug our hands deep into our pockets, kicking at dust on the floor as we realized that Sy was not joking. No one spoke.

"I'm serious, guys. What, you've never measured?"

"No, never," Davie said.

"Well, do you want to?"

Everyone was silent.

"My dick is ten inches long," said Sy.

"No way!" Micah said. He was lying in his bunk, with his feet crossed at the ankles, his face buried in a copy of a semipornographic magazine.

"Yes way," said Sy. "Ten inches of Hebrew Hammer. When hard."

Sy reached under his bunk and fished around in his bag. The room was filled with a dreadful silence as Sy withdrew a two-foot ruler, decorated with the faces of all the presidents of the United States, ending with George W. Bush himself. "Who's in? Manboobs?"

Benji looked like he might burst into tears, right there. The crickets were shrieking, not only metaphorically: it was a North Carolina summer night. I cleared my throat, and Sy and the other jackals turned away from Benji to look at me, licking their chops.

"Jonathan?"

I looked at Sy, and then down at the wooden floor, and swallowed my fear like it was a lump of dry mashed potatoes. "Yonatan. But sure."

An impressed murmur seeped from the collective lips of the others.

"Micah?"

"Fuck off."

"Anyone else?"

Davie took a bow. "Indubitably, your Dickness."

"Fine," said Sy, "so here's what we do. The three of us will go into the bathroom, each of us makes ourselves get a boner, and then we measure. Cool?"

I gulped again, mashed potatoes, and walked like a man condemned after Sy and Davie. Once inside my own stall, I had no trouble getting a boner. I still, at that point, was trying to figure out where exactly the bone came from, whether it slid from my lower stomach, or just rested dormant and horizontal inside my pelvis until I started thinking about all the forbidden parts whose very names sent threads of electricity weaving downward through my rib cage. I waited, my nostrils flared, and listened to the sounds of tugging and grunting as Sy and Davie beckoned their mysterious bones out, in the stalls next to me.

"What now?" I said, my eyes squeezed tightly shut.

"You come out," Sy said, and I heard the squeak of his stall door swinging open.

"Like, with nothing on?" Davie's voice was a tadpole.

"Yes, you dickhead. How else can we measure?" Sy said.

Davie and I opened our stall doors, and poked our heads out of our safe, if slightly stinky, fortresses. Davie's face was twisted and strange.

"You guys," he whispered, "I couldn't get it hard."

He was near tears. I couldn't help but feel a flood of relief. It felt tasty and wicked, my relief, but it was not just schadenfreude. It was also self-protective: now there was a zero percent chance that Davie would be established as having a bigger dick than me.

"That's all right," Sy said. "It happens to all of us."

"It does?"

"Nope," Sy said. "Now scoot. This bathroom is for hard dicks only."

Davie slunk out of his stall and then out of the bathroom itself. No mercy rules here. I looked over at Sy and felt a series of quick pulses run through my boner, which was still buried under a thin layer of cotton

T-shirt. Sy was standing completely naked. There it was, huge and swollen, with dark tufts of hair bursting in thick curls from the bottom of its shaft. Its head was enormous, puffy; it looked like the kind of boner I'd seen on the Internet, except that Sy's curved off to the left. It was just past Abraham Lincoln on the ruler that Sy gripped next to it: ten inches and a bit of Jewish manhood. If only the guys from Everbrook Middle School could see this.

"I told you," Sy said. "Now what about you? Are you gonna measure or just stare at my dick all night?"

I took the ruler from Sy and placed it next to my own still-throbbing boner. I squeezed with all my genital might, hoping that the bone would stay fully in place. Sy leaned close.

"Five and . . . six. Let's call it six," Sy said. "Six is solid, Jonathan. I mean, Yonatan."

I wanted to weep with gratitude.

Instead I laughed giddily and flung my hand forward to high-five Sy. The smack of our hands meeting reverberated through the bathroom, and the two of us began jumping up and down, our boners flapping against our taut bellies. Then Sy grabbed his own massive boner and began whipping it against mine. I laughed with no breath. I whipped my own boner back against his. Sy brushed his boner up and down mine, hard and then soft. I rubbed mine underneath his, my fist bumping against his thigh. And then, as soon as it had started, it was over. We pulled our boxers and pants back on and walked out into the main room of the bunk, where everyone else was waiting.

"It's true," I said. "Sy Sudfeld's boner is ten inches long."

———

Small rooms with bunk beds, filled with young men. Tal and Gadi and Eviad and I fell in love with each other in a room like that. We had all joined the Second Platoon of Battalion 202—the "Viper" battalion—of the Thirty-Fifth Brigade of the Israel Defense Forces: the Paratroopers. The Paratroopers, who had taken part in every war in Israeli history and in almost every fantasy I'd had since Camp Samaria. The first few months of Basic Training were pure effort, Laith. Running, night marches, predawn wake-ups, endless push-ups, fuzzy-eyed exhaustion, burning tendons, aching lungs: searingly hard, but easy too. All we had to do was to do as we were told.

I swallowed the gritty chicken we were served with a hardened relish, not wholly unlike the way I'd clenched my jaw and made myself almost-enjoy the stringy meat of the pigeon I'd watched your grandfather slaughter in Beit al-Asal. Its wings flapped wildly and its neck spurted such stunning red, but I had a choice about what to focus on then, in that moment, as in every moment, and so I held my breath and doused it in a pail of warm water, as instructed by your grandfather, and pulled the feathers out of its still-warm body, one by one, trying not to focus on the reverse sharpness of the feathers' ends, on the little holes their extraction left in the creature's limp corpse, ignoring both Nimreen's giggling and your taking my picture with your flip phone, watching as the dead animal grew to resemble the skinned supermarket birds, whitish-pink and only faintly distasteful, and then, later, as it started to look delectable, browned and sizzling in the oven. A delicious disgust, a transcendence of mortal queasiness, of human weakness. A manliness. My teeth tore into the flesh and clicked up against the little bones, chomping down on the Arab village pigeon and the IDF-issued chicken alike. Meanwhile, with each tear of my own muscles, I could feel myself surging forward toward something greater than myself. There were moments of difficulty in training, of course, but they were all shared. I didn't have to hold any of it alone. And I was so tired most of the time that I could barely think, could barely remember—the names Laith and Nimreen were like tiny bright balloons floating in a vast, empty sky.

Eviad, Tal, Gadi, and I quickly became a foursome. We'd stand as near to each other as we could, shoulders sometimes close enough to brush and then pull back, our guns snuggled to our bodies, shouting responsively to the commanders who stood faceless and nameless and ageless and flawless against the backdrop of darkness:

We are the Second Platoon.
We are Two hundred and two.
We are Paratroopers.

Part of the way through our training, Eviad and I, two of the best soldiers in the platoon, the fastest, the most serious, were given guns fixed with grenade launchers—which could also be used for tear gas canisters, although I didn't know that then. The launchers made our weapons heavier and clunkier, but we didn't complain. Tal became a combat medic and Gadi was trained with the Trijicon optical sighting device, which did seem pretty damn cool, we all had to admit. All this felt thrilling and breathtaking and great and good, but the highlight of our Advanced Training was the parachute jumps, and especially the first one, which took place on a clear spring morning—exactly a year after our afternoon in Ahihud, almost to the day.

The Paratroopers had only actually paratrooped into combat once, during the Suez Crisis with Egypt, back in 1956. Even though we'd probably never paratroop into combat ourselves, we all knew that we couldn't really be considered Paratroopers until we'd jumped. We had trained by hopping off a metal scaffolding, elevated maybe six or eight meters from the ground. We were attached to two heavy cords, meant to simulate the cords of a parachute. The whole thing was called the "Eichmann." I thought that this was because of the way it swung your body back and forth, back and forth, before finally releasing you onto the ground. It was a macabre nickname, to be sure, but I found it delicious (pigeon flesh). I ground my teeth together and jumped, smiling at the Jewish State's dark humor, at the very fact of our survival that enabled us to wryly repurpose the name of one of our people's most sadistic torturers, who we caught and tried and brought to justice. No fear and trembling anymore: now the name Eichmann is just part of the training regimen for our eighteen-year-old phoenixes, dressed in olive green and red berets, risen from the ashes to fly. When I shared these thoughts with Tal as he massaged a knot in his shoulder after our first jump from the Eichmann, he laughed and shook his head. "I think it's just called the Eichmann because it's scary and awful."

The Eichmann was just the beginning though. We had yet to jump from an airplane. I woke up the morning of our first jump shivering, nervousness zipping through my joints.

"So, which one of you sons of bitches is going to do something wrong and end up a holy puddle, fallen in the struggle for the Land of Israel?" Gadi asked, a grin pulled across his lips as he buttoned his uniform over his white undershirt. "America?"

I shook my head and put on a mock-determined face before hopping off the bottom bunk and crumpling onto my side on the ground below, my shoulder and hip pressed against the hardness, my heart pressed against the laughter that filled our room.

"Saddam?" Gadi said, still laughing.

Tal shook his head. "Can't. I have a date this weekend, remember? With your mom?"

Gadi slugged Tal in the shoulder and pretended to glare. He then turned to Eviad and cooed: "Eviaaad. It's up to you."

Eviad nodded, his handsome face solemn. "I volunteer for the selfless and noble mission of puddledom."

Gadi patted Eviad on the back. "You've been a good comrade."

We all laughed a little too loudly. Maybe everyone was as nervous as I was. We were, after all, going to jump out of an airplane. The night before, the conversation among the four of us was the most intimate we'd ever had: we spoke as if the night might actually be our last. Our voices were filled with such heated tenderness that I wouldn't have been entirely surprised if we'd all climbed out of our beds and glided toward one another; if we'd huddled at the center of the room, bare-chested as we always slept; if we'd snaked calloused fingers between fingers, pushed nipples into patches of new hair, gently slipped hardened cocks into opened mouths, not for the sake of sex, but just to prove to the world how fucking close we were, how goddamn one. We didn't, though. Instead we burnished our fervor into soft tones and wet eyes. Our words filled the darkness of the small room the four of us had chosen to share at the jump site.

Eviad, our leader without rank, had talked about his sister, Maya, and how he'd been mad at her for finishing the Kariyot cereal, wheat pillows stuffed with chocolate, the morning before the bus exploded. Tal told a story about his dad, how he had another family, another child, a brother whom Tal had never met, but how he was still married to Tal's mom too. We talked about sex, which we all claimed to have done one hundred graceful times.

I didn't talk about you or Nimreen that night, although your names floated back into the center of my mind. I'd started to give a skeletal summary of it all a few months earlier, when everyone was talking about ex-girlfriends and past loves, but even with caution restraining my tongue, I'd miscalculated, badly. My first statement—so anemic and downplayed as to be, almost, a falsehood—that I'd "had a crush on this girl named Nimreen" had quickly become the sole focus of the conversation—"Nimreen, as in . . . *Nimreen?*"—and had metastasized into an endless wellspring for jokes and ridicule, like Gadi's "Arab booty call" comment, months later, out in Suswan. There was no way I could even try to tell them the actual truth, the truth that I'm trying to tell you now, Laith. So I stayed silent. Gadi told a story that none of us believed, about how he'd showered with two of his older sister's friends, at once, back when he was sixteen.

"Not a chance, you asshole," Tal snorted. "You're so full of shit."

"It's true. I don't mind what you sons of bitches think"—Gadi's voice floated, unruffled, through the darkness—"I remember their tits like it was yesterday. Melons, really. Like four wet cantaloupes."

We all laughed and salivated and chose to believe him, despite.

"What about you, Yonatan?" Gadi said. "You've been quiet. Don't you have any stories?"

Did I? My biggest complaint against my dad was that he was tender and a little dorky. I didn't personally know anyone who had died, except for a few of my grandparents, and that barely counted. And I understood by then that the stories about you and Nimreen were stories from a different universe, stories I couldn't share that night or at all, not even in the safety of the darkness surrounding our bunks, not even with my adoptive brothers. You set me apart, kept me just out of reach from what could have been a seamless self-subsuming unification with these three angelic, chiseled youths, soon to float down from heaven, and after that to bring light to the land, crackling seraphim, wild beasts of the divine. I don't say that accusatorially, habibi, that you and your sister forced a space between me and the others, kept me from fully claiming the spot saved for me, by my people, in that bunk. It's just the truth.

"Not really," I said, "although there was this anti-Semitic fucker back in America. He was saying shit about Jews, all the time, and he wouldn't stop until I threatened to pound him."

"So what happened?" Gadi asked.

"I did," I said, my mouth sticky, "and then he stopped."

"You did what?" Gadi asked. "You pounded his ass?"

"Yep," I said, and the encouraging whoops that filled the room made me feel a little queasy, but what is truth, anyway?

"How about you, Gadi?" I pivoted, still off-balance. "Any other stories?"

"So, this one time, I fucked this other woman," Gadi began, "and she was so hot—"

"What did she look like?" I asked, overeager. "Big boobs also?"

"I think she'd look familiar to you," Gadi said, "because it was actually your mom."

"Go fuck yourself," I said, and laughter was everywhere, pouring out of the mouths and chests and bellies of my friends, so I started laughing too.

"Gadi, that's funny that you mention that," Tal said. "I didn't realize we were talking about moms. I didn't know how to tell you this, but your mom is actually expecting a baby, and you're going to have a little half-Iraqi brother soon."

More laughter, and a soft thump as Gadi's scratchy army-issued blanket—which we called a "scabies blanket," and which all of us kept stored away under our beds—landed on Tal.

"You fucker!" Tal laughed, and hurled the disgusting cloth back at Gadi.

"Guys, shut up," Eviad said, and everyone went quiet. "We're jumping tomorrow. We need to get some sleep. If one of you dies because you fall asleep in midair—"

"Yonatan's mom will cry at my funeral," Gadi said.

Everyone laughed again, Eviad included.

"Now really, though," Eviad said, "shut the fuck up and go to sleep."

I rolled over onto my side, my chest swelling with a certain kind of love.

From the plane's open belly, Laith, everything below seemed to fit together naturally. It looked like a reasonable, well-organized land, from up there. The air was cold and crisp and tasty in my lungs, and I felt so alive that death seemed like an impossibility. And anyway, it wouldn't be so bad, I thought, to die and be remembered by Tal and Gadi and Eviad. Saba Yehuda would be devastated but proud. Maybe you and Nimreen would've come to that funeral even, jumping out of an airplane being largely noncontroversial, nonviolent, nonpolitical, even if I did it as a soldier in the IDF.

We stood in a line, attached by yellow cords to a pole above us, and when the plane's belly opened up, the air flooded crystalline and sensual around us. I pressed my body gently into Eviad, standing in front of me, and I felt Tal press against me from behind. And then it was time to go: we were pushed out of the plane, one by one. Just like that: boy falling, parachute up. Boy falling, parachute up. Then Eviad was gone from in front of me, disappeared into the blue. Then I stepped forward, and everything was forward momentum, and I became a falling boy and there was no time for fear. My parachute grabbed itself a huge handful of air and everything slowed, my heart and my thoughts, and the sky around me felt so peaceful and I thought about you, Laith. I wished you could have been there with me. Then I remembered that you hated heights. So Nimreen, I thought. Nimreen would have joined me. She wasn't afraid of anything. I longed for her then, up in the air, but it was a puffy sort of longing and it didn't hurt anywhere in my body, coddled as I was by cloud fragments and silence and Technicolor sunbeams.

I tried to yell what it was I wanted to say, but the air swallowed the sound, and so I just floated down in silence, gazing around the sky at the other floating dots, and when I landed, less than a minute later, the weight of the whole earth echoed through my kneecaps, and I fell to the side, just like I'd practiced on the Eichmann, and everything hurt but nothing was hurt, and I folded my parachute back into its sack, quickly, and started running to our meeting point, adrenaline surging in my calves. I saw Eviad running, fast, a few meters ahead of me, and I pushed until I caught him, my lungs on fire, my eyes laughing, and we started running together. Then I saw Tal running, from the other direction, and I called to him, and we slowed and he glommed on to me and Eviad and our hands grabbed for the bristled backs of each other's heads. Right before we arrived at the spot where the Commander was waiting for us, at the edge of the sun-dappled field, Gadi ran over, and we slowed again to absorb his body into our tangle and he said, "What are you homos doing?" and Tal punched him in the shoulder and pulled him toward us. We ran the last paces together, and even the Commander couldn't suppress his smile. Everything was glowing.

———

Laith. I think in another context, in another place, you would have liked Eviad and Tal and maybe even Gadi. I didn't love them the way I loved you and Nimreen, but I did love them a lot. The four of us huddled close to each other for the rest of our training, our shoulders brushing and our rifles sighing and our hearts beating in arrhythmic unity.

We were huddled together like that as our platoon set up on July 25th, before the demonstration began.

Righteous Arabs, Gentle Jews

FOUR

THE FIRST TIME I MET YOU AND NIMREEN was a year and a half before that July morning in Suswan. A slush of winter rain was falling on the Galilee. Three space heaters glowed orange around the edges of Jamila and Raed's living room. It was cold in Beit al-Asal. My mom and I were perched on a springy red couch, sipping steaming hot coffee. I didn't like the bitter taste at all, but I liked the warmth and how sophisticated I felt drinking it. I'd been studying Arabic for four months by then and Jamila was impressed with my accent.

"You sound like a fallah," Jamila said.

"Remind me what fallach means?" my mom said, *ch*ing the end, as in "chanukah."

"Falla*h*," Jamila said, stretching the final *h* into a layer of sandpaper across the top of her throat, correcting her friend's pronunciation. "A peasant."

"Is that a good thing?" I asked.

"It depends who you ask." Jamila smiled.

"What Jamila is saying," Raed said, in Hebrew, his huge hands resting on his round belly, "is that you speak well, for a Jew."

I could feel my mom beaming next to me.

Raed continued, "You don't sound like the soldiers at the checkpoints who mangle the language so severely that I almost feel sorry for them."

"I don't," Jamila said. "The other day, we were driving back from Hebron—"

"Shopping," Raed said, as if offering an explanation as to why they were driving back from that other world commonly known as the West Bank, just a few kilometers away from us, but also a world apart; a world that even I, bleeding-heart Yonatan, associated with shadows and threats; a world that I had never before associated with something as banal as shopping.

"Right, shopping," Jamila said, in English. "Anyway, we were returning from Hebron, and I was stopped at the checkpoint, of course."

She rotated her hands so that her palms were facing upward toward the ceiling, as if she were holding an invisible tray. She then moved that tray toward her husband, Raed, dark-skinned and bald and nearly two meters tall. He was a high school Arabic teacher here in Beit al-Asal. Jamila was a professor of sociology at Haifa University. She and my mom had met at a Women Stand Up vigil in Haifa. My dad had been less than enthusiastic when my mom first announced her intentions to attend the vigil, right after we returned to Israel.

"The war just ended, Raphaela," he said, meaning the war in Lebanon that had wrapped up two days before we arrived. "Can't you wait with your pro-Arab demonstrations until at least after the dust has settled from Hezbollah's missiles?"

"It's not a demonstration, Paul," my mom said. "It's a vigil."

"A vigil for what?"

"A vigil against the occupation."

"So . . . a demonstration."

"Don't be smart with me, Paul."

And so on. Of course, my dad's opposition to her attending made my mom even more determined to go, especially given the fact that they were hosted by a group called Women Stand Up. She told us over dinner that first night that she'd stood with twelve other women, holding black hand-shaped signs, with wooden sticks protruding like skinny arms from the signs' backs and slogans emblazoned in white type across their palms. Toward the end of the vigil, a bus had passed too close, driving—intentionally, it seemed, although who could be sure—onto the curb where the women stood, and my mom had grabbed the nearest woman's arm, hard, and they had both stumbled backward into a patch of flowers. Standing amidst the broken stems and scattered petals, purple and pink and red, the two had looked at each other, surprised, and then burst into laughter. That woman was Jamila.

Over the following months, my mom and Jamila met at the weekly vigils, from which my mom would return home buzzing with stories about the men who would drive by and yell things like "Whores! Why don't you go get fucked in the ass by the Arabs if you love them so much?" She often talked about Jamila, who wore red-rimmed glasses and a short-bob haircut and elegant dress pants. My mom said that she'd only realized Jamila was an Arab once they started talking, after their laughter had died down and they had stepped out of the flower patch, and she heard Jamila's rolling *r*s punctuating her Hebrew.

After a few months, Jamila had finally insisted, in a more serious tone than usual, that it was past time that my mom came to her house for coffee. For all her left-wing political proclamations, my mom had never actually been inside an Arab village before, car mechanics and hummus restaurants situated on the outskirts notwithstanding. She dragged me, her Arabic-speaking son, along with her, pulling the planet of my life deep into the midst of your orbit, habibi. (Do I wish that she hadn't? I can't answer that.)

"I was nervous," Jamila said. "I always get nervous at the checkpoints. It's strange. Something about being stopped there makes you feel like you're guilty of some unnamed crime, like you should apologize. Then I heard this big crash—"

Jamila smacked her hand down on the coffee table. The stack of small porcelain plates and half-empty coffee cups clanked together. I jumped. Jamila noticed.

"Sorry," she said to me, "that's what I did too. Except I also screamed, a small scream, but still. I looked up at the soldier next to me, and he was laughing. His friend had slammed his hand on the back of my car, just to scare me, or to entertain himself. I'm not sure why. I looked up at him, and I wanted to say, in Hebrew, 'Titbayshu lekhem,' you should be ashamed of yourselves, but what came out of my mouth?"

The rain pattered frantically outside.

"'I'm an Israeli citizen.'" Jamila laughed, a small, sad laugh. Raed sat still, his bald head gleaming in the bright light, his hands folded over his belly. My mom and I were both silent.

"Anyway," Jamila said, "that's all. Sorry for the heavy story so early in the morning."

"Don't be sorry!" my mom said. "It sounds really terrible, what happened to you."

"Thanks, Raphaela," Jamila said, "but it wasn't so terrible. It was normal, for a lot of people. I'm just lucky I don't have to go through that every day. Anyway, how did we get there?"

"We were talking about Jonathan's excellent accent," Raed said.

By the time I stood at a checkpoint, I promised to myself, my Arabic would flow as easy as breath. And I would never bang on women's cars just to scare them. I wanted to say this out loud, but instead I said, "Badaber haali."

Jamila and Raed both laughed. I smiled. I'd just learned that phrase a few days before from Tom, the Arabic teacher at my high school in Pardes Ya'akov. Tom had spent over a decade working for the Shabak, and his Arabic seemed extraordinary to me, although I didn't have much to compare it to back then. This expression, "badaber haali," Tom said, was a slangy way of saying something along the lines of "I can take care of myself" or "I get by."

"I told you," I saw my mom mouth to Jamila in Hebrew, out of the corner of my eye.

Jamila and Raed were still laughing when two people walked into their living room, a girl and a boy, around my age or a bit older. I felt three things, in quick succession, as I looked up at them from my couch perch: jealousy, desire, and confusion.

Jealousy: I had been in the middle of basking in the compliments about my Arabic, my eyes fluttering with pleasure like those of a sun-hungry reptile the moment after clouds had cleared. I wanted to be the only young Jew in this Arab room, not to mention the fact that this young Jewish couple was clearly cooler and more beautiful than me. The girl was tall, around my height, five-ten—a meter seventy-something—and had long black hair.

Desire: She wore a bulky sweatshirt and faded jeans that hugged the curves of her long legs. Her skin was light brown, and her left eyebrow was pierced. Her irises were the color of a sidewalk after a misty summer rain, and her posture was almost straight, except for a slight tilt toward the boy who stood by her side. The tilt was nearly imperceptible, but I noticed it, the way it seeped comfort and intimacy. I noticed it because I wished, immediately, that she'd tilt like that toward me.

The boy was knobby-thin and even taller. He wore a red T-shirt, and his hair was wet, as if he'd just walked in from the downpour outside, only his clothes were dry. His chin and cheeks were covered with dark dashes of stubble, and he jutted his bottom lip out to one side and blew a stream of breath upward, as if to dry the droplets of water clinging to the edges of the mop of his hair. His posture was more slumped, but his eyes were the same light, his hair the same dark, his skin the same glow as the girl tilting toward him. They both looked so at home as they stood in the doorway. I should have put it together—they didn't *look* at home, they *were* at home—but I didn't. Instead, I thought to myself how amazing it was that I'd been back in Israel for half a year and I still couldn't get over how confident and beautiful Israelis were. The boy was smiling. The girl was not.

Confusion: What was a young Jewish couple doing here in Beit al-Asal anyway?

"Raphaela, Jonathan," Jamila said, "meet Laith and Nimreen."

"Nice to meet you!" my mom said, and then turned to Jamila. "Remind me which one is yours?"

"Both, remember?" Jamila said, her smile pushing dimples into her cheeks. "Tuwam. Twins."

You smiled with all your teeth, Laith, and did a little hand gesture near your soggy head, rotating your wrist forward, your thumb almost touching your curved forefinger, as if tipping an invisible hat. Nimreen glanced at you and then rolled her eyes, exhaling through her nostrils, a smile playing at the corners of her lips.

"Of course! Yes. Sorry! Tuwam," my mom said. "It's almost the same word for twin in Hebrew, teom."

"Ana ismi Jonathan," I said, pulling myself up from the couch, trying to surreptitiously brush wrinkles out of my shirt, which was not my best shirt, but which I hadn't worried about when my mom told me she wanted to take me to her friend Jamila's house in Beit al-Asal. My possibility-of-sex radar was generally turned on extra high, almost all the time, but we were going into an Arab village. What possibility of sex could there possibly be for me there?

"What's up, man?" you said in your marvelous, slightly accented English, pivoting toward me and reaching out a large hand. "I'm Laith."

Your smile wrapped around my chest like a cocoon.

"I'm Nimreen," said your twin sister, standing right behind your shoulder. Her English sounded completely American, as it always did except when she got upset, and then her rs would grow sharp like cactus spines.

As her hand gripped mine, I felt a shiver rush up my spinal cord and into my ears.

"Ana bahki 'arabi, shway," I said. "I speak Arabic, a bit."

Nimreen nodded. "That's nice," she said, in English.

"Ahlan wa-sahlan, dude," you said. "Welcome. Glad to meet you."

"Me too," I said.

"Laith and Nimreen both study at Haifa University," Jamila said, "which is great for me, because that way, I can embarrass them on campus regularly."

My mom laughed too loudly. She was overenthusiastic, though not usually. Usually, with my dad and with her dad and with other Jewish Israelis, she was combative and flinty, and my friends back in the States found her intimidating, a little terrifying even, and called her Robo-Mom. Only here, among the Arabs, was my mother so eager to please.

"We arrived recently," my mom said, addressing you and Nimreen, "for the year. Jonathan's in his last year of high school."

I clenched my jaw. I wasn't back for a year, for a long visit. I was back for good. Right before starting eighth grade at Everbrook Middle School, I told my parents that I wanted to move back home to Israel.

"'Back home'?" My mom snorted. "Jonathan, you haven't lived there since you were a little smush."

I glared at her. "You don't get it, obviously, *Imma.*"

I'd called her Mom growing up, rather than the Hebrew "Imma." This was her choice, the choice of a "yoredet," Hebrew for emigrant, which literally means someone who has descended, or gone down, from the land of Israel. I glanced at my dad. Maybe he'd get it. He had made "Aliyah"—had moved to Israel, had *a*scended from America—once, back then, had met an Israeli woman even, had had an Israeli child. But he had given in so easily when his wife said that it was time to go, that this place was gnawing away at her flesh, that she couldn't take it anymore. Together, as I saw it, they had robbed me, their little Yonatan, of the chance to grow up in the State of the Jewish Warriors.

"What don't I get, Jonathan?" my mom asked.

"Klum," I said, in Hebrew. "Nothing."

———

Half a decade after that conversation with my mom, we were back in Israel, albeit in an Arab village called Beit al-Asal. One point for me, as I liked to credit myself with sowing the seeds of my family's return, and one point for my mom, who had stated a few times over the years that she would only move back to that "semifascistical place" if her kids would learn Arabic. Of course, the move ultimately had less to do with either of our goals or ideologies and more to do with my grandfather's leukemia and the fact that Saba Yehuda, who almost never asked anything of anyone, had directly asked my mom, his only daughter, for a chance to get to know his grandchildren better, before.

This tie between my mom and me resulted in an uneasy truce, both sides armed and suspicious, cooperating now and then despite ourselves, like that visit to your parents' house. When my mom had invited me to come with her to one of the vigils, though, I looked at her as though she'd suggested I chop my arm off with a nail file.

"Mom, are you high?"

"Jonathan."

"What? Just checking. You did just ask me to join a women's demonstration against the IDF, in the middle of Haifa, right?"

"That's not what our vigils are about," my mom said.

"Yes it is!" Zehava, my little sister, said. She had started going with our mom to the vigils, even though she was only twelve. Now Zehava started twirling around the kitchen singing, in an operatic voice, "Free free Palestine! Free free *Palestiiiiine!*"

I looked at my mom. She shrugged.

———

There, in your parents' living room, Nimreen looked at me. I could feel her eyes scanning my face, and wondered if she could pick up on the thought storm raging behind my eyes.

"Are you going to go to university back in the US?" she asked, in English.

"Maybe," I lied, and then switched back to Arabic. "What do you study?"

"Political science," said Nimreen.

"How?" I asked, in Arabic.

"How what?" Nimreen asked.

I blushed and gave up, switching back to English. "How is it?"

"Interesting," Nimreen said. "It was helpful for me to learn how apartheid fell in South Africa."

I tensed. You snorted. Nimreen narrowed her eyes at you, but her irises were dancing like little flames behind casings of smooth-wet glass. "This dork studies biology," she said.

"Guilty as charged," you said, scratching your cheek. "If you ever need, like, some extra mitochondria, just give me a call, yeah?"

"Okay." I laughed.

"Anyway, dude," you said, "Nunu and I are going to go out with some friends tonight, in Haifa. Do you wanna come?"

My heart jumped. I did want to come.

And then my heart sank, as I remembered that I'd been invited to a party that night at Meron's house. His parents were in Eilat for the weekend, so it was just Meron, his family's dog, Booboo, and his meter-tall bong, which Meron had dubbed "President George Bubbly Bush." Everyone was going to be there, Rinat included. I could almost hear the watery murmur of the bong, almost feel the static crackle of potential collisions, between tongues and palms and slender bodies.

I looked over at Nimreen, who shrugged her shoulders. "Why not?" she said. Her hair was the color of wet nighttime, glowing in the living room light. "We can practice our English."

"Pneumonoultramicroscopicsilicovolcanoconiosis," you said, nodding somberly. "It's a miner's disease. Which you're not likely to catch in Haifa. Don't worry."

I laughed again. "I think I might have—" I started to say, and then I looked at you two, and I felt it, like a drop of pomegranate juice spreading through a glass of bright-white milk, changing everything. Do you remember, Laith, how you drank a full glass like that, on a dare from Nimreen and me, a few months later, and then you threw up for the rest of the afternoon, your skin greenish, your knobby middle finger waggling at your sister and me? I kept apologizing, in between fits of laughter, and Nimreen just smiled and told you you'd make a great scientist one day.

"Can I let you know this afternoon?" I said.

"No problem, dude," you said, and held out your hand for my phone. I placed it gently in your palm, and when you returned it, I saw that you'd typed your name with an exclamation point at the end: "Laith!"

Nimreen picked at a cuticle. Your mom suggested we all go get some baklawa.

On the fifteen-minute ride home, coffee in our bloodstreams, pistachios and honey in our bellies, your family in our minds, my mom and I drove in silence as the windshield wipers whipped back and forth at full speed, squeaking as they splashed through the curtain of rain.

"You can have the car to go to Haifa tonight if you want," my mom said, waving to the guard as we pulled into the entrance of Pardes Ya'akov, the yellow metal gate sliding open to let us in.

"Thanks, Mom," I said, grateful she hadn't made me ask.

ON THE SECOND DAY AFTER I WAS BROUGHT IN TO JAIL, Saba Yehuda came to visit me. Sitting across from him, I could almost hear the cancer sizzling just beneath his papery skin. His corneas were rheumy clouds; his irises were no longer contained and circular: like two tiny broken yolks, they seeped gelatinous into the white. He was wearing a pressed gray shirt, against which his skin looked unusually pale and faded. I was wearing the surplus Marines uniform that they'd given me at the entrance to the jail. I couldn't hold Saba Yehuda's gaze. I couldn't speak either: my tongue was latched to the bottom of my mouth, a heavy-sad slug. After a long silence, my grandfather spoke.

"Our people are an extension of our family. We don't have the luxury of standing apart, each man following his own whims."

Saba Yehuda paused, his breathing shallow. I wanted to embrace him. For him to hug me.

"Loyalty to your family is all that there is," Saba Yehuda said, his face falling downward toward the table, his warrior bones turned fragile and brittle, his voice a ship at sail in an empty sea, with no coast in sight, anywhere, at all. "Your people are your family. Remember that, Yonatan."

Then he stood up and left.

FIVE

OH, HAIFA. CITY OF GLISTERING GRIME, smog hovering over foamy sea. Of blocky apartment buildings facing the coast, topped with white water tanks crowded together like flocks of squat storks. Of palm trees and pine trees and electrical wires, twisting green and black toward the chalky beachfront and rows of factory smokestacks. The way you put it once, Laith, your voice warped to mimic a radio announcer: "Welcome to Haifa: you may die an early and also agonizing carcinogenic death, but at least you'll have a killer view from your hospital room."

There was nothing sugar-coated about this city. I adored it in all its unadorned glory. I'd been there plenty of times before. It was the closest major city to Pardes Ya'akov (and to Beit al-Asal). I'd also spent a lot of time in Haifa in my mind, wandering there through corridors of decades long extinct. Exactly seventy years before my family moved back, my grandfather, then called Yuda Sadicario, dark-skinned and yellow-green-eyed and eighteen years old, arrived at the Haifa port directly from Salonica, Greece, not knowing the first thing about being a stevedore, educated boy that he was, son of a livrero and korex, a bookseller and binder.

But fierce. Broad-shouldered. He figured he could pull off the ruse when a Haifa-based pioneer sent word to Salonica that he'd scraped permission from the British to bring over a boatload of Jewish stevedores to Palestine to work at the port. I often imagined my grandfather fumbling his way through the first days, hands aching, legs wobbly, heart pounding as he unloaded crates and barrels, bringing supplies into the soon-to-be-born state, sweating in the gritty predawn of Zion in the 1930s.

In one of the old letters that Saba Yehuda gave me before my class trip to Poland, my grandfather's older brother, Jacko, wrote to my grandfather, whom he called Ninyo, kid, in Judeoespañol—"Shalom, Ninyo, how are you? Ke haber?"—wondering if he might consider coming home, as some of the other Salonican stevedores had done after realizing that they'd be forced to work on Shabbat by the Jewish port master. It was clear from the letter that Jacko missed his younger brother. But my grandfather didn't want to return to Salonica yet. He had come to the Land of Israel for a reason.

Before too long, Yuda left the ports and tumbled into the muscular arms of the Jewish paramilitary known as the Haganah. There, given a rifle and a new sense of worth—if only he could have faced, like this, the Greek swine who burned down the Bos del Pueblo neighborhood—my grandfather Hebraicized his name, *Yehuda* Sadicario, sloughing off Salonica like a snake shedding its old skin. He rose through the ranks, became Captain Yehuda Sadicario before too long, and was eventually annexed into the elite underground strike force, the Palmach. He was involved in a famous operation to liberate the Jewish refugees who were held as prisoners in the British detention camp in Atlit, for the crime of entering the land—their land—without Her Majesty's permission. These were stories he told me often. The other stories I had to scrabble harder to unearth, fingernails chipping against history's hardened crust.

But Haifa. I grew up thinking of the word Haifa as synonymous with new beginnings, Laith. I thought about my grandfather a few times on that first evening in Haifa with you and your sister. I parked my parents' car on a slanted side street off Arlozorov at the edge of the Hadar neighborhood, where you'd texted me to meet you. I turned off the igni-tion, and both of us, the car and I, shuddered. It was cold out and I was nervous. I can't speak for the car.

Right away, I saw you and Nimreen leaning against your family's silver Toyota, just down the hill. You were both smoking, and I felt, for a moment, disastrously uncool, my best pair of jeans too baggy, my coat reading too "family camping trip." I walked down the seaward slope, trying to look nonchalant, but my knees ached from the battle against gravity, and it is very hard to walk coolly down a steep hill. I wondered if you'd feel like you made a mistake in inviting me, wondered if I'd made a mistake in coming. I thought about the bong bubbling at Meron's place, Avichai opening a beer bottle with his teeth, Rinat laughing and rolling her eyes and singing along loudly with the music, her breasts pushing against the fabric of her tight turquoise turtleneck. I'd told them I had a family thing I couldn't miss. The lie sloshed around my stomach, mixing with apprehension and regret and other assorted thoughts as I raised my hand in greeting to you and Nimreen and then put it out to shake yours. You pushed my hand aside and gave me a hug, your long arms wrapping around me, and Nimreen kissed me on the cheek. I could smell the smoke on your jacket and the raspberry chapstick on Nimreen's lips, and my anxiety dissolved and was replaced by a swell of unvarnished lust: all the more exhilarating for what I assumed was its impossibility, like a dream of being able to fly, legs pumping against the air, arms flapping. And yet, somehow.

"Kifkum?" I asked, in Arabic. "How are you?"

You both laughed, surprised maybe, to recall that this green-eyed Jewish boy from Pennsylvania actually spoke some Arabic.

"It's been so long," you said, in English. "We missed you."

It had been about eight hours since we first met, in your parents' living room.

"What my twerp brother means to say is 'Hello,'" Nimreen said.

"Hi," I said, and I thought about insisting that we speak Arabic, so I could practice, but the words caught in my throat, along with the realization that I didn't want to miss or misunderstand a single syllable that tumbled out of either of your mouths.

"Smoke?" you said, pulling three cigarettes out of your pack, even though one was still lit and dangling from the corner of your mouth, half-smoked and with a long finger of ash that remained precariously attached, until you shifted to take out your lighter and it plummeted downward toward the ground like a tiny comet, breaking apart as it passed through the atmosphere, exploding into harmless fragments against the earth.

"I don't." I shook my head, and then hurried to clarify that it wasn't anything puritanical: "Not tobacco, at least."

You laughed. "All right then."

We started walking down a long staircase, trees hanging down on either side of us, our conversation rolled out before us like a length of carpet, covering Haifa's cold pavement with a fuzzy warmth. We spoke mostly in English, with some Arabic efforts stitched in, by me, for good measure—eager to impress.

"I did it three months ago, and people think I've gone nuts," Nimreen said, responding in English to my Arabic question about her eyebrow piercing—which, in retrospect, must have sounded something like "You when make this?" "They won't say it to me directly, but I can tell some people would rather I covered my hair and started prepping for marriage."

"But your mom doesn't cover her hair either, right?"

"Yeah, no, it's not pressure from our parents, just basically everyone else in the village. And this thing"—she rolled both her eyes upward and to the left, toward the metal—"is, like, definitely a step in the wrong direction. So. Maybe I'll do my tongue next." She stuck out her tongue at imaginary interlocutors. "They think it's because of the Jews at the university, bad influence, blah blah blah, but it's definitely not. It isn't like I'm deeply in love with the Jews at the university, anyway." She paused and looked over at me. "No offense."

"None taken," I said, wondering if I could manage to be different from the Jews at the university.

Nimreen ran her index finger over the little silver hoop. "I did it because I like the way it looks. My body is my own, not the community's, you know?"

"My sister, if you haven't noticed, likes to think of herself as a 'feminist,'" you said.

"A feminist?" I said, adjusting my expression into that of a stunned possum, frozen in the headlights of this newest revelation about Nimreen.

Nimreen cocked her head, and I saw in her eyes that it took a moment for her to notice the laughter quivering behind my lips. I'd banked on that moment. She laughed then, and I soared. I'd lived with my mom too long—seventeen robust years and counting—to be afraid of the word.

"I also might probably, like, be one," I said, lowering my voice to a whisper. "Don't tell my baseball coach."

"You play baseball?" Nimreen laughed.

"I did," I said, "but I was kicked off the team for being a feminist."

"Yeah?" You looked at me. "You also don't shave your legs?"

I laughed and then stopped myself in the middle—Nimreen wasn't laughing—and felt the blood vessels dilating in my face, my cool lost once again.

"Uskut, Laith," Nimreen said. "Shut up. That's not the only kind of feminism." She brushed her black hair back behind one ear and clenched her jaw. The tiny rounded muscles bulged softly on either side of her face, as if she were chewing her annoyance. When she looked over at me, her eyes were bright again. "Anyway, do you have any tattoos or piercings, Jonathan?"

"Me?" I said, still blushing a bit, cursing my genetics, wishing my skin were darker, like Saba Yehuda's, to better hide the constant waves of emotion that displayed themselves on my face, to help me blend in better here, in the middle of the Middle East. "No. None. Do you, Laith?"

"That, my friend, is a secret," you said, and I felt a tautness in my jaw, as I imagined dark shapes on goose-pimpled skin.

"This dork?" Nimreen snorted. "What do you think?"

Her lips, covered in synthetic raspberry, pursed around her cigarette.

I shrugged and glanced down the street at another group of kids, trying to shake off the whiplash of my thoughts. They were maybe a year or two older than me, eighteen or nineteen. They were walking toward us, speaking in Hebrew, wearing jeans and winter jackets. A few of them had their coats open—the morning's rain had cleared, and it was a cold but dry night—and I saw that they were wearing T-shirts with their necks cut by hand, low-sloping, advertising sparse chest hair and thick cleavage and how deeply they didn't give a shit about material things. I generally loved that style, so Israeli, so devil-may-care, but looking at them now—after analyzing silently, as I often did, how many of the guys I could take in a fistfight (in this case, two out of the three, almost for sure)—and then back at Nimreen, who was wearing an elegant black silky shirt under her wool coat, I thought their hand-cut shirts looked goofy. I noticed that one of the guys in the group (the third out of the three, whose chest was so muscular that his pecs almost looked like breasts) had an M-16 draped over his shoulder.

The casual power of this Jewish kid, just a year or so older than myself, walking the streets of the Jewish State, holding a slender gun, his posture cocked forward, was more or less the essence of what I'd dreamed about since the incident with Joey von Ribbentrop in middle school and onward through Camp Samaria, which, I'd told myself, had sort of felt like living in a miniature Jewish State for a month. We had Jewish cooks and Jewish kids like Sy Sudfeld, well-endowed enough to be a porn star, and Jewish girls with beautiful Jewish breasts, which three of the girls, Ariella, Denise, and Melanie, flashed for me and Sy on the second-to-last night of camp, under the Jewish stars by the Jewish lake, in exchange for me and Sy kissing each other on the mouth, with tongue, which I minded far less than I pretended to, the kissing Sy part. If dinky little Camp Samaria was so full of possibility, I could barely imagine what sort of redemption lay in wait in the actual Land of Milk and Honey and Uzis and Bamba and Eucalyptus Groves and Khaki and Tragedy and Redemption.

I never fought Joey von Ribbentrop, never felt again, so directly, the need to, but throughout high school, I imagined recurrently the feeling of returning to Everbrook after completing three years of service in the IDF. Everyone would be able to tell how I'd changed, how my skin had tanned, how my body had grown hard, rippling with lean muscle. During my service, I imagined, I'd have made friends who were as close as brothers, plucked from the melting pot of multiethnic Hebrew warriors: tough Moroccans and rowdy Ashkenazi kibbutzniks and agile Ethiopian immigrants, all Jews. While some of our platoon-mates might have gone off to Bangkok or the Himalayas after our discharge, my friends would accompany me back to the United States of America, to finish my unfinished business. We'd make quick work of Joey and his friends, sending them into cowering submission simply by looking at them, and then we'd roam all around the country, searching for bona fide neo-Nazis and Klansmen and other assorted bigots. We'd wear the Star of David on silver chains around our necks, in the open, for everyone to see. Maybe we'd have tattooed the Hebrew word "chai," life, onto our battle-scarred shoulders. When we'd be confronted by the packs of roving anti-Semites, as we inevitably would be, we would beat them expertly, savagely, gracefully, and they would howl with pain and whimper in fear, fear of us: the Jewish Fighters. Once we finished in the USA, we'd fly over to Europe and repeat. We'd probably start in Greece.

Nimreen pointed to the off-duty soldier. "Check out his big metal wanker," she said, in a mock-British accent of sorts: *'is big meh-al wainkah.*

You laughed, and I laughed too, startled, and then I felt guilty, both for the way in which I was associated with him, in my fantasies and future plans, but also for the way in which I was laughing at Nimreen's joke, subtly betraying this guy and my people.

Then you spoke. "We've arrived, dudes."

Our destination was located in the middle of Masada Street, nestled between a laundromat and a faded-orange apartment building. We walked into the restaurant, Nimreen first, then me, and then you, close behind.

"Esh, ya shabab," Nimreen said, walking toward three people, seated by the window. "What's up, guys?"

She leaned down to kiss each of them on the cheek and then gestured to me, as you greeted the group with your own kisses.

"This is Jonathan," Nimreen said, in English.

"Hello, Jonathan," all three of them said, almost in unison.

I laughed and waved, both relieved and a little disappointed that it didn't seem like I was expected to go through a round of kisses myself. They introduced themselves, one by one: Amjad, Murid, Qamar, all three of them students at Haifa University as well.

I sat down to your right, and Nimreen went to sit at the other side of the table, next to the thin, dark-eyed guy who had introduced himself as Amjad. I watched him kiss Nimreen on the cheek a second time; a smile fluttered onto her face as he made some joke in Arabic that I didn't understand.

On your left was the girl who'd introduced herself as Qamar. She wore a necklace from which dangled a metal cartoon boy with spiky hair, facing backward, his hands clasped behind his stumpy back. Qamar herself had frizzy hair and fair skin and was wearing a black sweater and black jeans. She noticed me looking at her necklace, and I looked away, hoping she didn't think I was looking at her breasts, which I mostly wasn't. I could feel her gaze running over my face.

"Where are you from, Jonathan?"

"Well," I said, "Pennsylvania, basically."

"You don't have to hide it, Jonathan," Nimreen said, from across the table. "It's okay. Qamar's not going to chop your head off."

A waiter, with a ring through his septum and the sides of his hair shaved and the top puffed into a plume, brought out a tray piled high with salads, vegetables, dips, and breads.

"Qamar only does beheadings in the summertime," you said, scooping up a floret of roasted tahini-drenched cauliflower with a sliver of bread. Qamar flicked you off and you nuzzled your head into her shoulder, chewing. In the silence that followed, I was surprised to hear snippets of Hebrew skimming over the surface of the Arabic filling the room. Maybe I wasn't the only Jew in the restaurant. A "Visit Palestine" poster was plastered on the wall.

"Jonathan was born here," Nimreen said, "and his family recently moved back."

"Ana bahki 'arabi shway," I said. "I speak a little Arabic."

"Yeah?" Qamar said.

"Ya'ani," I said. "Badaber haali."

I can take care of myself.

My accent was very good, even then. I could feel heads angling around the table, analyses shifting, surprised chuckles filling the air around us.

"We're sure he's not in the Mossad?" Amjad said, laughing with his mouth, but his eyes were uncrinkled.

"We don't think so," you said, still chewing. "Although we might have to get him super high later on and see if we can extract some state secrets."

Your eyes were two fireflies, Laith, in the dimness of the restaurant. I scratched the back of my head, hard. It was true: I was not in the Mossad. Nor did I think I ever would be. But was I sure? I still hadn't filled out my manila envelope, which had arrived in the mail a few weeks earlier, and in which I was supposed to indicate my preference for what unit I'd enlist into. I was pretty sure I wanted to be a combat soldier—Paratroopers, ideally—but Tom, my ex-Shabak Arabic teacher, had told me that the rapidity with which I'd picked up Arabic showed him that I was clearly gifted enough to consider Intelligence. And how far was the leap from Intelligence to the Mossad? I didn't know.

"Are you in university?" Qamar asked.

I shook my head, blushing yet again, but this time just with the universal shame of being embarrassingly young. "No, still in high school."

"Where?"

"Pardes Ya'akov," I said.

"Cool," Qamar said.

Everyone chewed in silence for a moment. Then Qamar looked up at me, an odd expression pulled across her pale face. "So, I just have to ask: How do you feel about the fact that you're invited to move here from Pennsylvania, and your family probably got, like, government Aliyah funding, right, because you're Jewish?"

We had.

"It's not exactly like—" I started.

"While at the same time," Qamar said, "millions of people, who are actually the real owners of this land, aren't even allowed to visit? I saw you looking at my necklace earlier. The little boy is named Handala. He symbolizes the Palestinian refugees' longing to return home. He was created by a Palestinian cartoonist named Naji al-Ali, who was shot in the face and killed. Probably by the Mossad."

I opened my mouth, and then closed it, like a fish.

"Qamar," you said, in English, your tone light, wispy, "we at least need to give Jonathan a decent meal and some good pot before asking him to make up for the Nakba."

Nimreen said something to Qamar in Arabic.

"Qamar here," said the third friend, Murid, a heavy-set guy with dark skin, curly black hair, and thick-rimmed glasses, "fancies herself a Palestinian freedom fighter."

"Murid here," said Qamar, "fancies himself an Israeli."

"Well, I am an Israeli citizen. I study at an Israeli university," Murid said. "Where do you live, ya Qamar? What university do you study at?"

"I'm not from Israel. I'm from before Israel, from beneath the Israeli towns and cities built over my homes and orchards and fields. I am an Arab Palestinian, not an Israeli."

"Sure, I'm a Palestinian too," said Murid. "A Palestinian Israeli."

"Can I ask a question that might be dumb?" I cut in, wanting to keep the conversation theoretical, political, nonautobiographical. "Does anyone say 'Israeli Arabs'?"

"Oh yeah, for sure," Qamar said, "lots of people. Prime Minister Olmert, Foreign Minister Livni, Minister of Population Transfer Avigdor Lieberman . . ."

Everyone laughed. I did also, even though I wasn't sure I was invited to. No one seemed to take issue with my laughter, though, and I felt something shift in the air as I laughed along with the group. Maybe I didn't need to take everything so seriously, so heavily. Maybe I could just laugh a little more. I searched for your eyes and then for Nimreen's. You smiled at me, and Nimreen made an expression that I couldn't totally read but that seemed nonhostile.

"Not really," Murid said. "At least no one our age. No one serious. Not since the October Events."

"October of this year?" I asked.

"October 2000," Nimreen said from across the table, her voice gentle, patient, almost like a teacher's, which both grated on me and made me feel grateful, at once, "when the Israeli Police murdered thirteen 'Israeli Arabs.' Ever heard of Israeli Police shooting live bullets at Israeli Ultra Orthodox protestors or Israeli Mizrahim or Israeli Israelis period? We got the message, then. Our parents' generation's plan—integrate, keep your heads down, beg for scraps, be Good Arabs—hasn't gotten us anywhere. And anyway, whatever strategy we use to survive, our identity is Palestinian. That can't be taken from us, you know?"

I didn't know. But I nodded anyway. Later Nimreen told me that Qamar's cousin had been one of the boys killed in 2000, shot in the chest by a police sniper. Murid's father, on the other hand, was the deputy mayor of his village and was seen as being affiliated with the Israeli Labor Party.

"Anyhow," you said, "in the meantime, dearest sister, darling comrades, if we've finished our history lesson for the day, let's eat."

The main course had arrived, a huge bowl of rice and lentils and tender meat, and we ate, in relative silence, everyone lost in thought and taste. Then I decided to go for it, my chest surging with a bravery and recklessness I still cannot account for, to this day. Maybe it was my assumption we'd never see each other again, that your and Nimreen's act of interethnic charity would end after this slightly tense night out with your friends. Maybe I decided that if I was going to go out, at least I'd go out flaming. Or maybe it was an effort to reassure you and Nimreen that I was worth keeping around. Whatever it was, I took a deep breath and informed everyone that I had a joke to tell.

Five pairs of Arab eyes fell on my Jewish face.

"Go for it," you said.

"So, ahem," I said. "There was once this kid, Mike, right? And Mike went to school. On Sunday, he got back from school, after a long day, and asked his mom what was for dinner. She said to him, 'Tonight, Mike, we're having pizza.' And so Mike goes, like, 'Yeah! Pizza!'"

I said this part loudly—*Yeah! Pizzaaa!* I saw startled expressions around the table. You smiled. Nimreen looked worried. I'd started, and there was no turning back now.

"On Monday, though, Mike gets back from school and asks his mom what's for dinner. She says, 'Pizza.' So Mike goes . . ."

I looked around, allowing a pause, and then said, "Yeah! Pizza!" again, a tiny bit less loudly.

You chuckled, Laith. Qamar was staring intently at me. Murid's face was gentle. Amjad, who was sitting close to Nimreen, and who had been mostly silent during the meal, wore a poker face, showing nothing.

Tuesday, when Mike's mom told him pizza was for dinner, Mike said, "Yeah! Pizza," a bit less thrilled. By Wednesday, when Mom told him they were having pizza for dinner again, Mike was deadpan: "Yeah. Pizza."

Now there was laughter, around the table, some grumbles—Come on, where is this going? You remember this joke, right, Laith?

Thursday, when his mom announced that there would once again be pizza for dinner, Mike started to sound worried: "Yeah. Pizza?"

By this point, Amjad was drumming his fingers on the table. Murid was scratching the side of his nose, his eyes glazed and distant. But I still had you and Nimreen, listening, and Qamar too, who had started laughing.

"Friday, though . . . Friday comes around, and it's a big family meal, a Shab—" I hesitated and glanced over at you. You nodded, telling me to go on.

"A Shabbat meal. But so Mike is like, 'Mom, tonight, please tell me what we're having for dinner,' and his mom goes . . ."

Silence. I noticed with a flicker of pleasure that Murid and Amjad had started to listen again, ready for a punchline.

"His mom goes, 'Pizza.' And Mike goes, 'Yeah. Pizza . . .'" Now my Mike voice was resigned, miserable.

"Come on," Amjad said, "is this even a joke?"

Nimreen smiled at me, and my heart soared.

"Saturday night—just wait for it—Saturday night, dinner is . . ."

"Pizza?" Qamar laughed.

"You got it," I said. "Pizza. So Mike goes, 'Yeah . . . pizza . . .'"

I made Mike's voice totter on the verge of tears. I wish I had a picture, Laith, of the looks on everyone's faces.

"So, Sunday comes around, right? And Mike comes back from a very, very long day at school, and he's extremely hungry, so he asks his mom what's for dinner, and this time . . . this time, she goes, 'Pizza,' and he goes . . .

"'*Yeah! Pizzaaa!*'"

I jumped out of my seat as I yelled this part, joyous, elated, and then plumped back down into my chair, sweat on my forehead, my heart beating fast, my mouth sealed shut. I lifted my hands, a bit, to signal "end of joke." There was a moment of silence so loud I could taste it; then Nimreen looked at me and burst into laughter. Such laughter, Laith. Startlingly loud, inelegant, perfect. A moment later, Qamar started laughing too, and the two of them were infected by each other's laughter. You laughed too, Laith, a little less wildly, but fully, from your chest. Amjad scowled. Murid smiled confusedly.

"I don't get it," he said. "What is different about Sunday?"

"Yalla guys," you said, "with pizza on our mind, let's finish up here and go smoke a jay or four. Who's in? J?"

You looked at me, and I nodded, realizing that you had just given me a nickname. That meant a disproportionate amount to me, Laith, then and later.

"Wa-intu?" you said, in Arabic. "And y'all?"

Qamar, at the tail end of her laughing fit, raised her thin hand. Murid sighed dramatically, and raised his hand also. Nimreen, still laughing, did a tiny flutter with her fingers, and Amjad lifted his own left hand with his right hand, and then looked at his left hand, suspended in the air, and made an expression to indicate that he was shocked to see it there.

We got the bill, and I reached for my wallet, but you snatched it out of my hand.

"Uh-uh," you said, "we're not in Kansas anymore."

I'd been so unprepared for a reference like that that I started to say, "Pennsyl—" but then cut myself off.

You tossed my wallet across the table, to Nimreen, who shook her head and pulled a two-hundred shekel bill out of her purse, placing it firmly on the table, and then tossed my wallet back to me.

"Come on, Jonathan," Nimreen said, smiling at me and meeting my eyes. "You're our guest."

I said thanks too many times, which I worried might diminish for you how overflowingly grateful I truly felt, Laith. Afterward, I stopped in the men's bathroom, and as I peed, I noticed some hand-scribbled graffiti, in English: "JONATHAN FUCKED ME IN THE ASS HERE THANK YOU HAIFA." I blinked hard to make sure I was actually seeing what I was seeing. Below it, someone else had written: "JONATHAN DIDNT FUCK ME BUT HAIFA IS STILL THE BEST." I shook my head and put my hands under the dryer, which you'd later tell me you called "the machine that prepares you to wipe your hands on your jeans."

Then I rejoined the group, and all six of us walked back up the steep slope, to where you'd parked your car.

"Let's all drive together," you said, and your eyes were so hopeful that no one had the heart to mention that we were all parked a few meters away and there were too many of us to fit. We piled into your family's Toyota. You drove, Laith, and Amjad sat up front, and Murid got in on the back left side of the car. Qamar went in after him, from the right, and

I noticed, with more than a little surprise, her small hand lacing its way between his pudgy fingers. Then Nimreen got in and gestured for me to squeeze in next to her. I could feel heat radiating through her jeans, the softness of her thigh pressed against mine. I didn't look at her, didn't breathe, we didn't buckle our seat belts, and you drove like a maniac, but I didn't want the car ride to end.

We arrived at the beach, and Nimreen put her hand on my shoulder and stage-whispered something silly about your driving, and I laughed and said that Jewish drivers, at least, were a bit more moderate, and Nimreen grinned and pushed me and called me a racist, and I said I might be, when it comes to driving, but at least I was a feminist racist. Then I noticed Amjad looking at me: his chest was a bit puffed up, his eyes were narrowed. I almost mistook his expression as having nationalistic undertones, but then I saw his eyes flit over to Nimreen.

Nothing else happened that night. We smoked, laughed, talked a bit, in a mixture of Arabic and English, and you gave an impromptu lecture about jellyfish, and we all stared at the stars, smoked another joint, got cold, decided it was time to go. You and Nimreen drove us all back to where we'd parked and dropped me off at my car last.

"Let's do this again next Friday," you said.

I laughed, not sure if you were kidding or not. "It's a date," I said, and only then did I realize how deeply I hoped that you were not.

Nimreen was smiling with just her lips, no teeth; her eyes were bloodshot and beautiful. She brushed a strand of hair behind her ear and looked at me. "Maybe pizza?"

I started my car and was startled to remember that I actually knew where I was going, that this was the same Haifa I'd been to so many times before. Because as the night went on, in the restaurant where most people spoke in Arabic, on the beach with you all, I'd started to feel that I was in a different place altogether. I didn't have a name for that place then. Today, Laith, I might have called it Haifa, Palestine.

I drove home, feeling a little too high, a little too alive, a little too aroused, a little too filled with contradicting pulls to be contained in my own skin. Driving down Zion's coast, along the Palestinian shoreline, my tongue tingled with all the potential gloriousness. I didn't think, that night, about all the possible disasters.

SIX

THAT MORNING, THE MORNING OF JULY 25TH, our pulses pounded in our wrists and necks like the frantic beat of an ancient war drum. I could almost hear the adrenaline surging around us, filling the mo'adon, the base's clubroom. It was almost beautiful. I don't think you'd be able to see that, Laith, and I cling fiercely now, to that "almost." But the line between mesmerizing and horrifying is so slender. Our whole platoon, thirty-six of us in total, was packed into the mo'adon, heat slithering around us, the early morning sun glinting off the TV in the corner, behind the Commander, our heads craning forward, trying to absorb the Commander's words not only through our ears but through our pores. Some of the guys were seated on chairs and the twin aquamarine couches, which had been donated to our unit by Marilynn and Maurice Adelman, via the Manhattan-based NGO Lions of the IDF. I was seated between Tal and Gadi, cross-legged on the floor.

"Today, you're going to put down a riot," the Commander said. His eyes were gray, his hair was nearly black and buzzed short, his cheeks were shaved smooth. He must have been about twenty-one or twenty-two, but to me he looked ageless: a demigod dressed in olive green. I listened as hard as I could, all the nerves in my body straining toward him.

"This is what you've been training for," he said.

A swell, a surge, a rush, my chest, my arms, my eyes.

"I'm sure you've all heard about the attack in Jerusalem," he said.

We nodded. Of course we had. Three days earlier, on July 22nd: a Palestinian man driving a bulldozer, King David Street. The severed leg, the injured infant, tiny beauty mashed by metal. We'd heard. There had been a similar attack a few weeks earlier: Jaffa Street, bus flipped, pedestrian bodies crushed by weight and speed. And in March, the shooting rampage in the Jerusalem yeshiva, the slaughter, the blood on the books, on the ground, in the hallways.

"Everything is connected," the Commander said. "You're out here to make sure more attacks like those don't happen in Jerusalem and Tel Aviv."

The room was silent. No one even coughed or snuffled. We were barely breathing.

"Anyway, practically speaking"—he cleared his throat, *huh-hem*, and even his dislodging of phlegm and spittle seemed elegant—"it seems like there will be a few smolanim, a few leftists, joining, so we'll keep the means of dispersal simple. Those of you who've been trained with the tear-gas launchers: this is your show."

Meaning me.

This was my show. Mine and Eviad's. We were the two guys in our platoon whose guns were fixed with the launchers. But we'd barely trained with tear gas. Mostly we'd thought of our weapons' launchers as being for grenades: we had trained for war with the enemy. You don't use tear gas to take down squads of militants, to neutralize terrorist cadres. No one had really talked to us about putting down riots in crumbly villages in the southern West Bank. I vaguely remembered a protocol about shooting the canisters into the air, in an arc, like teenaged duck hunters, idealistic Israeli Elmer Fudds. My mouth felt filled with fur and earth.

"The rest of you, stun grenades, arrests if necessary, and holding the line. No rubber bullets, this time, unless I say otherwise. Like I said, we'll keep it simple for the smolanim."

You'd think that that sort of comment would have snapped me out of my trance, Laith. When the Commander said "smolanim," leftists, and specified the "keep it simple" protocol, we all understood he meant leftist Jews. Arabs don't get to be left-wing or right-wing. They are just Arabs, acting and reacting Arabicly. Arabian riots, Arabesque unrest.

But it didn't, Laith. My focus on the Commander's instructions was unbreakable, was only broken a moment later, when a voice from behind me cut in: "What if it gets violent?"

I could tell immediately that it was Yotam, slender, wispy, heartbreaking, with pimples all over his pointy nose. Poor Yotam.

"It won't, most likely," said the Commander. "Not when the smolanim are there. Usually our cousins reserve their best behavior for when their Jewish friends aren't looking."

"But what if it does?" Yotam asked. His voice was strained. A few vicious giggles cropped up from the crowd.

"If it does," the Commander said, "keep your heads on straight. I'll tell you what to do. The Border Police will be there to back us up. Those guys know what they're doing."

Laughter from the crowd: everyone knew the Border Police's reputation as "the ones who get their hands dirty." I laughed too.

"What if they're armed?" Yotam wouldn't stop. Shut up, Yotam, I thought, we all have questions. We're being told what we need to know.

"Who, the Border Police?" the Commander said.

I turned around in time to see Yotam recoil, as if struck. He realized he was being mocked by the Commander. I tried to feel compassionate, but all I could think was that he'd brought it on himself.

"No," Yotam said, his voice barely louder than a whisper. "The Arabs. The rioters."

"They won't be," the Commander said, "not with hot weapons, at least. That's not how these kinds of demonstrations go. These are fallachim, peasants."

I could tell that my trance was broken by the fact that I was tempted to correct his pronunciation of the Arabic word: falla*h*. No *ch* sound. Obviously, I refrained from doing so, rolled my tense shoulders backward, twisted my head in a long circle, and refocused on the front of the room.

"Our goal is to set up a line and to prevent the rioters from passing that line, from getting within five hundred meters of Kerem El. You'll be fine. You've trained for this. Clear?"

"Yes, Commander!" I yelled, along with everyone else, almost back in the zone. The Commander said, "Clear?" and I barked yes. We all did. The Commander said stomp, we'd stomp; run, we ran; shout, we shouted; move, we moved. There was something disturbing about it, Laith, for sure, on a zoomed-out, macro level: yes, we were like robots, like machines, but no one ever talks about how incredibly fucking comforting it is to be a machine. Finally, since becoming a Paratrooper, I was freed from the postpubescent agony of having to decide everything on my own. Finally, there was someone—something—to help me discern between right and wrong, good and bad. Like God, only real.

"Clear?" the Commander said again.

"Yes, Commander!"

As we stood up, I noticed a squat, ugly, dark-feathered bird perched on the outside of the window. I imagined cutting its neck, letting its life pour out of its throat like syrup from a jar, pulling its feathers out one by one, dousing it in fire, tasting its stringy, bittersweet muscles melting along my molars.

SEVEN

WE DID SEE EACH OTHER THE NEXT FRIDAY, Laith, and the Friday after that, and the one after that, until it became like a quasireligious ritual that none of us wanted to desecrate. Almost every Friday for the next eight months. These Fridays with you and Nimreen became the highlight of my weeks, surpassing even the late evenings with Avichai and Rinat and the others, where our conversations focused more and more around our upcoming draft dates. The IDF was the golden calf around which we worshipped, glimmering in the darkness of the late high school nights. Don't get me wrong: I bowed and supplicated and debated beret colors and the relative prestige of different commando units with as much husky-breathed fervor as the rest of my friends, and I felt alive and exhilarated as I did so, but there was still something special about the Fridays with you and your sister.

I kept our Fridays—and my friendship with the two of you—secret from my other friends for a long time; it was months until you even met them. Maybe my secretiveness was precautionary, and I was open-eyed enough to foresee the ways in which ugliness could arise. Or maybe I tricked myself into believing that if I kept the worlds separate, then I'd never have to choose between the two. I walked on a tightrope—inventing stories to explain my absences, obfuscating, scuttling into occultation for a few or many hours each weekend—wobbling from the beauty of Pardes Ya'akov and all that we'd built to the remnants of al-Birwa and all that we'd covered up. From them to you, Laith, and to Nimreen. It wasn't all opposites, of course: it was also a walk from the quiver of potential sex toward the quiver of potential sex; from bong rips to joint puffs; from Haifa to Haifa; from curtains of rain to curtains of rain, falling on neighboring pavement-coddled swaths of this land. Maybe I hoped that if I stepped right, mindful not to breathe too hard, then I could stay welcome in both worlds forever, Yonatan the Border Crosser, Jonathan the Brave. I forgot to take the winds into account, habibi, and I forgot to take myself into account.

On those Fridays with you and Nimreen, I laughed constantly. We explored what felt like the entire Galilee, smoked, all in all, at least a kilogram of marijuana. A few times, we went back to Beit al-Asal, to your family's house, like the day I helped your grandfather slaughter the pigeon and you took that absurd cell phone picture of me holding the dead creature. You and Nimreen couldn't stop laughing all afternoon, kept showing each other the picture again and again, until I actually got upset and you noticed and finally stopped. Once, we had lunch at my family's place in Pardes Ya'akov, but my mom was exhaustingly enthusiastic the whole time, and I decided too much was too much. Usually we just wandered. We had so much fun during our wanderings and took care of each other, for the most part, even when we did stupid shit. Remember the hitchhike back from Ein Tzvi?

It was almost summertime by then. I was on the verge of finishing high school, felt poised on the brink of freedom itself, although in many ways, the opposite was true. You and Nimreen were just about to enter your first final exam periods at the university. Nimreen was the one who suggested we go down south to Ein Tzvi, a little oasis town on the edge of the Dead Sea. "It's beautiful there," she said, "desolate and lush and super fucking far away. Let's get out of the North, yeah? Do something different for once?"

You and I went along with her plan happily, Laith, like we always did. She was the visionary; all we had to do was obey. We weren't able to borrow either family car, so we decided to take what you dubbed "a disgustingly early bus" down from Haifa to Jerusalem, and to switch to the Ein Tzvi line in the Central Station there. You and Nimreen both slept on the first bus, Nimreen's head falling on my shoulder. I stopped moving and breathing each time it did, as though a butterfly had just alighted on me and if I breathed, it would depart. Inevitably, I would eventually cough or breathe or squirm, ever so slightly, and Nimreen, still sleeping, would shift her head back to her own headrest. You were snoring, Laith, and eventually I dozed off too. On the second bus, you took the right window seat, about two-thirds of the way back, and I sat next to you. Nimreen sat alone across the aisle, leaning her back against the opposite window, her feet up on the empty second seat.

"Don't tell me," I said, stretching, trying to meet Nimreen's eyes, hidden beneath her big sunglasses, "Ein Tzvi was probably called, like, Ein Salam, and you're going to enlighten me about the disaster that befell the people there, at the hands of the Jewish brutes."

"You're getting good, Jonathan!" Nimreen said. "It actually was called 'Aiyn Safa, and Bedouin were living there before they were expelled."

I clamped my teeth down on my bottom lip. I'd been mostly kidding.

"But don't worry," you said, to my right, "my sister's not going to recite any poetry about eating flesh this time."

"I don't need to," Nimreen said. "It seems like we're well on our way to making *Yonatan* here into an honorary Palestinian himself."

I didn't say anything but sank into my seat and wished I had a window to stare out of. I thought about how my friends or Saba Yehuda would react if they heard Nimreen say that, and worse, if they knew how part of me was elated that she had, felt complimented, validated. Another part of me, of course, felt strange and bad. I wasn't a Palestinian, and I didn't actually want to become one.

"Can we not do politics today?" I said, after a long moment.

Nimreen might have rolled her eyes. I wasn't sure though, because of her sunglasses; it could have just been a glimmer of sunlight bouncing off the lenses. She was wearing a tank top, and her shoulders were bare and smooth. She reached up with her left hand to brush her hair back, and I saw, for a moment, the faintest shadow of returning hair in her armpit. I imagined the sensations and tastes under my tongue: prickly, sour, sandpaper, salt. I didn't actually want to become a Palestinian, but I thought then, on the bus, that I might have been ready to convert, to trade my birthright not for a bowl of lentils on a hot afternoon, but for a chance to kiss the sweat and stubble beneath your sister's arm in the heat of the morning sun. My conversion wouldn't be from Jewish to Muslim, of course, because that would never have been asked of me—you and Nimreen both inherited your sociologist mother's Communistic views on religion. Just a conversion to Palestinian. I'd have considered it, Laith, in that moment, if your sister had been serious when she asked.

"Everything is politics, habibi," Nimreen said.

"Even swimming?" you chimed in.

"Even swimming," Nimreen said, now smiling. "You know, Arafat and Abu Jihad once went swimming together."

You were the only one who could get Nimreen to pivot like that. I was jealous, Laith, and also grateful.

We spent a long time on buses, that morning, but there was not even a hint of boredom in the stale air around our heads. We always had something to talk about, or some game that you'd make up for us to play. Remember, on the ride from Jerusalem, how we dubbed a conversation going on at the front of the bus, between the hirsute man wearing an Israel Police T-shirt and a comb-over and the two blond women in floral, ankle-length, spaghetti-strap dresses? We couldn't hear what they were saying, so you suggested we fill in the blanks.

"So, well, say, Svetlana, Cynthia," you said.

I laughed. "Cynthia?"

"Uskut," you told me to be quiet, laughing too. You continued: "Have you ever considered the benefits of . . . laptop computers?"

"Vy no, Morrison," Nimreen said in a high-pitched Russian accent. "I have never considered this. I spend most of my time . . . birdvatching, and so have very little time to consider such things as laptop computers."

At the front of the bus, one of the two blond women laughed half-heartedly at something the man said. You and Nimreen looked over at me, expectant.

"I, um, ahem." I cleared my throat, and made my Svetlana voice as deep as I could. "I don't believe in computers. Like my granddaughter Cynthia always says . . ."

You and Nimreen both giggled; the women at the front of the bus were both clearly in their midtwenties. Encouraged, I continued, my voice still a low baritone, "Like my granddaughter Cynthia always says about laptop computers . . . 'Abraham Lincoln.'"

It was a ridiculous ending, I know, and I could have come up with something better, but it didn't matter by that point. The three of us screamed with laughter, breathless. One of the blond women, the one I'd decided was Cynthia, turned around to look for the source of sudden noise, scanning the length of the almost-empty bus until finding us, the three young hooligans in the back. We all laughed even harder.

"Abraham Lincoln!" you said, between breaths. "You are too weird, J."

The first thing we did when we arrived in Ein Tzvi was to swim at the pool. I had to use every ounce of my willpower to look away from Nimreen, dizzying on the verge of vertiginous in her black bikini, with a line of paler skin barely visible, but visible, a few centimeters above where her nipples pressed against the fabric, the white shells of her anklet glowing against the brown skin of her legs. We then walked around the botanical garden, which was filled with trees that looked as though they'd been plucked straight out of a Dr. Seuss book, with silly names like royal poinciana and baobab, and an erotic-sounding one called the blossoming adenium. I always found plants to be a little bit boring, but we had so much fun there too: all any one of us needed to say was "Abraham Lincoln" and the three of us would be sent into a fit of uncontrollable laughter. We had lunch in the dining hall, eating schnitzels and cucumbers and low-quality hummus, speaking in Arabic. I savored the askance glances we got from the other diners. We ended up chatting with the guy clearing tables—your initiative, of course, Nimreen and I both being a little shy around strangers—who turned out to be a refugee from Darfur named Ahmad, and who was stunned when Nimreen told him I was Jewish and spoke Arabic like I did.

"Yahudi yahudi, ya'ani? Like, Jewish Jewish?"

"Lil-assif." I laughed. "Sorrowfully so."

"Why sorrowfully?" Ahmad said, smiling. "Kul al-ihtiram ilak. All the respect to you."

He shook my hand with his hardened palm and then moved on to clear another table.

"All the respect to you," you said, looking at me, "Abraham Lincoln."

I choke-laughed and the chocolate milk I was drinking came out of my nose and it was awful and painful and perfect and I hoped that Ahmad wouldn't think we were laughing at him. I got up to get a few napkins, to wipe my face and the table so that Ahmad wouldn't have to. I washed off in the sink, grabbed a whole handful of paper towels from the dispenser, by the bathroom, and then looked back. I saw the two of you sitting there, across from each other, mirror images, you shaggy, Nimreen elegant, both of you tall and thin and beautiful. My heart filled so full that I actually skipped back toward the two of you.

"Jonathan." Nimreen laughed. "What kind of hidden treasure did you discover among the napkins?"

"Let's go hiking," I said.

"Hiking?" You rolled your eyes. "Your Zionist indoctrination, I see, has still not left you, J. You know, that's the major problem with you Jews: your obsession with hiking."

"Come on," I said, "let's climb that little mountain—" I squinted my eyes and pointed out the window toward one of the reddish rocky cliffs jutting upward into the sky. "Right there."

"Okay," Nimreen said.

"Yahoo!" I skipped around the table. "Abraham Lincoln!"

———

The walk was exhausting. It was well after noon and so hot out, and we barely made it a third of the way up before you stopped, lit a cigarette, and suggested we go back to the pool.

Nimreen glared at you, took your cigarette from between your fingers, and threw it down the side of the mountain.

"Come on, Nunu," you said, "I was eating that."

I watched as the little orange ember tumbled at the end of the white stick, and cringed as I thought of forest fires, but there were barely any shrubs even, out here, it was all baldness and hardness, and the ember extinguished, and nothing caught on fire that day, or maybe everything did and we just didn't notice. Thirty minutes later, we were back in the pool, floating and splashing and laughing.

And then I remembered. "Oh fuck, you guys!"

"What?" you both said, at once, your four identical eyes trained on my face.

I didn't answer but instead swam over, quickly, to where the lifeguard was seated.

"Tagid, achi," I said, in Hebrew. "Tell me, bro, when is the last bus?"

The lifeguard, red-tanned and muscular and wearing fancy sunglasses, laughed. "The last bus? Three thirty."

"Oh. What time is it now?"

"Four twenty-three," he said.

"Fuck."

"It's all right," he said, "you should just hitchhike. It's cool. Everyone does. There aren't really any Arabs down here, nothing to worry about, bro."

I was glad that you and Nimreen were out of earshot, didn't hear my silence, my obsequious "Thank you, bro," the splash of shame as I dunked underwater and swam back toward you.

"What was that about?" Nimreen said. "Were you reporting two Arabs spotted lurking in the shallow end?"

"It is true we don't swim so well," you said.

"No reports," I said, pushing my hair off my forehead and to the side, in a motion I'd picked up from you over the past months. "We just missed the last bus, because of Shabbat."

"Fuck," Nimreen said.

"Oh God of Moses and Ben Gurion," you said, raising your hands above your head and looking skyward, "we are but two lowly gentiles, who know nothing of your ways. Spare us! Give us a bus home! And we'll sacrifice this one, out of gratitude."

"The lifeguard said that we should hitchhike," I said.

"Hitchhike?" Nimreen said, furrowing her eyebrows, the piercing catching a glint of sun refracted off the blue chlorine clearness of the water. "Mm-hm. Are you all right, Jonathan? Sunstroke, maybe?" She placed her hands on either side of my face and peered exaggeratedly into my eyes, and I wanted her hands never to leave, wanted her lips to move just a few centimeters forward. Instead, I laughed and squiggled out of her grip.

"What?" I said. "It's fine. It'll be an adventure."

You shook your head. "If we get chopped up into little pieces . . ."

"Then I'll make sure to collect all of them and put them back together. Come on, guys, what are you so worried about? Relax!"

You and Nimreen exchanged a look, one of those looks, one of your looks.

"It doesn't work like that, Jonathan. We don't hitchhike," Nimreen said. "This is not a safe country for us like it is for you."

"What?" I said. "Come on. That's what everyone says to Jews too, like, 'Don't hitchhike because you might get picked up and murdered by an Arab.' Anyway, I'm with you. I'll protect you!"

I flexed my biceps and made a scowling face, and then leapt into your arms, Laith, and you almost didn't catch me, but then you did, and held me like a baby, supported by the buoyancy of the water, and I felt the heat of your chest, rising and falling with laughter, and Nimreen laughed too, and it was agreed that we'd try, because fuck it, so we put our clothes on and trudged down the hill, toward the crystal shimmering blue of the Dead Sea and the bus stop across the street from where we'd been dropped off, and within thirty seconds, a black jeep appeared down the road, and I stuck out my thumb and ignored your eyes and the car slowed and then stopped.

I ran forward.

The passenger window rolled down, and I saw a very pretty woman smiling at me from the shotgun seat. She had dark eyes and heavy eyelashes and looked to be in her early twenties.

"Where to?"

"Well," I said, "around Haifa, but even—"

"You're in luck," she said. "We're heading to Akko. Hop in!"

Past her, holding the wheel, was a dark-skinned guy. I glanced at him and noticed that he had a small kippah on his head.

"Will you, uh, make it before Shabbat?" I asked.

"That's the plan," the guy said, smiling with all his teeth. He must have been about my age, maybe a year older. He was wearing a sleeveless shirt, and his arms were thin and covered with dark helices of hair. "Hop in."

"You have room for three?" I said.

"Of course!" the woman said.

"Come on," I said, in English, to you and Nimreen. I noticed now that both your faces looked strained, but there was nothing to be done at this point, right? We needed to get home, and these two were clearly not the type to chop us up into pieces.

Nimreen walked slowly around to the other side of the car and got in behind the driver. I slid into the middle, and you got in on my right. I liked feeling each of your thighs pressed against mine, but I could also sense the subterranean discomfort radiating from your bodies.

We started moving, and the woman introduced herself, in Hebrew, as Yael.

"And this is my brother, Shimon."

"Nice to meet you," I said quickly, skipping past the stage where we might say our names, eyeing Shimon's kippah a little warily, as if it were a creature that might lunge at us. I knew that this wasn't fair: my own father wore a kippah sometimes, and he was nothing but gentle. But still. You and Nimreen didn't say anything.

"What were you doing down here?" I asked.

"Hang gliding," Shimon said.

"Wow!" I said. "First time?"

"Yep, f-f-first time," Shimon said.

"Oh, fantastic," I said, not looking to my left or to my right. "And how was it?"

"Amazing!" Yael said. "It was like being connected to two giant birds."

"That sounds awesome."

"What are your—" Yael started.

"Do you live in Akko?" I cut her off.

"Shimon just moved there," Yael said. "I'm spending Shabbat with him. We're actually from Givat Avinu."

I swallowed. Givat Avinu, as in the Israeli settlement of Givat Avinu in the West Bank. Speaking of which, I realized that as Yael had said that, we had just crossed over the checkpoint, into the West Bank, from the South. On the way down to Ein Tzvi, which is on the Israeli side of the border, the bus from Jerusalem had glided through the West Bank, as was its route, but none of us mentioned it: somehow, being on a bus made us feel removed from the world around us. It had its path, and we could either join or not. Now, though, the crossing felt different.

"Oh, uh, what are you doing in Akko, Shimon?" I said, changing the subject again.

"I'm studying at the Yeshivat Hesder," Shimon said.

"What's that?" I asked.

"It's the Jewish military yeshiva in the middle of an Arab neighborhood that is trying to turn Akka into a place for Jews only," a fourth voice joined in, in Hebrew, low and familiar: Nimreen. The air in the car froze like dry ice, fragile and chemically strange.

Yael twisted around in her seat, and words began to pour out of her mouth. "Oh, wow, you, uh, you speak Hebrew? I thought you were tourists . . . I heard . . . Weren't you speaking English earlier?"

"I'm originally from the US," I said quickly, glancing over to Nimreen, trying to speak to her with my eyes, without words, the way the two of you always did, but she wouldn't return my gaze. I looked over to you, to ask for help, but your eyes were focused on something else also. Your eyes were exactly your sister's eyes, in that moment.

"We speak Hebrew," you said, your voice soft, your *r*s rolling like the hills on the Jordanian side of the Dead Sea. *Medabrrrim ivrrrit.*

"Where are you f-f-f-from?" Shimon asked.

I peered over his shoulder at the speedometer. We'd hit 140 kph. I didn't know what that was in miles per hour exactly, but it felt a little fast.

"Us?" Nimreen said, her voice too calm, which I recognized, by this point, as a sign that she was angry. Akka was to Akko as al-Birwa was to Ahihud, except that Arabs still lived in Akko/Akka. And this Yeshivat Hesder was implanted there, according to Nimreen, to make that not the case. Shimon and Yael didn't contradict her. I couldn't blame her for what she said next, but still I cringed, thinking, *Nimreen, there's so much left for us to live for*, thinking, *Nimreen, I adore you*, thinking, *Nimreen, let's move to Akka, teach our babies Arabic and Hebrew and English and Espanyol, for good measure*, thinking, *Nimreen, we're doomed.*

"We're from Falasteen," Nimreen said.

Yael laughed. Maybe she thought Nimreen was kidding. Shimon didn't laugh.

150 kph.

"Are you Ar-ar-ar-ar-ar—?" I looked at his eyes in the mirror, big and brown and shiny. He looked afraid. "Are you Ar-ar-arabs?"

"I'm Jewish," I said, my voice as gentle as I could make it.

"I wish I'd had a bar mitzvah," you said, chuckling as if nothing were amiss.

We were now going 160 kph down this thin ribbon of road.

"We are definitely Arabs," Nimreen said, "very much so. Is there a problem with that?"

"No," Yael said, "it's okay. Not a problem at all. We love all people."

"I think it-it-it-it-it is a prob-prob-prob-prob . . ." Shimon's stutter had grown heavier; he sounded like he was on the brink of tears. I felt a strange urge to climb up into the front seat and kiss both his eyelids.

165 kph.

The car had started shaking.

"I think it is a prob-prob-prob—"

"It's cool, my friend," you said, your voice steady. "Everything is cool."

170 kph.

"I promise you everything is cool," you said, and even I felt calmer, hearing your voice, Laith. "I promise."

Then there was a squeal of brakes, and the car wobbled and skidded and eventually pulled to a stop on the side of the road. There was a heavy silence in the cabin. I thought, for a moment, that Shimon might pull out a weapon and execute us, all three of us, right there, and the headlines would read, "Arab Brother, Arab Sister, Arab-Lover Found Dead in West Bank Desert." Sad, but not too sad.

He didn't move, though. It was as if he were frozen. A statue, but one from which pain and confusion emanated like static from an old radio.

"G-g-g-g—" he tried.

We were quiet.

"G-g-g-g-g—" he said. He was near tears.

He tried one more time: "G-g-get out of my c-c-c—"

"Here?" I said. "But where—"

"It's okay," Nimreen said, in Hebrew. "We wanted to get out here anyway. In fact, this was exactly where we'd hoped to go. Really, thanks so much."

"I'm sorry," Yael said. She sounded like she was on the verge of tears also. "It's just . . ."

You tugged your large frame out of the right side of the car, humming to yourself. I climbed out after you, quickly, just as Nimreen slammed the other door. I tried to close my door gently, but the Jeep sped off down the road, and I barely had a chance to shut it, and we were left standing there, in a patch of dust and scratchy bushes, our small backpacks in hand, stunned.

"Fuck you!" Nimreen yelled, in English, after the car. "I hope you fucking crash!"

I didn't. I didn't hope they'd crash. I hoped that they'd turn around and say that they were sorry and take us to Haifa, and that we'd have such a nice drive together that sweet, skinny Shimon would convince the others in his yeshiva that bigotry was not the way toward spiritual enlightenment after all. They didn't turn around. The sun was starting to set.

"Well, that went well," you said. I glanced over at you, an apology balanced on my lips, but when I looked at your face, I saw that your eyes were smiling. You winked at me. "Abraham Lincoln there was quite a driver."

Nimreen looked at you, paused for a moment, and then burst out laughing. I laughed too.

"Well, fuck," I said, "so maybe we'll find another hitchhike?"

"You're kidding, right, J?" you said. "Jokes aside, we got lucky there."

"Oh, come on," I said, "they weren't going to kill us."

"If he'd crashed that car, going four million kilometers per hour, it would have been a suicide-murder," you said. "What's the difference between that and blowing yourself up on a bus?"

I didn't say anything.

"Remember, Jonathan," Nimreen said, "you lose a bunch of your Jewish privileges when you're with us, especially out here."

"Where are we exactly, by the way?" I asked.

You both shrugged. Neither of you spent a lot of time in the southern West Bank, or in the West Bank at all, except for the occasional shopping trip with your family. I'd asked you once, a few months before, what Ramallah was like, and you both admitted to me, a little sheepishly, that you'd never been.

"Palestinians from 'forty-eight," Nimreen had said, referring to the Palestinians who had remained in Israel in 1948, after the Nakba and the War of Independence, and become citizens of the state, like your family, "don't always have the simplest relationship with Palestinians from the West Bank. They don't totally get us. They think that we're, like, soft and overprivileged, working and going to university with the Jews and stuff. They don't realize that we are living under an occupation of our own, really right in the heart of the occupation."

"And that you never hang out with Jews," I shot back, glaring and grinning at once.

I looked over to Nimreen now, as she stepped out toward the road to flag down a car. I started to ask her what she was doing but then noticed that the car had white license plates, with green numbers. Not an Israeli car: a West Bank Palestinian car. My breath caught in my chest as the car slowed. I looked at the driver, who had a gray mustache and was wearing a faded keffiyeh around his neck, and at his passenger, who was fat and tired-looking and dark-skinned. I could see the two men staring at the three of us, their expressions wary. They kept driving, slowing down without coming to a full stop and then accelerating quickly.

"Nimreen," I said, after the car had passed, "I thought we said we're not going to hitchhike."

"Do you want to stay here all night?" Nimreen said.

I didn't say anything, and she started to lift her hand to wave at the next passing car, but then lowered it as she noticed the yellow—Israeli—plates. A third car passed, a moment later, white plates. It had three men in it. Nimreen lowered her hand, but a moment too late.

The car stopped, the windows rolled down, and two bearded heads gazed out the front window; one more, clean-shaven, peered out the back-right window. Most of the eyes were focused on Nimreen. She looked downward and adjusted her tank top. One of the men whistled, shrilly, and licked his chapped lips, his tongue emerging small and pink beneath the sharp spikes of his mustache. You moved fluidly, steadily, to stand by her side.

"Salam aleikum," you said, and I saw surprise flash across the men's faces and realized that they'd assumed we were all Jews.

The man in the passenger seat said something in an accent that I couldn't decipher, and you said something back, quickly, and I picked up the word "Amrika."

One of the men looked at me, and I could feel his gaze pouring over me like sludge. He grinned wolfishly.

"Al-mawt l'Amrika."

Death to America.

His companions laughed, and this car sped off too.

You put one of your hands on my shoulder and the other on Nimreen's for a moment, and then took them off. The next car that passed was a Palestinian taxi, which you flagged down.

"Can you take us to Haifa?" you said, in Arabic.

"Sorry, brother," the driver said, shaking his head morosely. "I can't get inside. I can take you to the checkpoint, though."

"How much?" you said.

"Two hundred shekels."

"Two hundred!" You laughed. "We're in the middle of the desert, but we're not crazy. One hundred."

"One hundred and fifty," the driver said.

"Okay," I butted in, in Arabic. "One hundred and fifty."

You and the driver both looked at me, driver surprised, you irritated, and I looked downward so as not to have to hold either of your gazes. I was ready to go home. You sighed and ducked into the car, and Nimreen and I climbed in after you, all three of us squeezed together, once again. We rode in silence for what seemed like an eternity, passing hills and valleys and glimmering red-roofed settlements and small Palestinian villages nestled together, topped with black water tanks. Then we arrived at the checkpoint. Each of us put in fifty and thanked the driver and asked

God to give him prosperity. He returned the formality and then drove away quickly.

"So that's it, right?" I said, as we stepped out of the taxi. "There are racist idiots on my side, and scary creeps on your side. If only there were more people like the three of us, people who had each other's backs, maybe then things would be better here."

"Mm-mm," Nimreen said. "That's wrong, Jonathan."

"What? Why? Are you saying that those guys in the car would have given me a big hug if you'd told them I was an Israeli? Why did you say I was American then?"

"That's not what I'm saying. What I'm saying is . . ."

We walked into the checkpoint area, and Nimreen's voice faded. All three of us were quiet. I'd never been inside a checkpoint before. Everything was clanging metal and crackling loudspeakers, cold bars and corrugated tin. The smell of congealed urine and trash invaded our nostrils. But there wasn't a long line, probably because it was a Friday afternoon.

The soldier behind the glass said, in Arabic, "Permits."

"We're Israelis," I said, in Hebrew.

He looked up at me, startled, and then over at you and Nimreen.

I looked at you two also. You both looked tired.

"What are you doing here?" he said, in Hebrew.

None of us answered for a moment.

"Visiting," I said, and we handed him our ID cards.

"Late, and . . . Narmeen," he read, inaccurately. "Can you come with me please?"

I thought of Darwish.

Record, you are both Arabs, and together your identity card number is 100,000.

I moved to follow you two, but the soldier waved me off and snorted, "Not you." He glanced down at my ID card, a smirk on his lips. "*Yonatan.* You can go on through."

I should have followed you, but he spoke so authoritatively, and I was never good at disobeying orders.

You were gone for fifteen minutes, maybe twenty. When you finally came out, I was holding three sodas that I'd bought from the vending machine on the Israeli side and was pacing back and forth, chewing my lip, fraying, on the verge of frantic.

"What happened? What did he want? What did he ask you?"

You just shook your head slowly, your hair flopping from side to side.

"What I was saying earlier, Jonathan," Nimreen said, "was that, sure, maybe there are people on 'both sides' who suck—and yeah, fuck all those guys from earlier—but you guys have the checkpoints and F-16s and M-16s and Q-16s and whatever and . . . and the Most Moral Army in the Universe, which just so happens to be controlling and destroying the lives of fucking millions of people." She paused. "So no, Jonathan, it's not just about whether the Jews are more gentle or the Arabs are more righteous."

I didn't say anything. I was too tired and deflated to think, let alone to speak. I held the sodas toward you, placating, offering, hoping.

"Don't look so worried, habibi," you said, taking two of the sweating cans from my hands, handing one to your sister and opening the other one yourself. "You were half right also. We do have each other's backs."

You took a sip, and I could hear the saccharine liquid crackle and hiss as it collided with your tongue. You swallowed your sip and then smiled at me. "At least there's that, J. At least there's that."

AFTER MY TRUNCATED VISIT WITH MY GRANDFATHER, I returned to the holding room, so crammed with smoke that the air had turned a light shade of blue, and sat down. One of the other prisoners tapped my knee. I shifted my leg away from him, thinking he was trying to tell me I was in his space, but he tapped it again. I looked up at his face.

"What are you in for, man?" he asked. The prisoner had mucus in his voice, grease in his hair.

I couldn't tell him the truth. I'm still trying to figure out how to tell you the truth, how to tell myself. I was too tired to cower, though, so I lied in a way that felt, for a moment, anesthetic.

"We're doing fucked up shit that I don't want to be a part of anymore," I said.

"What do you mean, 'fucked up shit'? Like to the Arabs?"

"No, to the Chinese," I said. Now I knew myself as someone to be feared.

"Are you some kind of Arab-lover or something?" he said, his eyes bulging like those of an insect.

"Are you some kind of fascist or something?" I said. My lie had gelatinized in my mind, enough that I almost believed, for a moment, that this, all this, was just about politics, Laith.

He stood up. I stood up too. I could taste his sour cream breath in my mouth. A commander strode toward us, his hands splayed at his sides. "What's going on here?"

"Nothing, Commander," I said. "Me and him were just about to kiss, is all."

Laughter surged all around us and the Commander snarled at everyone to shut up.

A few minutes later, seated across the room from the other prisoner, I started to grow afraid of how he'd respond to the humiliation, what he'd do when the Commander looked away. I snapped my fingers until he looked up at me.

"What are you in for?" I asked.

He stared at me, his eyes unblinking. "Arikut," he said. "AWOL."

I wanted to laugh, Laith, or to say something smart or brave, but instead I just stared at the space behind his head, my two eyeballs sagging heavy in their sockets.

Al-Kalf

EIGHT

THE FIRST TIME WITH NIMREEN WAS IN THE EARLY SUMMER, the same night when the three of us sat on the beach, lapping up the salty air and sharing a joint and listing synonyms for love. "Al-Kalf," Nimreen said, staring at me.

"Al-Jouah," you said, humming tonelessly along with the rhythm of the sea.

Three-quarters of the way through the joint, which was supposed to be the first of many, Nimreen looked at me again and then stuck the embery end into the sand, like she was jabbing a tiny stake into the earth, and the joint, deprived of oxygen and surrounded by minuscule rock fragments, gasped for air and then fizzled out. Nimreen stood up and brushed sand off the back of her blue-jeaned thighs.

"Yalla, boys, I have to go study."

"There was still something left to smoke there, Nunu," you said, looking mournfully at the ground and then up at your sister. "And you have to go already?"

"Yes, Laith," Nimreen said, "some of us actually have to look over the material before finals."

"I do look over my material," you said, "every month or so. Check it out: tibia." You pointed to Nimreen's leg. Nimreen swatted your hand away, and you let the swat carry your hand in an arc upward and then rapped on my head with your knuckles. "Cranium."

I laughed. I was freed from finals. I'd graduated from high school three days before, and it felt significant, as if all of us were finally on the same plane, three adults on our own intersecting paths. You and I stood up too, dusted the sand off our bodies, slipped our shoes back on, and walked toward the parking lot, where we said goodbye. I hugged you, long and tight as usual, and then hugged Nimreen. Her hug was brief and chummy, none of the lingering embraces we'd grown into over the past months. I climbed into my parents' car in a haze of dull panic, trying to think of what I might have done wrong, but I couldn't. When she'd translated al-Kalf as "exaggerated love," I thought that she was looking at me, but maybe I was wrong. Maybe she'd been looking at the coastline behind me. I turned the car on with my jaw clenched tight, my mind racing in paranoid circles, made worse by the whispers of marijuana still dancing on my tongue.

I'd been driving for six minutes when I got the text message.

I looked at the front of my flip phone and saw Nimreen's name in tiny green letters. I opened it.

[Nimreen]: Come back.

22:56.

I stared at the phone, and then my car swerved dangerously toward the side of the road. Luckily, I was going tremendously slowly. You once told me about a study that found that people who drove drunk usually sped but that people who drove after smoking marijuana generally drove slower than the speed limit. I don't know where you found all these weird studies, Laith, and I don't know if this one was true for all people, but it was definitely true for me. I steadied the wheel, scrolled for Nimreen's name, and called.

"What?" Nimreen picked up almost immediately.

"Everything okay?" I said, trying to catch my breath, steady my hands, straighten the car out, straighten my thoughts out.

"Yes, you idiot. Are you coming back or what?"

I laughed, and felt like I might cry also, and did a wildly illegal U-turn, and then hit the gas and saw the speedometer kissing 150 kilometers per hour: al-Kalf. I pulled into the parking lot on the outskirts of the dorms and ran up to the guard booth.

"Ahlan, gever," I said, thickening my voice and my r sound and my slang as I addressed the Ethiopian guard with long eyelashes and tired eyes. "Hey, man. I forgot something and am just running up to the dorms . . ."

He glanced at me, at my light skin and green eyes and button-down shirt, and nodded me through, and the metal detector beeped because I had left the keys in my pocket, but when I looked back at him, he just shrugged, and on that night, I didn't have time to feel guilty about my privilege.

I bounded up the stairs, two, three at a time, and then stood for a moment, trying to catch my breath and slow my heart, sweat prickling on the back of my neck. Then I knocked. Nimreen didn't say anything when she opened the door. Her dorm was filled with a dim orange light, seeping from the reading lamp lit by her bed. The wall was covered in posters: there was Bob Dylan, grinning in one corner; another one had a silhouette of Jerusalem and said "Visit Palestine" across the bottom. It was almost the same as the one that had been on the wall of the restaurant on Masada Street, except that on Nimreen's, an image of the Separation Wall mostly obscured the view of the Old City. But I didn't spend too much time thinking about the posters that night.

Nimreen was barefoot, wearing the same jeans she'd had on at the beach, and a threadbare white T-shirt with the sleeves cut off. She wasn't wearing a bra, and I could see the echoes of her dark nipples through the fabric. Her face was lit up, flushed, familiar but different also. Her eyes were unblinking as they scanned my face. After an infinite moment, she reached for the collar of my shirt and pulled me toward her. I wrapped my arms around her waist, feeling the warm softness of the skin of her lower back. We kissed, with our mouths closed, and then our tongues pushed forward, anxious and hungry.

"Finally," she said, leaning back and taking a deep breath, taking one hand off my chest and moving it behind her back. She pulled the elastic band out of her hair and the room filled with the smell of her shampoo, mixed with the salty beach air still clinging to both our bodies.

I inhaled deeply, my nostrils trying to store away some of the scent for later. She peeled my arms off her waist and took a small step backward, and I stood there, trying to steady my breath. She crossed her arms over her torso, grabbed a corner of her shirt with each hand, and then lifted it up over her head. It caught on her hair, and she laughed, and so did I, and then she freed the shirt and dropped it in a pile on the floor, and stood like that for a few moments, her arms by her side, the light casting shadows on her skin, diagonal slants dividing pale from dark, her hair pouring over her shoulders, her breasts bare and soft and glowing.

(Blossoming.)

"Stop staring and get over here, you idiot," she said.

"Okay," I said.

"Wait," she said, and I froze, awaiting new orders. "Take your shirt off."

I complied, fumbling with my buttons, flexing my stomach muscles as hard as I could, blessing the push-ups and sit-ups and long-distance runs I'd been doing all year, in preparation. Not in preparation for this, of course. I couldn't have predicted that I'd be standing here—in Nimreen's dorm room, the air filled with dried salt and shampoo residue, the wall plastered with posters about Palestine—when I started the regimen in the early fall, just after moving back to Israel. The preparation then, of course, was for my draft date. I felt the thought stab into my trachea like I'd swallowed an opened safety pin and I looked down at the ground, stuck on the last button. After a moment, I looked back up at Nimreen. She had noticed something on my face, like she always did, and her eyebrows knitted toward each other, her ring catching a bead of light, like it always did.

"You okay?"

I nodded, "I think so. You?"

She nodded.

"Come here, Jonathan," she said.

I dropped my shirt to the floor and moved toward her.

"Nimreen—" I said, but she put her fingers over my lips.

"Uskut," she said, and I obeyed.

Then our chests touched, glowing hot, surging desperate, colliding. I'll never have words for that moment; it was as short and staticky as a flash of heat lightning over an empty field, in a rainless summer sky. We tried to stretch the moment over the whole night, over the whole world, palms kneading flesh like holy dough. Nimreen's nails dug into my back, and her breasts reached for me, nipples puffed up and gentle, pushing forward through the tangled curtain of her blackbird hair. I shimmied my body downward and brought my mouth around her breasts, one and then the other, and she hummed and grabbed two handfuls of my hair and pulled my head up, hard, and stared into my eyes, and I stared into hers, and there was wetness in both of ours, and the room was filled with smoke and cinder that we couldn't see or smell or taste. We didn't put any clothes back on or take anything else off, and we never succeeded in resuscitating that moment that night, but we tried pretty goddamn hard, and kissed until our lips were exhausted and our jaws sore, and then kissed some more and shared a cigarette and a delicious cup of lukewarm water from the tap in the bathroom sink, and we looked out at the black night tinted with morning gray, and then I buttoned my shirt and Nimreen pulled a hoodie over her bare torso, and as soon as we were dressed again, we both became shy, and we hugged goodbye. I slept in my car for two hours, to maintain the "sleeping over at Avichai's" alibi I'd texted my parents, and then awoke when the sun punched me awake, nauseated from exhaustion, confused by the tastes and textures bouncing around the edges of my mouth. Before I could turn the key in the ignition, a single racking sob surged from some depth in my chest. Then I snuffed my snot inward, wiped my eyes with the back of my hand, let out a laugh, which came out more like an animal's bark and frightened me, but I didn't linger too much, just adjusted the mirror and drove.

NINE

EVIAD, TAL, GADI, AND I ALL HUDDLED NEAR EACH OTHER as we set up on Friday, July 25th, early, before the demonstration began. I noticed that Eviad was eyeing the launcher fixed to his gun, and I wondered if he was also trying to remember exactly what the fuck we were supposed to do. I knew neither of us was going to risk looking stupid by asking the Commander. We wouldn't even ask each other. Gadi drummed his fingers on his Trijicon scope. Tal smoked softly. It was so hot out. Saline rivers snaked down from beneath the metal mushroom of my helmet. Thirst and dust knit the beginnings of a web around my tongue. I was uncomfortable and jittery, but I also felt sharpened, and alert, and unalone. And excited, if I'm being honest. If I'm trying to tell you something like the truth. I took a pair of binoculars from Eviad and watched as the first bus pulled up to the outskirts of Suswan. Its passengers were mostly skinny twenty-somethings, many of them dressed in black T-shirts and cargo pants. Some had dyed hair.

Next to me, Eviad spit on the ground. "If there's anything I can't stand, Yonatan, it's leftists."

I put the binoculars down and looked at him.

"Not leftists like you, bro. Leftists like these guys. Traitors, really. I mean, I can actually understand the Arabs, in a way. We're at war. I even have a certain amount of respect for them, standing up for their people. But Jews who come out to support the Arabs against other Jews? That makes me sick."

I didn't say anything, but as I looked out into the crowd, I could feel my stomach twisting, and I wondered if maybe I knew what Eviad meant.

"At the same time," Tal chimed in, "I sort of get why Jews would join the protests."

As soon as he said that, I felt a surge of jealousy. It was my job to be the most tolerant. Tal had one-upped me, even though I hadn't spoken.

"Are you kidding, Tal?" Gadi said. He'd been unusually silent this morning, his trademark class-clown antics dulled, pocketed away.

"No, I mean, I'm not justifying it or anything, but, like, these people have the right to protest if they think something isn't fair, right? And so why shouldn't people from Tel Aviv join them?"

"America, do you agree with Saddam's nonsense?" Gadi said, taking the binoculars from me and peering again at the group, his mouth curved downward.

I shrugged and mumbled, "Probably."

"Right," Eviad said. "Let's see how you feel when they start calling us Nazis." He spit again, shooting saliva between his teeth with a *tsst* sound.

None of us spoke for a few minutes, each of us lost in our own thoughts, our shoulders gently brushing against each other's, our hands sporadically leaving the smoothness of our weapons to run up and down each other's napes, or to take a sip from our water bottles, trying to blunt the desert thirst.

Another bus pulled up. Its human content was mostly young, red-shirted, keffiyeh-draped protestors. Arabs? I wondered. Or Germans and Austrians?

Or Jews?

I remember once, during the one week in which everything still seemed possible, I put on Nimreen's keffiyeh, in her dorm room. She laughed and said, "Take that off immediately, Lawrence."

"Lawrence?"

"Of Arabia, Jonathan. Give me that." She pulled at the front of the scarf, and I let my body move along with the inertia of her tug, until our faces were close enough that I could feel her laughter on my lips, and her eyes were sparkling and her teeth were reflecting the overhead light and her eyebrow was glowing and her body was made out of heat and I didn't want to take the scarf off or to move at all. I wanted to stay like that forever.

The Commander called for everyone to gather for a final briefing.

"Like I said," he said, standing tall and jagged in the already brutal sunlight. "We hold the line here, and no one gets within five hundred meters of Kerem El. Clear?"

"Yes, Commander!"

"Tear gas on my order. Rubber bullets only if I say so. Clear?"

"Yes, Commander!"

We fell into formation, quickly, fluidly, gracefully. We were a barrier of hardness, an impenetrable row of force. Across the desertscape, the crowds from the buses had begun mingling in between the shacks of Suswan. Through the binoculars' lenses, I could see a man stepping up onto a rock. He began to speak into a megaphone, in choppy Hebrew. He was wearing a purple shirt, and I couldn't tell for sure, but I was confident it was the same man from before.

"You are welcome in Suswan." His voice echoed in the bullhorn: *Suswan . . . wan . . . wan.* "Thank you for coming to support us today (*day, day*). As you know, the apartheid Zionist government wants to destroy our village. My name is Mustafa Mohammad al-Suswani. I have lived here since I was born. My father too. His father too. But now the Zionists tell us we need to leave our homes (*homes, homes*)? So they can give our land to settlers? Build another colony? But we will not leave (*leave, leave*). We will die before we leave. Thank you (*you, you*)."

There was sporadic clapping, and then drumbeats started. *Dum dum dah-dah dum dum dum dah-dah.* I scanned the crowd until I found their source: a group of shaggy-haired drummers in T-shirts. One was holding a cowbell. Mustafa al-Suswani's bullhorned voice crackled over the thumps and thuds emanating from the drummers' circle:

"We will march toward Suswan's lands, which were stolen by the Kerem El colony."

His bullhorn clicked off, and there was a pocket of swollen silence. Then the crowd began to advance, walking through the empty landscape, toward us, nothing in their way but some shrubs and stones. After a moment, some of them started chanting responsively after Mustafa al-Suswani, in Arabic:

"Ali ali ali sawt, ili bi'yasrach mish ha-yamut!"

Raise raise raise your voice, whoever shouts will not die.

Which didn't totally make sense to me. The meaning of the next one, in English, was clear enough: "From the river to the sea, Palestine will soon be free!"

Eviad was on my left, Tal on my right, close enough that I could hear both of them breathing. I spit onto the ground in front of me. I was stretched thin over the drying rack of history. I was nowhere but present. The crowd was moving closer. One of the Druze Border Police officers spoke into a megaphone, in Arabic-accented Hebrew: "Stop. This is an illegal march. If you do not turn around, we will have no choice but to disperse you forcefully."

His voice was calm. Laconic, even. He repeated himself in Arabic. The crowd did not stop moving forward, a slow-motion, horizontal human avalanche. At the front of the crowd were the Palestinians from Suswan and some of the red-shirted protestors and a few of the black-shirted protestors as well.

"Listen up." The Commander's voice cut clearly into the growing noise. "Hold the line. No one gets through."

It felt like a game of red rover, my team facing off against a crowd with at least ten times as many people. Only they weren't chanting about who they wanted to send over but about freeing Palestine from the Jews. And I was holding a gun. A new chant started.

"Hurriyeh, hurriyeh, ikhlikna n'eesh bil-hurriyeh."

Freedom, freedom, we were created to live in freedom.

By the time the crowd got within about fifty meters from us, it began to waver, human pieces breaking off and falling back like some amoebic being crumbling into particles. I nudged Eviad, who looked over at me.

"We haven't done anything," I said, "and they're already scattering." Eviad nodded.

A smaller, tighter group kept walking forward.

Thirty meters away from us. The chants grew louder.

"B'rooh, b'dam, nafdiq ya filisteen."

In spirit, in blood, we will sacrifice for you, Palestine.

"Stop, now. Stop, now," the Border Police officer repeated lackadaisically. He didn't sound stressed at all, but I could feel the tension surging in the air around us. Or maybe it was just in my own head. I touched my finger to the trigger, stroking its perfect metallic curvature.

Ten meters away.

I found myself gasping for air. I'd forgotten to breathe for some moments. *Breathe, Yonatan. It's cool. Everything is cool. I promise you. Just breathe.*

Then the Commander was standing next to Eviad and me, his voice soft and steady as it pierced our eardrums, entered our hearts, trickled down into our forefingers:

"Ten l'hem," he said. "Give it to them."

And like that, the tension snapped, like a rubber band stretched until it finally broke. Eviad aimed his gun into the air. I did the same. On my left side I heard the recoil as Eviad shot his canister into the sky. A moment later I shot too, and the echo reverberated through my body. Eviad shot again. Some of the Border Police officers shot as well.

The tear gas canisters *fffpp*ed upward and I could see them whirling through the cloudless sky like black metal birds. Then, a moment later, they came crashing down into the middle of the crowd, releasing clouds of noxious smoke into the desert air. The wind was blowing toward Suswan, away from us, but after a few moments, even I could taste the echo of the gas's spice, and it felt like tiny pins were poking at the bottom of my eyes. People in the crowd started bellowing and screaming, running in every direction, aimless, crazed. They looked like frightened animals.

And then, from one of the clusters in the crowd, where a group of young men had covered their faces with keffiyehs, it came, ripping through the air, toward us. It landed on the hood of one of the jeeps behind me, and the sound of stone crashing on metal reverberated around us.

Another one flew a few meters over Gadi's head, and I saw him duck, next to the jeep, his face melting into a frightened, childish expression. I looked over at Eviad, standing next to me, his face placid, his hands steady.

"Sons of bitches," Eviad said, loud enough for just me to hear, and shot another tear gas canister into the sky.

Another rock, small, sharp, singular, came at us from the cluster of men, obscured by smoke clouds and dust.

"Aiiy!"

I looked over, and saw Yotam—poor little pimply Yotam—reach his hand up to the side of his face. Red surged between his splayed fingers, glistening in the bright sunlight. Tal rushed over toward him and ushered him back behind the Wolf, parked next to the jeeps.

"All right, everyone." The Commander spoke loudly, his voice steady. "Hold position. Let's give them a few stun grenades and more tear gas, soldiers. Clear?"

"Yes, Commander!" came the reply, and I tried to shout along, but my voice was lost somewhere in my chest.

Then there was an explosion. Were they attacking us with hot weapons after all? It took me a moment to realize that it was a stun grenade, one of ours.

"Get it together, Jonathan," I whispered. Fear crackled in my nostrils.

"Tear gas, let's go, let's go! Ten l'hem!" the Commander yelled. "Give it to them!"

My weapon was hot in my hands, burning into my hands, my hands felt so soft, so fragile. Eviad was breathing hard now, next to me. Another rock came sailing toward us and I ducked and everything was salt and sweat and my tongue was immobilized and I was soaking and I couldn't see right with the sting in my eyes and I couldn't breathe right with the dust in my nostrils and the spit clogging my throat and I wanted to push them back, I wanted to make them go back into the shacks of Suswan, I didn't want to have my face opened up and made sticky and syrupy red and wet from a shard of sharpened stone, and I didn't want to be here anymore, and then there was a cracking sound, metal slicing through the desert air.

Three minutes later, I was lying flat on my back, next to Tal's reddish boot, next to flecks of my own vomit, seeping into the cracked earth. I looked over to the side and saw that there were beetles and bugs all over the ground near Tal's boot: A flint-gray one, frozen in place, with a bulbous body and whisker legs. Another was balanced on a dry weed, its black head gleaming like the polished tip of a tiny dress shoe. A third was bright red, minuscule, like a speck of blood, running in harried circles, around, around, around. All these beetles and bugs on this little sliver of land, and I hadn't even noticed. I turned away from them and looked up at the huge blue sky.

Laith, what a big sky.

TEN

WE DIDN'T HAVE A PERFECT RECORD: you were gone on one of the Fridays, maybe studying or out with other friends. I assumed you didn't know yet about what had happened between me and Nimreen. She was wearing her huge sunglasses, and with her long limbs, she looked like a praying mantis, striding through the streets of Beit al-Asal, green Doritos bags and yellow Pesek Zman chocolate wrappers bumping by us like Technicolor tumbleweeds in the early-summer wind. I told her that.

"You're too weird, Jonathan. I think I should be offended. I'm a walrus, I'm a praying mantis . . ."

"You're beautiful," I said. My chest felt like a crumpled juice package, sucked clean of sweetened fluids and air bubbles.

She stopped walking and turned to look at me. I couldn't see her eyes, only two miniature reflections of myself, puffy-haired, squinting in the sun.

"Jonathan," Nimreen said.

"What? It's fine. No one here speaks any English."

"Everyone here speaks some English, you colonialist."

I laughed.

"FinemaybebutnoonespeakswellenoughtounderstandmewhenItalk-fastlikethisandtellyouhowbeautifulIthinkyouare."

"Huh?" Nimreen said. "Sorry. I just wasn't able to understand you. I think you said something about how you'd like to drive a fast car?"

"Yep," I said, "I would. I've always dreamed of driving a Toyota Camry."

"Careful, now, Jonathan," Nimreen said. "If you insult my family's car, I'll have to have you killed. My brother, Laith, he is a very scary man."

The only silliness in our conversation that morning was my Hollywood platitude, "You're beautiful"; the rest was the fluent language of our late-teenage love. It was glistering and burnished, but it was also precarious, I knew, we both knew. The second after our lips met that night in Nimreen's dorm, the whole world took on a new flimsiness. This made each word taste sweeter, each syllable stuffed with the knowledge of how easily it could all collapse, burying our thin pretty bodies alive.

I would have felt more at ease if you were there, that afternoon. I knew it was strange for Nimreen to be walking around, outside, in Beit al-Asal, with me, alone. I imagined the rumors: *The girl with the mutilated eyebrow and the uncovered hair walking alone with an* Ajnabi, *a foreign man.* And of course, gossipy suspicions of lasciviousness weren't wrong; if they flared their nostrils enough, I was sure they could smell the smoky crackle of the exposed wires strung in the air between your sister and me. At least we were speaking English, rather than Hebrew. *The girl with the mutilated eyebrow and the uncovered hair walking alone with a* Yahudi, *a Jew.* I wondered, though, if they looked hard enough, could they see that I was one and was almost eighteen? Almost an eighteen-year-old Jew in the State of Israel. Tryouts for the Paratroopers in late July.

It was already June, by then, Laith, and we'd managed to never speak of it, not even once. That was the beauty and the danger of our Fridays: they were islands, filled with palm trees and clear water and drugs and fantasies, stripped of context. We could talk about anything we wanted, but we didn't have to talk about anything either. It felt like it was up to us to create the borders of our shared reality. Only, of course, it wasn't.

———

Nimreen and I had both taken Friday morning buses to get to the movie theater in Haifa, had met alone, in the cavelike darkness, and sat keeping our eyes fixed on the screen—an upsetting American movie in which Justin Timberlake kidnaps and murders his rival's younger brother—our fingers threaded so tightly that sweat squelched audibly between them each time one of us would shift. It hurt, after a while, keeping my hand in the same position for so long, but there was no chance in the universe I was going to remove mine from hers. After the movie, Nimreen suggested we take a bus back to your family's house, in Beit al-Asal. "Friday afternoon maqlubeh, dude."

"Are you sure it's okay for us to walk through the village together?" I asked Nimreen, as we stepped out of the theater, each of us wiping our hands on the back of our jeans. Nimreen's eyes narrowed. "You don't need to protect me, Jonathan."

"No, yeah, I know," I said, "but still."

"'But still'?"

Nimreen shook her head and punched me in the shoulder, hard.

———

At lunch with your parents, I insisted that we speak Arabic the whole time. I had a hard time looking at your father, his big face an unreadable mask, seemingly even more than usual. I wondered if your mother's talkativeness and huge smiles meant something. My Arabic was faltering and shy. I was grateful to be able to focus on the language. I barely looked at Nimreen, but I could feel her pulsing next to me, her heat, like a fire lit in the middle of a hot day, making the sticky-thick air seem cool and barren by comparison. You were somewhere else still; you missed a great lunch, the maqlubeh, especially: the chicken tender and rich, the pine nuts moist and chewy, the rice fluffy and perfect. Why weren't you there, Laith?

"You haven't met my grandmother yet," Nimreen said, after lunch. It was not a question. It was also the first time she addressed me directly during the whole meal.

"No," I said, "right. I haven't. I'd like to."

I thought I saw a shadow of a look cross over your father's face.

"Yalla, let's go," Nimreen said.

"Now?"

"Yes."

"Jamila, Raed, thank you for the meal," I said, in Arabic. "It was delifioush."

"Delicious," Nimreen corrected.

I blushed. "Delicious."

"Saha wa-'afiya," your mother said, smiling. "To your health and well-being."

Nimreen and I got up from the table.

"Have some coffee," your father said, in Hebrew, and I started to sit back down.

"It's okay, yaba," Nimreen said. "We'll drink with sidti."

"You okay?" I asked, as we walked next to each other, a good amount of space between us, across the courtyard that separated your parents' house from your grandparents'.

"Mm-hm," Nimreen said. "Super."

I wanted to ask her more, but we'd already arrived.

"Sit down," Nimreen said to me, gesturing to a white plastic chair. I sat, and she went inside. Through the thin walls, I heard her speaking, softly, in Arabic, and I couldn't quite make out the words. A moment later, your grandmother came out. She was wearing a plain blue thobe, with long sleeves. A white hijab rested loosely on her head; her white hair was visible at the front, combed into a part. What I really noticed, though, was her face, Laith, how her wrinkles spread like a delicate spiderweb, how her eyes were so dark, in the scattered shade of the fig tree outside her house, that their irises looked to be almost black, as if her eyes were only gaping black pupils and yellow-white corneas.

"Salam aleikum," I said, standing up. I hesitated, keeping my hand close to my side, ready to extend it if called for, ready to submerge it in my pocket without excessive awkwardness if not.

"Wa-aleikum a-salam wa-rahmat Allah wa-birkatuhu," your grandmother said. "May peace be upon you, and God's mercy and his blessings."

She put her hand out. I took it in mine, and it was bony and flaky and warm. In that moment, I glanced over at Nimreen, who was smiling, her eyes focused on your grandmother, and I wondered if maybe I'd get to hold her hand when she was bony and flaky and warm like this. If maybe, if maybe, if maybe. We'd name our kids Amir and Sara, neutral names, names that could work in both, could be both. Our grandkids would have new names, names no one has heard of yet. We'd live in a little house in Akka-Akko, under a fig tree, and read poetry and drink coffee in the evenings. Maybe we'd even make love, still, every once in a while, our familiar bodies disintegrating toward the end, but it would be beautiful, because we'd be disintegrating together. And you'd be close by, of course, Laith, laughing all the time.

"This is Jonathan." Nimreen's voice cut through my reverie, in Arabic. I allowed myself to imagine that the tenderness in her voice was at least partly due to her saying my name. "A friend of Laith's and mine, from America."

A friend from America.

"Ahlan wa-sahlan," your grandmother said. "Ahlan wa-sahlan fii falasteen."

Welcome to Palestine.

I thanked her, and we sat down.

Then she put her hands on the chair's plastic arms and began to hoist herself upward again, and I heard her say something about "qahua," coffee.

"It's okay, sidti," Nimreen said. "I'll make it."

Nimreen stood lithely and walked into your grandmother's home. I heard the hiss of gas, the scrape of matches, the *tfff* of a flame igniting.

"Ahlan wa-sahlan fii falasteen," your grandmother said again.

She looked at me, her eyes unblinking. Nimreen would be a few minutes, I knew; the water needed to boil, then the coffee added, then more boiling, then the cardamom, then still more boiling. She wasn't making the instant Nescafé my mom drank in the mornings. I tried to think of something to say.

"Have you always lived in Beit al-Asal?" I asked, in Arabic.

Your grandmother looked at me, a vacant look in her eyes, and then she shook her head violently, as if jolted from her silence. "Always in Beit al-Asal? No, no, no, no . . ."

She was quiet for a moment. I was quiet also. I knew better than to try to fill that silence; I could sense a story beginning to boil inside her, alongside the coffee being prepared by her granddaughter, inside her home. The story was ready before the coffee was. You've probably heard all this before, Laith, a thousand times, but I want to tell you again. That afternoon, I was trying to listen for Nimreen's sake, which became harder and harder as the story went on. I'm trying to recall this story, now, for my own sake.

———

Your grandmother Selsabeel Ziad was eighteen years old when she married. Her new husband, Marwan al-Shiltawi, was a very thin man, nineteen years old with large, dark eyes and an already-thick mustache. He was from Kufr Qanut, by way of another village, called Shilta. Kufr Qanut was far away from Beit al-Asal but had become home to a shepherd named Musa al-Shiltawi, a dear friend of Selsabeel's father, your great-grandfather Ahmad Ziad. Ahmad Ziad and Musa al-Shiltawi had fought together in a makeshift brigade, against the Zionists, eight years before, in 1948. Both had been reluctant to fight; both were peaceful men. But once they heard what had happened in Deir Yassin, where the Jews had lined the villagers up in the streets before slaughtering them like animals, and then, a few months later, in Lydda, where the Jews had massacred frightened refugees huddled in a mosque, they realized that they had no choice. Each man took hold of a rifle. To steel their hearts, they would imagine their beautiful families, lined up against a wall.

But they were untrained and barely armed, compared to the Zionist forces, and most of Musa's and Ahmad's comrades' bodies fell lead-ridden and limp along the plains of central Palestine. The Jews crashed forward like a wave. Musa's tiny village, Shilta, was subsumed and destroyed. Most of the villagers were expelled into Gaza, but Musa's family managed to escape the forced march into exile and found refuge with distant relatives in Kufr Qanut. Ahmad Ziad's village, Beit al-Asal, was spared thanks to the intervention of a Druze leader who had pledged allegiance to the Jews but who remembered fondly the evenings in which he would sit for coffee with his Muslim neighbors in Beit al-Asal, before.

Your grandmother spoke in an even tone, slow, measured, choosing her words carefully. I don't remember each word, but I remember the meanings, thanks to your sister, who brought the coffee out and sat down next to me, so quietly that I almost didn't notice her, until she leaned close to me and began murmuring in English, translating any word or phrase she thought I might not know. I thought then about how her tongue had snaked into my eardrum as we pushed into each other in the orange light of her dorm room, and I wanted the feeling of her breath in my ear to stay there forever. My desire contrasted, at first, uncomfortably with the words of your grandmother's story, and I tried to rein it in, to listen as well as I could. Later in the story, when I found a way to weave my desire into its threads: that was when everything began to crumble.

Selsabeel was only a girl then, in 1948, just ten years old, but she remembered noticing the cold eyes of the Jews as they patrolled Beit al-Asal, their rifles heavy and sharp like the tusks of some frightening beast. They had let Beit al-Asal remain but had taken two boys, Selsabeel's cousins, Ghassan and Mahmoud, off into the olive groves. The younger of the two, fourteen-year-old Mahmoud, had spoken back to a Zionist soldier who was roughly ushering the women and children and elderly men into the center of the village. The soldier, a tall man with dark bags under his strangely colored eyes, had barked something in a tongue that sounded both almost familiar and utterly foreign to Selsabeel, and two other soldiers had started punching Mahmoud in his rib cage. Ghassan, fifteen, had run to help his brother. A swarm of soldiers had descended upon the boys then. Selsabeel remembered the sounds: the thud of their rifle butts driving dully into the two boys' lean bodies, the cries of their mother, the thick silence of the rest. And the sounds, also, that followed, when the two boys, semiconscious, were dragged out to the olive grove:

———

"*Tff.*

Tff.

Like small bursts of thunder echoing over a distant hilltop."

———

The Jews returned alone from the olive groves, their eyes even harder than before. Selsabeel looked away as Mahmoud and Ghassan's mother collapsed into a pile of wretched screams that Selsabeel wished she could unhear. Some of the other women kneeled to the ground with her, their bodies flanking hers. Everyone else was silent. The boys' bodies were never found, even later, when the villagers went to look, once the siege had been lifted, once the fighting had stopped, once Baba had returned home, gaunt and sad like he never had been before, once the Zionists had turned Palestine into "the State of Israel."

"It's still what they call our land, today, you know?" your grandmother said. "'The State of Israel.'"

I nodded.

But that was all years before Selsabeel's marriage to Marwan, in 1956, when perhaps enough time had passed that things could be mended and renewed. At least life could continue. Ahmad and Musa decided that Selsabeel and Marwan would marry, their eldest children of disaster, survivors of siege. It was strange that Selsabeel would marry so far from home, but these were strange times in Palestine. Musa al-Shiltawi was not truly a local in Kufr Qanut; he and his family were locals of a ghostscape, gliding over the scorched land, land so familiar, being made ever less familiar by the year, by the month, by the day. The Zionists had made those who remained "citizens" of their new country but had kept them under military law—curfews, sieges, closures—even as they built new towns for the Jews imported on planes and boats from Poland and Morocco and Romania and Iraq. "Tajri a-riyah b'ma la tashtihi a-sufun," Selsabeel's father would often murmur, stroking his neatly cropped beard.

"The winds do not blow as the ships wish them to," Nimreen said softly in my ear.

I nodded again.

Selsabeel was afraid to go so far from her home, from her mother and her brothers and her father. She had only met Marwan a few times, when they were both preteenagers. Then Selsabeel had paid little mind to the skinny shepherd boy. This time, though, when their families met for more solemn purposes, Selsabeel looked at Marwan, sitting across the room, and saw that his dark eyes were kind and laughing, his jaw square. She felt a little bit less afraid.

———

"He was a handsome man," your grandmother said, "a thin man, but strong. Maybe even a little bit like you."

I blushed, and Nimreen laughed softly.

———

The night after the final day of their weeklong wedding, a celebration amidst darkness, a candle burning in the murky shadows, Selsabeel moved into the home she and Marwan were to share, next door to Marwan's father and mother.

Here, Laith, I imagined the two of them sitting up for hours in the darkness—child-adults, my age, Nimreen's age—a newly married couple now quickly becoming friends, stifling laughter so as not to disturb Marwan's parents or siblings, talking about everything they could think to talk about. Perhaps they too had left some of their clothes on, despite being expected to peel them off. I imagined their faces flushed from the lingering heat of the first time their torsos touched. I imagined Selsabeel's breasts blossoming like Nimreen's. I imagined Marwan's body, thin and strong, a bit like my own. I imagined them finally dozing off into sleep, in the bed they now shared, having no other home to return to, each on their own side, their hands intertwined in the middle like a bridge over a river of sheets. I imagined the sun beginning to coax the purple of the night into gray, silhouetting its way into the Palestinian morning sky.

Within weeks, your grandmother told me, she began to feel more at ease in the village, and she walked the streets and alleyways of her new home with a greater calm. She'd learned that Marwan's favorite food was maqlubeh, which she happened to know how to make well from her home and was trying to perfect, using different amounts of garlic and onions, and that Marwan wrote poetic songs in his mind during the long days alone with the sheep.

He hadn't told her this at first, when she'd asked him what he thought about during his time with the flocks. At first, he'd only laughed and said, "What do I think about? Well, mostly about sheep."

Only later had she learned about his songs.

Selsabeel was shy but hoped that she would soon befriend the women in the village, who still looked at her a bit crookedly. Perhaps, with time, she thought, they could feel like the older sisters she never had. When her parents and brothers came to visit in the fall of that year, in late October 1956, she and Marwan welcomed them into their new home along with Marwan's family. Selsabeel's father sat outside smoking with Musa—with Abu Marwan—and with Marwan himself, and Selsabeel's mother, Leila, spoke with Marwan's mother, Fatmeh, as the three of them chopped vegetables inside Fatmeh's house.

"I've heard talk that there is going to be another war, now against Jordan," said Fatmeh.

"I don't think so, sister. The Jews are cruel, but they are not crazy," said Selsabeel's mother. "And anyway, we are now part of this country. We have to make do with the lot we have been given."

"I am not a part of this country. I am its prisoner. Perhaps you can say that more easily because you are still in your village, still in your home," said Fatmeh, her tone turning stony.

"Perhaps you're right, sister," Leila said, "but it seems that you have made a beautiful home here."

"We've had no choice."

"Well, I wanted to thank you, sister. My daughter seems to be happy and well cared for, al-hamdulilah," Leila said, her hand rubbing the small of Selsabeel's back, the way she had since Selsabeel was little. "She has become such a woman."

"We are blessed by God to have Selsabeel as part of our family. She is decent and smart, and Marwan is the happiest we have ever known him. He returns with his flocks singing. He didn't sing before. I'm sure he sings at the thought of arriving home to your daughter."

Selsabeel watched out the window as her brothers ran around wildly, maniacally. She thought she saw a new admiration in their eyes as they looked at her, when they arrived, their sister now a woman. They all ate together, a big and beautiful meal. Her family stayed almost until the 9:00 p.m. curfew began, the risk being worth it. They made it home safely.

———

"The next morning," said your grandmother, "began as any other morning."

———

Marwan left the house early with his flock. Before he went, Selsabeel gave him a package of maqlubeh from the night before, a big piece of round bread, two cucumbers, and two tomatoes. His days were long, and he was usually gone from early morning until evening. Sipping his coffee before he left, Marwan turned to Selsabeel, and said:

"I am very grateful to you."

"For what?" Selsabeel laughed.

"For being so good."

"You're just saying that because of the maqlubeh in your hands," Selsabeel said.

"I'm not. I think you are a good and holy woman. God willing, we will have many, many more years . . ."

"Until a hundred and twenty," said Selsabeel.

"Until a hundred and twenty."

"Which means you'll get there a year before I do," said Selsabeel. "I may have to find a new husband when I am a hundred and nineteen."

"That you may." Marwan laughed, his brown eyes sparkling. "Until then," he said, "I'll see you this evening."

"Unless I have other plans." Selsabeel smiled and waved her thin hand at her husband.

Marwan walked off, humming to himself, in the direction of the pen, where he kept his flock overnight. At his approaching footsteps, the ardent chorus of bleating began.

——————

"He seemed like a holy and good man to me too," your grandmother said. "I did not have a chance to get to know him well."

——————

Selsabeel moved slowly in the mornings. She cooked a little bit, cleaned the house, and then sat to read. On this morning, like many mornings, Selsabeel started by leafing through the Quran, from a sense of obligation, but before long she hungrily grabbed from under the bed the book she had been given by her mother. Her mother, in turn, had gotten the book from a friend of her cousin's, a man named Sufyan who somehow managed to get his hands, every now and then, on books from Beirut and Cairo.

——————

"The Jews didn't allow us to have books in Arabic," your grandmother said, with a small smile, "but Sufyan wasn't afraid of the Jews."

——————

The book was a novel, *Bidaya wa-Nihaya*, *The Beginning and the End*, by the Egyptian writer Naguib Mahfouz. By the late afternoon, Selsabeel was still reading. She realized, with a start, that she had nearly finished the book, and decided that she would savor the ending later, for the next day, or at least for that evening. Perhaps Marwan would want to read it too, after she finished—if he ever grew bored thinking of his sheep. Selsabeel laughed to herself and placed the book back under her and Marwan's bed. Then she went outside, to walk around the village, to taste some of the crisp afternoon winds tumbling through Kufr Qanut.

As soon as she stepped outside, though, Selsabeel could sense that something was wrong. The voices around her were raised and strained, and there was a sticky pulse in the air. Startled, Selsabeel called to a young boy she recognized, running down the street.

"Wait! Abdallah, wait."

He stopped and looked at her, his eyes darting in every direction, his fingers twiddling wildly at the ends of his hands.

"What's happened?" Selsabeel asked.

"The Jews have started a war with Egypt."

"With Egypt? Very well," Selsabeel said, her stomach clenching at the word "harb," war, "but why are you running? What does that have to do with us?"

"The Jews said that the curfew here will begin tonight at five p.m." The boy hopped on either foot, anxious to get going but respectful of his elder.

"Where are you running?"

"I have to go tell my brother. He doesn't return from the fields until evening!"

With that, the boy was off.

And then, the thoughts started to fall in place in Selsabeel's mind: the Jews had declared that the curfew would begin at 5:00 p.m. It was already past 4:00 p.m., certainly. Marwan did not have a set time that he returned each day, but the standard curfew did not begin until 9:00 p.m., so he would often take his time, singing songs in the hills as he walked. And he would almost certainly be alone, as he usually was. Who would tell him that the curfew was beginning at five? Certainly, the Jews must know that there would be some who would not have heard of the new curfew. Selsabeel stood still for a moment. Would they arrest Marwan? All around her, the village seemed to be sliding into pandemonium, people running in every direction.

Selsabeel began to run also, until she realized that she had very little idea where Marwan went in the mornings. He could be anywhere, on any hilltop or in any valley. How would he know that there was to be a curfew at five? La ilaha ill-Allah, Selsabeel murmured to herself. There is no God but God.

She made her way toward the western entrance to the village, in the direction she guessed Marwan might be. As she reached the entrance, she froze at the sight of the Jews, piling out of their jeeps, dressed in the uniforms of the Border Police, setting up along the road into the village. Selsabeel scrambled up a small hill, away from the Jews. Once she felt she was out of sight, obscured by a cluster of thin trees, she turned around to look down on the scene unfolding. She saw a small group of young women approaching the soldiers, carrying water on their heads. Selsabeel recognized one of them, Farah, a beautiful, haughty girl who lived not far from Selsabeel and Marwan. Farah had not been warm toward Selsabeel, and Selsabeel's first thought as she watched Farah walking along with the other women, looking tiny and meek as they approached the armed Jews, was a vengeful, ugly one: perhaps the Jews would taunt her, she thought, spill her water. She quickly chided herself and said a prayer to God for Farah's well-being.

The Jews called for them to stop, in their strange language. The women did not stop. The Jews switched to Arabic, and the women stopped.

"Do you know that there is a curfew at five?"

The women were silent. Farah stepped forward.

"No, we didn't know, sir."

"It's ten minutes after five," one said. "You are violating the curfew."

The women were silent. Another one of the soldiers toyed with his weapon. Selsabeel had stopped breathing.

"Go," one of the soldiers barked, motioning for the women to go back into the village. The women did as they were told, walking fast, a few of them running. The jug fell from Farah's head and shattered on the earth. She did not stop to pick up the shards.

Selsabeel tried to regain her breath and to decide if she should attempt to sneak past the Jews and find Marwan out in the field, but a few minutes later, her decision was made for her. Four shepherds approached, with their sheep and goats trailing them. Three of them were a father and his two sons, and along with them was a thin, mustached man, whose singing faded as he saw the armed Jews standing at the entrance to his village: Marwan. Selsabeel stayed quiet. She was sure that the soldiers would let Marwan and the other men pass, just as they had with Farah and the women. There was no way that they could have known about the curfew, and the soldiers could surely see that they were not armed men but rather simple shepherds.

"Where are you from?" one of the soldiers said.

"From Kufr Qanut," the oldest shepherd answered.

"Jib al-hawiya," another soldier said, demanding ID cards from the men. Each of the shepherds handed the soldiers their ID cards.

"Stand here," one of the soldiers said.

The four men stood as they were told. Selsabeel noticed that Marwan's flock was beginning to wander off. The soldier holding the ID cards asked, "Where were you?"

The older shepherd spoke. "With our flocks."

The soldier asked them again, "You're all from Kufr Qanut?"

One of the older shepherd's sons spoke, in a deep voice. "Yes, sir, all of us."

Marwan still hadn't said a word. Selsabeel wondered if she should call out to him.

The she heard one of the soldiers say something in Hebrew, "Tiktzor otam." Only later would she understand the meaning of these words. Now, perched on the hill, her fingernails digging into bark, she did not understand them.

—

"I think he was a holy and good man," your grandmother said again. "His body was so thin, but so strong. He sang beautifully. He stood there, and the Jews raised their weapons.

<blockquote>

"Tuh

tuh   tuh

tuh   tuh tuh

tuh."

</blockquote>

Your grandmother's face was blank, Laith, as she made these sounds, her tongue pressed against the back of her teeth, her hands folded in her lap.

"Then, after this, the shepherd and his sons fell onto the ground."

———

Marwan too. His body stained with flowering reds. There was no sound in the air except for the wild bleating of the flocks. One of the soldiers cocked his weapon and began shooting at the sheep. One of the animals was hit in the neck, and fell to the ground with a gurgling scream trapped in its throat. The rest of the flock ran off, and other soldiers dragged the bodies of Marwan and the other men off to the side of the road.

"Tiktzor otam."

Cut them down.

Selsabeel drew in her breath to scream, but the scream was muffled by a hand flung over her mouth, and she felt herself pulled toward a body behind her. She wrenched free, and whirled around, prepared to face the soldier who had come to slay her, to take her back to paradise, along with her Marwan. But it wasn't a soldier. It was Marwan's mother, Fatmeh. She had also come to look for her son. Selsabeel thought about him, lying there, how she had remained silent, and she wished that Fatmeh had been a Jewish soldier, had killed her then and there.

"Quiet, habibti," Fatmeh said. "You must remain silent. They will kill you if they hear you."

"But—they killed—they killed Marwan," Selsabeel said, sobs ripping their way through her whispers. "It's my fault."

"It is not," Fatmeh said, and drew her eighteen-year-old daughter-in-law to her breast. The two women stayed like that, Selsabeel sobbing into the soft fabric of Fatmeh's thobe, until they heard the sounds of more voices approaching. It was a group of laborers returning from work on bicycles. Some were singing, others were chatting, the bicycle tires were crunching along the dirt road. All sounds died out when they saw the soldiers standing at the entrance to the village.

Fatmeh and Selsabeel watched as the fifteen or so bicycle-riding day laborers were told to stand in a line, and then cut down, their bodies and bicycles crashing to the earth in a combination of flesh and metal. The same thing happened when a truck filled with women arrived. One of them was pregnant. One was a little girl. Surely, Selsabeel thought, they wouldn't. But they did. *Cut them down.* Another truck approached, and Fatmeh grabbed Selsabeel's hand, and they ran down the hill. They hid behind a tree near the road, and watched as the truck pulled to a stop.

"Where are you from?" a soldier asked.

"From Kufr Qanut," said the driver.

"Follow me," said one of the soldiers, climbing into his jeep.

As the truck shifted into gear and began to follow the soldier's jeep, Selsabeel and Fatmeh climbed into the back. Selsabeel saw little Abdallah, whom she'd seen running earlier, whimpering in the corner, snot running down onto his lips.

"Where is your brother?" Selsabeel asked.

"I couldn't find him. I don't know where . . ."

"Shh," Selsabeel said, and pulled the boy toward her, patting his hair softly.

In the meantime, Fatmeh leaned over the side of the truck bed, and got the attention of the driver, whose named was Ismail, and said, "Al-wihda kheir min qarin al-sua'a."

———

"Loneliness is better than bad company," Nimreen said, and then I understood.

The driver, Ismail, who must have felt that something was not right, understood right away. As the jeep made its way into the village, he veered quickly to the right and sped off down the narrow streets that he knew so well. The soldier tried to give chase, but all the passengers in the truck, nearly thirty people including Selsabeel and Fatmeh, scrambled into houses and survived, in body at least.

After, Selsabeel returned to Beit al-Asal and married Hassan Ziad, a stocky, moody cousin of hers who worked as a butcher in Beit al-Asal. They had three children—three sons—and many grandchildren, including two twins.

"Why did the soldier in the jeep ask him to follow?" I asked, in Arabic. I needed to latch on to some detail, to try to make sense of any of it.

"They wanted to put them by the border, to make it seem as if they were trying to sneak over the border, or perhaps to throw them over the border. It doesn't matter," said your grandmother, her dark eyes dry, buried in wrinkles, almost unblinking. I realized that she was not as old as I had thought, not even seventy.

I nodded, trying to keep my face blank. I am ashamed to admit this, now, Laith, but I did not believe her when she told me this story. I couldn't. This account of Israeli soldiers executing unarmed Arabs, citizens of Israel, didn't align with anything I'd ever heard before. Surely there was some context being left out here, some plot by the residents of Kufr Qanut against the State of Israel, some act of treachery, something.

"You must be merciful, like God is merciful," Selsabeel said, looking at me. "Tell the Jews this."

I didn't say anything.

She shut her eyes, forcefully, significantly, as if to say, "We are done here."

"Shukran," I said, not knowing what else to say. "Thank you."

Nimreen kissed your grandmother's wrinkled cheek, and we stood up to leave.

As we walked away, the silence pulsed between us like something alive. I was the first to break it.

"I don't understand," I said. "Why would the soldiers do this?"

"They were following orders," said Nimreen, and we stopped walking, standing just on the other side of Selsabeel's home.

"What kind of orders?"

"Allah yerhamu."

"What do you mean?" The phrase, I knew, meant "God have mercy on him" and was usually said after someone died.

"Those were the orders they were given," said Nimreen, glancing back toward your grandmother's house. "When one of the soldiers asked what to do if someone coming home from work didn't know about the curfew. Allah yerhamu."

"But is that really what happened? Isn't there . . ."

My voice trailed off as Nimreen whipped her head back around to look at me. Her eyes were flickering. I was startled by how panicked she sounded when she said my name. "Jonathan?"

I was silent.

"How dare you."

"Nimreen." I reached for her arm.

"Don't."

I dropped my hand back to my side.

"It's just, everything is always more complicated than it seems, right? Nimreen?"

"No."

I was silent.

"Are you joining the army?" Nimreen's voice sounded like it was coming from far away.

"What?" I said. Nimreen was staring at my face as though it were some strange item or creature she'd never seen before. I looked away. "That's not what we're talking about right now."

"Now it is. Are you?"

"I—I don't know."

"Tell me the truth, Jonathan."

"You know the truth, Nimreen. You know the answer."

"Say it."

"Yes."

"Yes what?"

"Yes, I am. I have to."

"You have to?"

"Nimreen, it's not a choice."

"Do you hear what you're saying, Jonathan? It's not a choice? It's a choice. At least own that. Just—" Her voice shifted, the anger melting into something softer, more awful to hear. "Just, please don't, Jonathan, okay? Just fucking say you're, like, crazy or something."

"I can't do that, Nimreen. You don't get it. It's not—"

"Just go back to the States."

"Is that what you want?" I said, after a moment.

"I want to be able to love you," Nimreen said, looking away.

"I'll still be me, Nimreen," I said. "I'll still be the same person."

"I'll drive you to the bus, Jonathan."

I IMAGINE YOU AND NIMREEN HERE WITH ME. I imagine what it would feel like for this land to consume us all together. Inside, there'd only be light and cumulus clouds and marijuana smoke and the three of us. Outside, the sea might drink itself. Birds might die shrieking in tiny rooms. Rifles might wilt and clusters of dust might dance in abandoned fortresses. Little sand creatures might crawl dazed and frightened to the edge of the woods, meeting only darkness there. History would try to breathe in the back of our faces, to gaze through the emptiness of our eye sockets, to murmur through our open mouths. But we wouldn't be afraid, Laith. We'd be okay, right?

We'd be together.

ELEVEN

"SABA," I SAID, AS MY MOM LOWERED A PIECE OF SALMON onto my plate, drawing my breath inward, tapping into a courage which I thought would make Nimreen proud, "what do you think about Shahar Admon and Sophia Gold?"

"Who?" Saba Yehuda said. He was seated across the table from me, which was our usual Shabbat dinner arrangement, with my parents on either end, and my little sister, Zehava, on my left. He looked good this evening. It fluctuated, the leukemia did, and on that night, his skin looked less faded and his eyes were bright, flicking back and forth around the room but mostly scanning my face and Zehava's.

"The two kids from Tel Aviv who refused to—who didn't enlist this morning."

I'd read about it online, in the *Jerusalem Times:* seventeen high school seniors, from all over the country, had publicly declared their refusal to enlist. Two of them, Shahar and Sophia, both from Tel Aviv, had had the earliest draft date, and had each been sent to the military jail known as Jail 7 this morning. I didn't usually read the news, and I didn't know them personally, of course, so I might have missed the story, but Nimreen had texted me their names earlier that afternoon.

> [Nimreen]: shahar admon & sophia gold.
> 14:01.

I had texted her back—"?"—and she just wrote, "google it." Things had been strained between us since the afternoon with your grandmother, a few weeks earlier.

Now, over dinner, I watched as recognition spread over Saba Yehuda's face. He read the paper every day. I was prepared for him to say that they were wrongheaded, misguided, silly.

"They should be hanged," he said.

"Abba!" my mom said, dropping the serving spoon, which clanged loudly on the edge of the glass fish dish. She looked straight at her father and spoke in a barbed voice that only manifested when she spoke Hebrew. "What an awful thing to say. They're kids."

"An eighteen-year-old is not a kid, Raphaela," Saba Yehuda said, his eyes focused somewhere behind my mom's head. My chest swelled, despite the churning of my stomach and convulsions in my heart: I was almost eighteen. Almost not a kid in my grandfather's yellow-green eyes.

"Right," I said.

My mom looked at me significantly. I might have been able to decipher the look, if I'd wanted to, but I didn't want to. We'd never spoken directly about the possibility of my not enlisting, mostly because it wasn't really a possibility, and also because silence was part of my family inheritance. Genetic, even: you were the one who told me once that family history—trauma, in particular—can actually alter genes.

"They're narcissists," Saba Yehuda said, "betraying their people for a few seconds in the spotlight, Raphaela, or for God knows what."

"I think they're brave," my mom said.

"Brave?" Saba Yehuda snorted, and I looked at my mom and saw that her nostrils were flared. "I think they're cowards. Especially the boy."

"Why?" my mom said, her voice thin and sharp like the edge of a blade. "Because it's okay if the girl is a coward, but the boy has to be a man and a hero?"

"Wars aren't led by women," Saba Yehuda said, his voice steady.

"I'm going to lead a war," Zehava said. "I want to be a pilot."

Saba Yehuda's face softened. "That's right, Zehava. You're right. And you are far more brave, more of a man, in fact, than these boys who shirk their duty."

Zehava beamed.

"Jesus Christ," my mom said, in English.

"Raphaela, it's no way to win an argument, getting emotional," Saba Yehuda said.

"Don't tell my daughter that she is a man," my mom said.

"He didn't mean it like that, Raph," my dad said, in English, his voice hesitant.

"I don't need you to speak for me, Paul," Saba Yehuda said, and my dad put down his fork, slowly. Only he had touched his salmon. Zehava too had started eating, but she'd decided three days earlier that she was a vegetarian. The slabs of pinkish fish were getting cold on my grandfather's plate, on my mom's plate, and on my own.

I cleared my throat, and all the eyes at the table turned toward me, the one who had initiated this conversation, the boy with a birthday coming up, with a Paratroopers tryout at the end of the month, a draft date in four. The candles flickered in the window; the smell of the lukewarm fish, blended with the humid summer air, almost made me gag. I generally really liked salmon.

"Anyway," I said, wanting it all to stop, wanting, like always, for everyone to be on the same side, "who cares, right? It's just a hypothetical question. Who knows why they even did it anyway, right? Like, what their actual motives were?"

I saw Saba Yehuda open his mouth and then close it again, censoring himself, a rarity.

It was my mom who spoke, looking directly at me. "I think that these kids probably meant what they said, when they said that they don't want to oppress the Palestinians."

"It's fine to respect the Arabs," Saba Yehuda said, "to feel sympathy for them. But to love them more than your own people? That is too much."

"That's an absurd way to—" my mom began.

"When are your tryouts for the Paratroopers, Yonatan?" Saba Yehuda said, cutting his daughter off, cutting a thin sliver of the soft pink fish flesh with his fork and knife.

"At the end of the month," I said, looking up at him.

"You'll do great," Zehava said.

I glanced over at her, to see if she was being sarcastic, but it didn't seem like she was.

"Thanks, Z," I said.

"I'm proud of you," said Saba Yehuda, from across the table, still sawing at the fish, although the cut had been long completed.

I felt tears spring into the corners of my eyes and blinked them back. It wasn't strange for me to cry in general, as you know, Laith, but I didn't cry in front of my grandfather, not then, not ever. Silence folded around all five of us like a blanket. Then my mom spoke.

"But you'd be proud of him no matter what he did, right, Abba?"

Saba Yehuda looked at my mom, met his daughter's dark-brown eyes. Then his yellow-green eyes, which had skipped a generation, met my own, unblinking. Then he looked back down at the fish once more. Then he spoke:

"No."

"But Abba . . ." My mom's voice was thin and reedy.

"Mom, stop," I said.

"It's not a question we have to ask, Raphaela," Saba Yehuda said.

I didn't say anything. Not anything at all.

That night, after Shabbat dinner with my family, it was just you and me on the beach, Laith. By then everything between Nimreen and me was thrumming guilt and pounding confusion swirling around our two bodies that had once, so recently, seemed to fit together so well. I don't think either Nimreen or I expected that it would happen like it did: the moment our most important shared secret, our love, was spoken, articulated not so much through our words as through our bodies, it was as if we couldn't keep anything else silent anymore, and we were forced to move onward to the second unspoken secret, my draft date and all that it held. And it was too much, Laith, and we couldn't hold it together.

Sitting with Nimreen in the air-conditioned dimness of the movie theater, our nostrils filled with the scent of stale popcorn, sweat squelching between our interwoven fingers, it had felt like we might have a chance to become Nimreen and Jonathan, letters $N + J$ etched into the bark of some ancient tree, at least for a little while. But then we sat with your grandmother in the dappled shade of a tree laden with soft fruit, the air around us filled with torment, and then Nimreen drove me home in the heaviest silence I've ever heard.

The Friday after that, we all went out to lunch at a pancake restaurant in Haifa, my choice, and you did ninety-seven percent of the talking, Laith, trying to be a peacemaker, trying to make it better. The next week, Nimreen texted me to say that she was not going to join us on our drive up to the Lebanese border to try to spot UN towers. That one was your idea, of course, Laith, and we ended up deciding, you and I, when we were halfway there, that maybe it wasn't such a good one, and so we stopped and got falafels instead, munching on the greasy chickpea balls in shared silence. I'm sure you felt how sad I was, Laith. I couldn't finish my falafel sandwich. You finished it for me.

That night, after the tense Shabbat dinner, when I texted Nimreen to see if she was going to come with us to our usual spot on the beach, she spelled everything out more directly:

[Nimreen]: Jonathan, stop. I can't, and you know why I can't. What's the point? You've made your choice.

21:18.

[Me]: It doesn't have to be like that, Nimreen. It doesn't have to be either-or.
21:21.

[Nimreen]: How can it not?
21:46.

[Me]: It's us Nimreen. We are stronger than everything else. No?
21:47

[Nimreen]: I don't know. Maybe I'll see you next week. I can't tonight.
22:11.

By the time that last text came, you'd already told me your sister wasn't coming, and I was already sitting next to you, Laith, facing out toward the water, angry and hurt by Nimreen's absence. I didn't think about the generosity then of Nimreen's not telling *you* not to come. If she had, you would have stayed home too. You were my friend, Laith, but you were her brother.

You lit the joint and passed it over to me without smoking from it.

"Abraham Lincoln?" you said, a grin playing on your stubbled cheeks.

I tried to smile, but it felt as if there were fish hooks stabbed into the flesh on either side of my mouth, each strung with a heavy weight. I felt my mouth tugging downward, and I think if I hadn't inhaled the smoke as hard as I could, that instant, I might have started weeping.

Instead, I started coughing, and tears sprung into my eyes, but they were THC tears, and you put your big hand on my back and rubbed in gentle circles, and then I laid my head on your bony shoulder, and you pulled me closer to you, and the sea sizzled and coughed, and the wind whistled and shrieked, and I wanted to tell you about everything but couldn't find the words, so I turned my head to look up at you, and saw that your face was smiling, and you were humming something unrecognizable, and you turned your neck and looked at me, tilting your head slightly downward, and I then moved my mouth toward your mouth, quickly, and your mouth was soft and felt so familiar, which made me feel guilty and hungry at once, and I tried to push my tongue forward through your lips, but you laughed again, just as my tongue lurched forward, and it scraped against your teeth and then dangled, suspended in warm open space, and I withdrew it, ashamed, but then you leaned toward me once more and kissed each of my eyelids, Laith, and I let the smoky grace of your breath cover my eyes, guide me to darkness, and in the darkness, I rested my head back on your shoulder, and let my nose and eyes run wet onto your T-shirt, the joint still burning between my fingers.

And eventually, after some minutes or hours or lifetimes, we turned to walk back home, together and alone.

And I took your hand and squeezed hard, Laith, and you squeezed back, and by the next Friday, I was gone.

I didn't see you or Nimreen. I was fleeing from this land of sharp teeth and cackling stones, from my grandfather's eyes and my mom's voice and from you and your sister, molten twins, mournful and wild, silly and sacrilegious, sharp and stoned, gentle and beautiful, whose love was burning through my flesh, threatening to scorch and disfigure my past. To engulf my future.

By the next Friday, I was already in Greece.

IV

The Most Beautiful Man in Salonica

TWELVE

I HAD ANCESTORS TOO, LAITH, and I decided that it was time that I go visit them. My veins were heavy with their blood, bulging with blood, and the moment I stepped off the plane in Salonica, I had the sense that everything around me was familiar and that everything around me was stolen: flags cockily fluttering Greekness over what once was, not so long ago, our city, my grandfather's city, his brother's city. I thought I saw the eyes of the border control agent flicker when he looked down at my passport, saw the word "Israel." I could have given him my American passport, but I didn't want to. I wanted him to say something, dared him to say something. He didn't say anything. I passed through quickly.

The buildings were tall and blocky, huddled closely together, as if to hide something from my gaze. The streets sloped downward toward the sea, and I could taste the salty balm pulsing throughout the city, and it was nauseating. I walked down to the coast, before heading to my hostel. Across the water, white-capped mountains stood as silent witnesses to all that had transpired here. It wasn't their fault, the mountains, but I was startled by how much I despised this modern Greek city, so soon after arriving, even the mountains, even the sea. I felt a fire urge surging through me, dark and ashy and tingly: I wanted to burn down the buildings, to turn the mountains into gravel, to wipe some of the smugness off the faces of all the passersby. As I walked toward my hostel, I passed a homeless man, shaking his head and mumbling to me in Greek. His skin was leathery and his clothes were dusty.

This is what you get, I thought.

I looked at him again, his mustache drooping over his lips, and I felt ashamed by my thoughts. I pulled out a ten-euro note, placed it into his palm, said, in English, "Sorry, here you go," and walked on, feeling like a scream was welling up in the bottom of my chest. I didn't blame the homeless man or even the pedestrians—chubby children, busy-handed women, crumpled old men, who I told myself were the most likely to have been guilty, but still, Laith, even they were so pitiful and frail—so instead I focused my anger toward the buildings, imagining them in flames as I walked. And then I entered the hostel.

"Welcome to Thessaloniki. Where you from?" The guy behind the desk at the hostel had strangely, almost cartoonishly round eyes, tattoos snaking up both arms, cigarette smoke drifting out of his mouth, gauges in both ears.

"Thanks," I said. "I'm from Israel."

"Oh," the guy said, "Israel?"

"Yep." I nodded and then looked down at the form and started filling in my name, my address, Rehov HaKovshim 18, Pardes Ya'akov, Israel.

"Well." The guy cleared his throat. "I have to say, what you guys are doing to the Palestinians is pretty fucked up."

I whipped my head up to look at him. He was staring at something behind my head. As I tried to meet his eyes, I thought about mentioning the fact that my girlfriend was Palestinian, but I realized that'd sound apologetic and that I was pretty sure the chances of Nimreen actually becoming my girlfriend were almost zero. I didn't need to apologize to him anyway, and definitely not to lie. He looked back at me, and I didn't say anything, just stared. Soon he spoke more, as people usually do when faced with the prospect of extended shared silence.

"I don't have any problem with Jews, you know. I just don't like Zionists."

"You're kidding now, yeah?" My pulse was pounding in my ears.

"Not kidding. I have a good friend who is a Jew. He also says that Zionism is, like, the worst kind of colonialism. You look like a decent guy, though. You're not a Zionist, right?"

I was really glad that I hadn't told him that my girlfriend was Palestinian.

"Do you know where my grandfather was from?" I said, slowly, loudly, as if he couldn't speak English well. His English was just fine.

He didn't say anything.

"Here," I said. "Right here. From Salonica. And you know why he wasn't killed?"

Silence. I continued: "I'll give you a clue. It wasn't because of the intervention of his Greek neighbors. No thanks to your grandparents, who were probably thrilled to see the Jews go. By the way, do you know who lived in your house sixty-five years ago? Or in this hostel?"

The air was spoiled pudding, slimy and rancid all around us. He was bigger than I was, and I was completely alone in Thessaloniki, Greece, and now out as being a Jew and an Israeli. Still, I couldn't stop.

"It was Zionism. Zionism is the only reason my grandfather wasn't gassed alive and then burned to ashes."

"Whatever," he said. "Do you realize that you're coming to my city and trying to make me feel guilty about something that I wasn't even there for? I wasn't even born. And anyway, what you're doing in Palestine is just like what the Nazis did, maybe worse. You Jews are—"

"We Jews are what?" I stepped closer to the desk, the swooshing of blood in my eardrums now arrhythmic, wild. I begged silently for him to say something else. I was ready to climb over that desk, to rip his earrings out of his earlobes, to flail fists into his flesh, right here, inside his own youth hostel. Because it wasn't really his. This wasn't really his city.

I felt like the hostel worker was looking at me as though I had horns growing out of my head, although I get now, Laith, that maybe he was just nervous. I was pushed up against the counter, and my question—"We Jews are what?"—hung in the air like a cloud of smoke.

"Nothing," he said, his voice wispy and thin. "You're being oversensitive. I was trying to have a political discussion, but clearly you're too brainwashed to listen."

"Oversensitive?" I almost laughed, but I was too mad to laugh. "You know what? I'm definitely not staying here."

I picked up my hiking backpack and walked out into the salty summer air, my heart pounding, wondering if he'd come after me, maybe with a few of his Greek friends, to kick my ass, to grind another Jewish body into the Greek pavement. Or maybe he'd come out and apologize for what he said, for all of it. But he didn't do either. The door swung shut behind me. I stood still for a moment, trying to slow my pulse, alone in the middle of Thessaloniki. This wasn't his city. It was my grandfather's city. And it was Jacko's.

According to my grandfather, Laith, his older brother, Jacko, was the most beautiful man in all Salonica. Jacko's skin was smooth and brown, like my grandfather's, and his eyes were an odd yellow-green, like my grandfather's, like my own. He was lithe, his body tall and slim and sloping, all coiled muscle and springing steps. Jacko grew his hair long, down to his shoulders and then beyond, even though that was a strange thing to do, in Salonica, back then. By the time Jacko was fourteen and a half years old, in 1931, and in the ninth class at the Alliance Israélite Universelle school for boys, where he and my grandfather studied, Jacko was aware of the effect his presence had on a room, the way women's voices would grow lower and plumper, and their eyes would follow him, glinting with something that resembled hunger, only sharper. That year, a new, short-haired Greek teacher took Jacko into one of the classrooms after school, unbuttoned her dress, and asked him, in Espanyol, if he would like to touch her breasts. Jacko politely declined in Greek, and the teacher, Miss Azouvi, hurriedly refastened her brassiere and warned Jacko not to tell anyone, her eyes those of a cornered animal.

Jacko didn't tell anyone, except for his younger brother, Yuda, because he told Yuda almost everything. Yuda was thirteen, just a year and a month younger than Jacko. Yuda knew he looked a lot like his older brother—everyone said so, asked even if they were twins—but Yuda felt "as if the Artist had grown tired the second time around."

———

This was exactly how my grandfather put it, Laith, and I looked at him sideways when he said that: even in his eighties, it was hard for me to imagine a man more handsome than my Saba Yehuda.

"It's true," Saba Yehuda said, smiling softly. "Jacko's ears were elegant conch shells, while mine felt like ungainly flaps, and where Jacko's chin was a proud cleft, I could feel my own sinking back into my neck."

My grandfather touched his chin tenderly, his face bearing an expression I'd never seen before; his face looking for a moment, Laith, like that of a thirteen-year-old boy.

———

Jacko was not boastful, and Yuda did have similarly smooth Sadicario skin, his own pair of startling eyes. Still, Yuda felt pangs of envy surge through his chest as he compared the image he saw of his older brother with the image he encountered gazing back at him in the washroom's mirror. Jacko, for his part, guessed at some of what Yuda felt, and wished he could give his brother just a bit of his own beauty, to even out the load. Jacko, in my grandfather's stories, in my imagination, and in his letters that I read, Laith, was really gentle, really good.

Yuda did not believe his brother when Jacko first told him what had happened.

But when he looked at Jacko's eyes, yellow-green mirrors of his own, flickering and troubled in the moonlight dripping into the room they shared, Yuda could see that Jacko was telling the truth.

"So why didn't you touch?" Yuda asked, groaning, his heart pounding in his chest, "Miss Azouvi is legendary. Are you crazy, Jacko? Or are you just a xamor?"

They learned Greek in school but spoke to each other in Judeo-español, which my grandfather just called Espanyol, and which had Hebrew woven through it like a thin snail-blue thread. "Xamor," for example, in both Espanyol and Hebrew means donkey.

Jacko kept silent.

"What did they look like?" Yuda asked.

"What did what look like?"

"Her pechos, you donkey!" Yuda said, and giggled.

"Oh," Jacko said, scratching his head. "When she leaned over to pick up her dress, after I told her no, they swung like pendulums. And her nipples were very long."

"How long?" Yuda whispered.

"Maybe as long as my fingers," Jacko said, "like this!"

Jacko pulled off his sheets and jumped up on his own bed, wiggling both his index fingers in front of his chest, waving his hips back and forth as he did so, a goblin's grin smeared across his face.

Saba Yehuda, when he told me this story, Laith, the day before my class trip to Poland, stood up from the table and began to mimic the motion, and I was worried for a moment that he was losing his mind: it was the strangest, most vulnerable, most joyful thing I had ever seen my grandfather do.

Then he sat back down, his face growing heavy again.

A few months later, in the early summer of 1931, Saba Yehuda told me, the Greeks burned the Jewish neighborhood known as Bos del Pueblo to the ground. Christian men, immigrants from Asia Minor, eager to prove their patriotic fervor, had begun spreading rumors about the Jews betraying Greece. In the middle of Salonica, of La Madre de Israel, their lies spread like a disease. Then one day three young Jewish men grabbed a handful of flyers from a group of Greeks. The Jewish men took the papers between their fingers, pretended to read, and then ripped them to shreds, tossing the shreds back in the faces of the Greeks, spitting, thrusting fists and shoulders forward, brave and tall and unhesitant. That night, other Greek men swarmed to attack the Jews in their houses. In the 152 District, where my grandfather lived, Jewish youths took to the streets, eyes gleaming, veins pulsing swollen on oily foreheads, Adam's apples bobbing in svelte throats. My grandfather wanted to join them right away, but his parents refused to let him out of the house.

"They are attacking us, in our own city, and you want us to stay inside and cower?" Yuda said.

Jacko was silent.

"You're thirteen years old, Yuda," Mrs. Sadicario said.

Mr. Sadicario nodded slowly.

"I'm not a child," Yuda said, turning around sharply and walking toward his and Jacko's room. Jacko walked after Yuda, and Yuda heard their parents sigh, relieved, and he felt, for a moment, sad for them, picturing the way Mr. and Mrs. Sadicario's faces would crumple, some time later, when they would enter the room, after knocking, and find it empty, the window of their second-story flat open, the smell of cinder seeping in on the back of the Salonican summer breeze. Yuda and Jacko shimmied down the side of their house, ran toward the smells and sounds, and saw the streets of the 152 District, churning and chaotic.

Yuda's eyes darted from sight to sight, his nostrils flared, absorbing the scents. On one end of the street, Yuda saw a group of Greek youths throwing stones through the windows of the synagogue. On the other end, a group of Jewish boys walked quickly, holding sticks and rocks, their fists clenched as they approached the Greeks. Yuda smelled smoke, metallic echoes of blood, ashes. He heard screams, thuds, cracks, a howl.

"Take this," Jacko said, licking his lips and reaching downward toward a stick he'd noticed, discarded. He wiped it on his shirt, a smear of dark staining the blue cotton, and handed it to Yuda. They walked a few more paces, and Jacko bent down again and then stood upright with a glass bottle in his hand. He smashed it on the edge of a building, small flecks of green glass flying in every direction. In Jacko's hand, the half-broken bottle glinted sharp and savage, like the many-toothed maw of some discolored beast.

"Come with me," Jacko said.

Yuda did as he was told, biting down on his lip, sprinting after his brother down a back alley, quickly running out of breath as he strained to keep up with Jacko's loping strides. The sounds and smells faded behind them, as they arrived at the back entrance to the Matanot Le-Evionim welfare building at the edge of the district, where hungry travelers and poor students could always expect a warm meal. There was no one else there. Yuda looked around and then at his brother.

"We must protect this entrance," Jacko said.

"Why?" Yuda whispered.

"Because," Jacko said, "this is where all Salonica's wealth is hidden. We have to keep the Greeks out of here."

Yuda nodded, grasping the stick tightly with his right hand. The two brothers stood at the back entrance to the welfare building, each of them shaking delicately, their throats clenched, their shoulders pressed firmly against one another's, gripping their makeshift weapons. Yuda hoped he would know what to do when someone came, that he would be brave enough to fight well, to defend Salonica, to make Jacko proud.

But no one came, and soon enough most of the noises died down. Jacko pulled his arm around Yuda's shoulder. Meanwhile, Bos del Pueblo was being set on fire, and all of it was just a dress rehearsal for the decimation that was to come, which no groups of stick-wielding Jewish youths, no matter how brave, could fend off. But the brothers didn't know any of that then. They walked home, with their arms around each other's shoulders.

"You were brave, Ninyo," Jacko said.

"Grasyas, Jacko."

"Why did the Jews keep all their wealth in that building?" I asked.

"What?" Saba Yehuda's eyes focused on me, and he slid back into the present. "Oh, no. There was no hidden wealth in the Matanot Le-Evionim building, Yonatan."

And then he started laughing again. His chest rose and fell with laughter: a gorgeous sight.

"Jacko just told me that to keep me away from the fighting. If it had been up to him, we would have stayed home. He was just taking care of me . . . He was scared I'd run off on my own if he tried to bring me home, so he made up this fiction, about hidden wealth, and why we needed to guard the entrance. He was right: I might have run off too. I was a stupid boy, reckless, too brave."

Hearing that, Laith, all I wanted was to be a stupid boy, reckless, too brave.

That night, the mobs continued to rampage through Salonica, searching for Jews. They were forced away from big neighborhoods, like my grandfather's 152 District, by groups of Jewish youths, but eventually they fell upon the destitute Bos del Pueblo neighborhood and turned it into ashes. There they murdered a round-faced, broad-bellied baker, a man with a fine mustache and flour still on his hands, his screeches and cries drowned out in a chorus of boots, of dull thuds, laughter in the air, blood and dust on the streets.

"The attackers didn't even know how to identify their victims, and in that sense, they were less clever than the swine who would come later: every Jew in Bos del Pueblo knew the baker there was a Christian," Saba

Yehuda said, but a Christian who shared his life and bread with the Jews of the city.

After Bos del Pueblo, my grandfather joined the local Zionist group, Beitar. Members of Beitar had been prominent in the defense of 152, and they spoke of the need for Jews to stand tall and proud. At the first meeting Yuda and Jacko attended, a woman named Raquel gave a speech that my grandfather remembered, almost word for word, more than seven decades later:

"Who are we? Are we Jews or are we Greeks? Of course, there are some among us who say, 'We are Greeks now.' Salonica is now, of course, part of the noble country of Greece. But ask the people of Bos del Pueblo how Greek they feel. And the real question is: Do we want to be welcomed into Greece? Matityahu Ben Yohanan killed the Jew who slithered forward to sacrifice to the Greek gods. We hope these Greeks will be different, but it is a foolish hope. They won't be.

"But right now, in Eretz Israel, the land where our people were born, Jews are taking up arms, men and women, to throw off the yokes—British yokes, Greek yokes, Amalek's yokes. We used to say, 'Muestra Palestina esta aqui.' But our Palestine isn't here any longer. Our Palestine is in Palestine. Our brothers and sisters are waiting for us to join them. Will we heed their call?"

Yuda could barely sit still, waves of excitement pulsing through his body. He looked over at Jacko, who mumbled something about how he didn't understand what the biblical story of Matityahu Ben Yohanan had to do with Bos del Pueblo or Palestine. Jacko was distracted. Jacko was in love.

That day at the kitchen table, Saba Yehuda gave me an envelope. It was brown and worn, and when I opened it, I saw that it was filled with letters and poems. "These were Jacko's, Yonatan." I picked one up, hungry, but my heart fell: it looked, at first, like the letters were penned in sloppy Hebrew, but I realized after a moment they were all written in a script

I couldn't decipher. But that afternoon, Saba Yehuda and I sat around his kitchen table, and he taught me how to read Solitreo, the cursive handwriting that Jews in Salonica had used to write in Espanyol. With a combination of my grandfather's help, three years of high school Spanish from back in Everbrook, and my Hebrew, I found that I could chisel my way through the language, bit by bit. The first thing we translated together was one of Jacko's poems, written to someone named Rafi.

por Rafi, mi alma, mi amor

The moon is like a tender egg
In the charcoal cough of the night
My chest quivers as I dream awake
And drink the air that slithers in tight
Your voice, my love, is minor key mist
All mourning, moistness and right
How many times can your eyes I kiss
Before they melt into puddles of light

Reading that, I imagined Jacko with Rafi, on top of the White Tower, the old Ottoman Fortress, looking out over the sea. The sky dribbled with stars, soaking with stars, two teenaged bodies pressed against each other, hands stroking waists, lips meeting lips, eyes closed, eyes open, running fingers through each other's hair, Jacko deciding then to grow his hair long, to let it become as a field for Rafi's plowing fingertips.

Jacko was in love with Rafi. My grandfather was in love with Zion. Jacko didn't go back to the next meeting; Yuda was soon put in charge of one of the local Beitar groups. Jacko finished school and started working with their father, binding and selling books. Yuda left school before he had finished, and set sail for Palestine.

This was a story I heard dozens of times, Laith: the Haifa pioneer, the port workers, the ruse, the boat, the departure. In Palestine, after leaving the ports and joining the Jewish paramilitary force, the Haganah, Yuda—who became Hebraicized, became Yehuda—mostly stopped using Espanyol, except in the letters to Jacko and his parents. By mid-1938, I gathered from one of Jacko's responses, my grandfather had begun urging Jacko and his parents to join him in Palestine. Jacko wrote:

> Everything's fine, here. Todo bien, Ninyo. We know that
> from Palestina, everything looks like a crisis, that over
> there you are filled with ema lemilxama, but here things
> are normal. Salonica is our home.

Ema lemilxama: War-terror.

As far as I could tell, Jacko never explicitly mentioned Rafi, except in one letter, dated November 5, 1940, just after Mussolini's Italians first attacked Greece. My grandfather explained to me that thousands and thousands of Jewish men from Salonica joined the effort to defend the country that had treated them like dirt, spit on their heritage, burned their neighborhoods and synagogues. In this letter, Jacko started by wondering, Did Yuda remember Rafi, the tall, thin boy from the Alliance school, with the dark eyes? He had been killed, Jacko wrote, by a bullet through his eye.

> Rafi's eyes were like the earth, Yuda. To think of one of
> them missing, replaced with the hungry flower of blood
> that flows behind all our eyes, is to think of the world
> diminished by half. Half of the world is missing, Yuda.

The Greeks held off the Italians for a period, in part thanks to the brigade nicknamed "the Cohen brigade," who fought more fiercely, according to my grandfather, than anyone else, but then the Germans came, of course, and the Jews of Salonica thought they might be fine for a while, but they weren't, of course. Most of the Jews of Salonica, of

La Madre de Israel, were to be scattered like dark snowflakes in sickly Polish skies. Jacko's final letter to his little brother, Yuda, was written on the last day of 1940.

It began, "Shalom, Ninyo . . ."

———

After I left the hostel, Laith, I stood on the sidewalk for a few moments, breathing hard, and as the adrenaline faded, I felt such sadness pour through my body that I thought I might vomit. I didn't vomit, though, and I managed to make myself start walking. With my heavy bag pulling on my shoulders, I walked for half an hour until I got to the Jewish Museum of Thessaloniki, which was one of the three or four places I planned to visit on this trip. I had asked my parents to buy me the tickets to Salonica as an early present for my eighteenth birthday. My mom got teary-eyed and offered to come with me, but I said no. I was holding out hope that when I told Saba Yehuda I was going, maybe he'd offer to come with me, if he felt up for traveling, a grandfather-grandson journey. He declined.

"There's nothing left to see there, Yonatan."

So I went alone.

After spending a distracted half hour in the museum, I left and found another hostel nearby. This one was run by a round-faced, merry-eyed woman, who just blinked and smiled when I said I was from Israel. I felt relief flood through me, and gratitude. She handed me a brochure of "What You Should Do in Beautiful Thessaloniki."

I went into the room at my new hostel, put down my bag, sat on one of the beds, and opened the brochure. On the first page I read the sentence: "Thessaloniki is a home to three religions, Christianism, Islam & Ancient Greek!"

It was like I'd been punched in the face, Laith.

Ancient fucking Greek.

I felt like I was going to cry, and I wasn't ready to cry, wasn't willing.

Instead, I pulled open my laptop, connected to the Wi-Fi, and logged into Skype, hoping she'd be online, and she was.

Boop bop boop badu bop. She picked up after six or seven rings.

"Hi, Nimreen!" I said. I was so happy to see her face, even if it was discolored and pixelated and the size of my palm. I missed her so much right then.

"Hi, Jonathan." There was less tension in Nimreen's voice than the last time we spoke on the phone, two nights before I left, when I'd called again. Neither of us said much, we just wallowed in silence and hurt, attached across the chasm by the static in our eardrums. Maybe it was the safety, now, of distance, that allowed both of us to let our guards down, the knowledge that even if we wanted to hang up the call and drive to see each other, we couldn't. My heart bounced in my chest like a tennis ball. She was home, in Beit al-Asal, rather than in her dorm, and she was wearing a gray long-sleeved shirt. A black-and-white checkered keffiyeh was wrapped around her neck, covering the perfect dents of her clavicle. Her hair was pulled back into a heavy bun; her earbuds hung down in twin strands of white plastic, disappearing into the folds of the Palestinian scarf.

"Kifek? How are you doing?"

"Fine," Nimreen said. "I just realized that I forgot to tell you about Mahmoud Darwish's reading in Haifa last week, where he—"

And then she froze, her mouth hanging open, her eyes stuck in a heavy half blink, as if she were falling asleep, hit with a sudden wave of narcolepsy.

"Hello? Nimreen? Ergh. Fuck."

I clicked the little red-phone icon and ended the call. I grimaced. The hang-up sound always struck me as unsettlingly wet. Skype asked me if I wanted to give feedback.

"Fuck off," I murmured, scrolling my mouse down to the chat box.

> **YonatanISR2002:** You froze.
>
> **NBintFilastinyya1948:** Oh no. Did u not hear anything I said? It was really important.
>
> **YonatanISR2002:** It was? Shit. No. About the Darwish reading? What did u say!?

NBintFilastinyya1948: lol nothing. I'm jk, Jonathan.

YonatanISR2002: Grrr.

NBintFilastinyya1948: Don't u growl at me, little cub.

YonatanISR2002: Little cub!?! I'm a huge tiger. Or wildebeest.

NBintFilastinyya1948: lol uskut.

YonatanISR2002: Can we try video again? I miss your face.

NBintFilastinyya1948: shut up. You've been gone for like seven hours.

YonatanISR2002: Aw, you've been counting! Someone, quick, inform the PFLP! Operative Nimreen, aka NBintFilastinyya1948, misses her little Jew-cub.

YonatanISR2002: jk

YonatanISR2002: Nimreen?

YonatanISR2002: I was kidding. Come on. Call me back. Please?

I answered the incoming call by pressing the little green-phone icon. Nimreen's face looked pinched. I tried to tell myself it was just the Skype quality again. The Internet in this hostel was shitty.

"I was joking, Nimreen."

"I know," she said. "I didn't say anything. How are you doing? How's Thessaloniki?"

Her tone was formal, awful.

"Salonica," I said, maybe a little sharply.

"It isn't it called Thessaloniki?"

"That's the Greek name, yeah. The Jews called it Salonica or Salonico."

"Sounds familiar," she said, and started humming the marching-band melody of "Mawtini," the Palestinian national anthem.

"It's actually been pretty fucked up, being here," I said, ignoring her humming.

"Fuck—e—e—ed up? Ho-o—ow?" Nimreen's voice was choppy again, slowed and molasses thick, like in some frightening fever dream.

"Can you hear me?"

She nodded, her head moving downward in a cluster of pixels, her eyes suspended where they had been a moment before.

I looked away.

Mostly I wanted to tell Nimreen about how I'd felt reading the brochure and about how I missed Jacko as I walked around the streets, how strange it felt to miss someone I never knew, how viscerally I did. I didn't get to tell her any of that, though. I started with the story from the first hostel, and as soon as I told her what the worker said about Zionism, she cut in.

"He sounds like a jerk, Jonathan, but he's partly right."

"Nimreen, come on . . ."

"No, I'm just saying, like, maybe not the 'worst kind,' because there's no Colonialism Olympics, but Zionism is for sure colonialism."

"No, it's not, Nimreen," I said, breathless, each fiber of my body frozen, and it felt like there was much more at stake here than just our different interpretations of history.

"Jonathan, it is. Jews came to Palestine, displaced and murdered the indigenous people," Nimreen said. "They turned us into refugees and took our land, closed the borders, turned al-Birwa into Ahihud, and Palestine into Israel . . . Khalas. That's it. That's colonialism. It's not so complicated."

"My grandfather didn't come for gold or cheap labor, Nimreen. He *was* cheap labor, actually. For my grandfather, Zionism wasn't about greed or getting rich. It was about survival. Without Zionism, I probably wouldn't be alive."

"Okay. But think about it: for us, what does it matter if it's gold or if it's fear?" Nimreen said. "The results, on our backs, in the Nakba, in Kufr Qanut . . . It's the same either way, Jonathan."

We can't be together, Jonathan, she didn't say.

"It has to matter, Nimreen! How can you not have compassion for someone seeking refuge from genocide or someone trying to save their people from extermination?"

How can your love for me not conquer everything, Nimreen? I didn't say.

"It's hard to have compassion for someone who is trying to steal your—"

"What else were we supposed to do, just march passively into the—"

"We weren't the ones killing—"

"What about Hebron in 1929? People with axes and—"

"We did fucked up things, but that's true for all people who resist colonization—"

"Whole entire families! Not Zionist militias. Little kids, their heads smashed open and—"

"I bet you didn't know that the ANC exploded cafés in Johannesburg—"

"We were trying to save our—"

"I actually can't believe that you're—"

"People. Why are—"

"Blaming us for things like—"

"I was trying to tell you about—"

"It's actually insane—"

"You were the one who started on the nationalist path—"

"I was—" Nimreen froze again. I looked around me. The blinds were letting streaks of late afternoon sunlight into the dim hostel room. It smelled like feet and tuna fish. I was alone with nine other empty bunk beds.

I clicked the red-phone icon. I sat in silence, staring at the screen. A minute later I saw in my chat box: *NBintFilastinyya1948 is typing*. I took a deep breath.

> **NBintFilastinyya1948:** I'm the one on the nationalist path? You're not serious.
>
> **YonatanISR2002:** I'm serious. You're wearing a keffiyeh to skype with me as if you're at like a demonstration or something Nimreen. Am I your enemy all of a sudden?
>
> **NBintFilastinyya1948:** How can you tell me that I'm on a nationalist path when you're the one who just took yourself on a self-designed Holocaust memorial trip to reinforce your victimhood so you can feel better about joining the army?

YonatanISR2002: Holy shit, Nimreen. Come on.

NBintFilastinyya1948: What.

YonatanISR2002: That's not what this trip is about.

NBintFilastinyya1948: No? So why now?

YonatanISR2002: It's about learning about my family who was murdered, Nimreen. And seeing where they used to live.

YonatanISR2002: Nimreen?

NBintFilastinyya1948: One sec.

I pressed the green-phone icon and answered the incoming call.

"I'm sorry," Nimreen said. She'd opened up her keffiyeh so that it was now draped over her shoulders rather than wrapped around her neck. "That was a little mean. This is just really hard for me, all of it. Anyway," she said, brushing a strand of her hair behind her ear. "My brother just got here. He'll probably want to say hi to you."

"Nimreen, wait," I said, but she'd already taken out her earbuds and walked out of your parents' computer room. I looked out the window, toward where a Greek flag was fluttering in the wind, toward the sea. When I looked back at the screen, I saw your face, Laith, big and way too close, one eye squinted shut, as if you were inspecting something through a magnifying glass. You were wearing a pink baseball cap, backward, and gnawing on the edge of your lip as you screwed the earbuds into your eardrums. Then you looked into the webcam and smiled.

"Hey, J," you said.

"Hey, Laith," I said, too loudly, my face flushed, remembering the beach. "What are you wearing, dude?"

"It's the new style, ya habibi," you said. "Thing's've changed in the Roly Poly Land since you've been gone."

You sounded entirely like yourself. I laughed.

"So, have you engaged in hand-to-hand combat with any Nazis yet?"

"Laith, that's not . . ."

"It's cool, it's cool. Just, if you see them, tell them that I say, 'Salam aleikum, dudes. Chill out. Smoke a joint. Maybe try meditation.'"

"Ha."

"I'm not kidding, J. I've been trying to meditate over the last few days."

"Yeah? How's that going for you?"

You closed your eyes and put on a mock-pious face and said, "Om . . ." And then went silent.

I wanted to hug you, through the screen. Our conversation felt so normal. I was able to follow your lead, then and always. Almost always, at least.

"Can I tell you something?"

"Sure," you said, "tell me lots of things."

"I went to the Jewish museum here, and I read this plaque about how the Jews in Salonica would go to their cemeteries before holidays."

"Mm."

"And guess what they called the visits?"

"What?"

"Ziyaras!"

"Yeah?"

"Yeah!"

"Makes sense, habibi. Jews and the Arabic language weren't always enemies."

Ziyara: Arabic for visit, or pilgrimage. The plural s was the Espanyolization. The museum was empty except for two German women, probably in their midtwenties, with intentionally messy haircuts and strained faces, speaking in whispers to each other. Under a grainy black-and-white photograph of people walking through a graveyard, I saw the description of the communal Ziyaras in Salonica, which would take place before the high holidays.

"A chance to talk with the dead and the living," the plaque read.

A Ziyara. Was that what I was doing? Nimreen had been mean, but I realized, even then, that she wasn't totally wrong. This was my Ziyara to my family's—my people's—sprawling cemetery, a chance to talk with the dead in the haunted city of Thessaloniki, in the usurping country of Greece, in the hellscape known as Europe, on the eve of what was for me and for so many other Israeli teenagers the highest holiday of all: my draft date.

I didn't tell it to you like that then, of course, Laith. I just wanted you to know about the Arabic, about how I felt like we could be on the same side of history after all.

"Anyway, Laith, I have to go. I'm going—I'm heading to the synagogue here."

It was Friday afternoon, by this point, and as much as I wanted to keep talking to you, I didn't want to be late.

"Achshav hegzamta," you said, in Hebrew. "Now you've gone too far, J. You're not going to come back all religious on me, are you?"

"I am. Beard and big hat and everything."

"Sexy."

"Uskut," I said, trying to force a laugh.

"Anyway, have fun, I guess?" you said. "You know, I haven't been to mosque since I was thirteen. I don't do God."

"Me neither. That's not why I'm going, Laith."

"So, what will you think about while you're there, if not the Big Guy?"

"I dunno. The past. My family. I'm not sure. I'll tell you when I see you. Is Nimreen there?"

You were silent. I didn't want to give the silence the chance to grow, so I spoke again.

"Never mind. I—just tell her I—I want to see you and Nimreen as soon as I get back."

"Inshallah," you said. "Bye, Jonathan."

"Bye, Laith," I said, but I felt uneasy about the way you said my full name, which you almost never did. I tried then to continue the conversation, like when I was a child and I'd stall my mom before she turned the lights off, struggling desperately to think of something, of anything else to say, to ward off the darkness for at least one more moment. "Wait, Laith—"

But it was too late. The call had already ended.

MY GUN WAS SO HOT IN MY HANDS, LAITH, and my vision was filled with salt and my tongue was a dry, swollen creature filling my mouth and I was afraid I would choke on it and poor little Yotam was leaking blood from his face and the stun grenades were so loud that they smashed the air around us into pieces and there were throngs of people everywhere and I wanted them to not be close by anymore, just for a moment, just so that I could catch my breath, and then there was a cracking sound and the reedy song of metal parting the desert air.

A faucet is leaking somewhere, here, and I want to imagine rain and mist and dark pines and wild horses but I can't. Instead, I just gnaw on the nothingness around me. Down the hall, another prisoner is screaming and slamming his body against his cell's door. I hold my hand between the fluorescent light and the dead-egg wall and squint my eyes, and for a moment, I can almost see the silhouette of something holy and good, but then it disappears.

THIRTEEN

IT WAS AT THE SYNAGOGUE IN SALONICA that I finally had a chance to talk with the living as well as the dead. As I walked in the direction of the synagogue from my hostel, the sun was setting, and Thessaloniki looked softer than it had earlier. I grudgingly admitted to myself that the Ancient Greek ruins in the middle of the gridded streets looked pretty in the fading light. Before too long I arrived near the market where the *Guide to Jewish Thessaloniki* that I'd picked up at the museum told me to go. I walked around the side streets and the main streets, looking for some indication, a sign, a star, but I saw nothing. Ten minutes passed, and then fifteen. I was beginning to worry that I'd miss the Shabbat services entirely, when a man in a black leather coat called out to me in English from a darkened corner.

"It's here."

I looked at him and then looked around me, to make sure he was talking to me.

"What . . . uh, what is?" I asked.

"You're from Israel, right?"

"Yeah," I said, "how did you—"

"Come in. The synagogue is here."

I looked past the man, to the unmarked door of an unmarked building, and followed him inside, past an unmarked desk, but when he opened the door to the room for me, everything lit up. There were four chandeliers hanging from the ceiling, and the wall was lined with white marble plaques. I looked at one of them, which was inscribed in Hebrew letters:

Kehilot que existían antes de la guerra en Salonico 1941.
"Communities that existed before the war in Salonico 1941."

And then it listed all of them. One was there before the Common Era; a few more, from Majorca and Hungary and Sicily, were founded in the 1300s, and then the list took off after 1492, following the expulsion from Spain, community after community after community, from Spain, from Portugal, from North Africa. The plaques wrapped around the room, until 1941.

There the list of communities stopped. Almost all the Jews who lived in Salonica that year, I knew, were taken by the Germans to Poland.

But the stop wasn't actually complete, Laith. The room wasn't just old chandeliers and plaques on the walls. There were also people seated on the benches, mostly men, mostly older, but some women also, on the other side of the divider, and some younger people too, and a rabbi in the center of the room. The singing was warm and resonant and the melodies rose and blended and the room sounded full. I didn't recognize most of the Sephardi melodies; they weren't familiar from Temple Beth Shalom, in Everbrook, where I'd been bar mitzvahed.

I took a white kippah from the basket and rested it on my head. It didn't sit well, because of all my curls. I took a prayer book and tried, in vain, to locate where we were in the service. After a moment, a shriveled old man sitting next to me, with a thin mustache and tired eyes, sighed and took the prayer book from me, leafed through some pages, and handed it back to me, his gnarled finger resting on a line in the middle of the page, its Hebrew words curling like black fire on the white paper.

"Bevakasha," he said, in Hebrew. "Here you are."

We were halfway through Shir HaShirim, the Song of Songs, and because I didn't know the melody, I paid attention to the words.

K'migdal David tzavarekh, banui l'talpiyot, elef haMagen talui alav, kol shiltei haGiborim.

Like the Tower of David is your neck, built as a citadel, one thousand shields hanging from it, all of them signs of the warriors.

Oh, Saba Yehuda.

The singing wrapped around me like a cool sheet on a hot summer night, and for a moment, I felt almost at peace. After a few more moments, though, my trance broke, and with no God to think about, I started to grow bored, but before too long, the services ended, and I was approached by a number of the men.

"Shabbat shalom," they said to me, shaking my hand.

"Shabbat shalom," I replied.

"Where are you from?" one said, in English. He was younger than the rest of them, by a lot, maybe in his early twenties. He was tall and slender, with bright eyes and light-brown skin. He wore a short, stubbled beard, and his mustache was fuller than the rest of it, a dark smoothness crinkling over his upper lip as he smiled.

"Israel," I said, looking into his eyes.

"Fantastic," he said, laughing softly. "I've never been, but I've heard it's beautiful." His laughter was a cool alpine lake. "Welcome, my friend."

"Thank you," I said. "I'm Yonatan."

I gripped his hand, firmly, and felt the smoothness of his palm against my own, felt a current of electricity dance through my gums.

"Yonatan, shalom. I'm Rafi," he said.

I looked at his face. I didn't say anything for a long moment.

"You'll stay to eat with us, yes?"

I nodded, and Rafi and I followed the others up flight after flight of stairs. Once in the dining room, I sat next to Rafi, sat close to him, and the rabbi made kiddush, and some got up to wash their hands, and others remained seated, and we all blessed the bread and were served guevos haminados, their beautiful brown shells spiraling and surging with such patterns that I was almost surprised and a little disappointed to see, once I'd cracked mine, that it was still just a regular hardboiled egg on the inside.

"How old are you, Yonatan?" Rafi asked.

"I'm eighteen," I said. I was overcome with a sudden urge to tell him everything. To fill the empty spaces inside me with his smile. To fill another member of my people in on my plans to serve my people. "I'm going into the army in a few months."

"Of course," Rafi said, "you must. You're eighteen years old, and you live in Israel." He cracked his egg gently on the edge of a bowl and then rolled it between his palms, and the shell fell off easily. "You'll be safe, though, Yonatan. Yes?"

He looked at my eyes directly.

"I will," I said.

"Promise?" Rafi said.

"I promise."

"Are you afraid?"

"Afraid?" I said, locking my jaw, locking my heart. "No."

"It's okay if you are," he said.

"I'm not," I said.

"Okay," he said, and scooped another portion of cucumbers and pickled cabbage onto my plate.

"Grasyas," I said, and Rafi laughed.

"We don't speak Espanyol anymore, Yonatan. In Greek it's efharisto."

"Oh, right, yeah," I said, deflated. "Efharisto."

"But you know what?" Rafi said. "Grasyas is okay too."

"What's it like here, today, in Salonica?" I asked. "Can you wear your kippah outside?"

Rafi touched his hand to the crown of his head, where the white kippah rested, a puffy half dome on the spikes of his buzzed hair. "No," he said, "it's not safe."

Anger surged from my chest, into my throat. "How can you stand it?"

"I don't wear a kippah full-time anyway," he said, touching his hand to my forearm, and then I felt a wind blow through my body, remembered that this anger wasn't mine to hold on to, so I tried to breathe it out of my nostrils and was distracted when Rafi spoke again. "Do you play chess?" he asked.

"What?" I said.

"Shakh mat."

"Ah, yeah. Sort of," I said. Saba Yehuda had taught me when I was young, during the summers we spent at his house in Pardes Ya'akov. "I'm not that good though."

"At least you're honest," Rafi said. "Or maybe you're being falsely modest, to force me to let my guard down . . ."

After dinner, he and I stayed in the synagogue until midnight, playing, talking softly, drinking leftover Shabbat wine. He destroyed me on the board, five out of five times, and it got worse the drunker I got.

Afterward, we walked out into the street. The night was chilly, and we walked next to each other, Rafi and I, and our bodies bumped against each other and then ricocheted off one another, back out into the almost-empty street.

"Can we go to the White Tower?" I asked.

"Sure." Rafi laughed. "But it's a long walk."

"That's okay," I said.

After a long walk that didn't feel so long, we arrived at a big, circular fortress-looking building, with turrets and small windows, pine trees leaning toward its base and away from it, supplicating, retreating, bowing.

"Do you want to go up?" Rafi asked.

"Can we?" I said.

Rafi smiled. "Not technically."

We walked around back, and he pulled a small pocketknife out of his front pocket and fiddled with the lock for a moment, until there was a click, and the lock fell open.

"Come on," he said.

I followed him, my heart pounding, as we walked up a steep ramp in the almost pitch-blackness, lit only by slivers of moonlight trickling in through the tiny windows. And then we were outside, and the air was colder, and the stars above us were brighter and the city looked smaller and everything looked more beautiful.

"If it weren't dark," Rafi said, "you could see Mount Olympus out that way."

I nodded. "It's so beautiful up here."

"It is," Rafi said, and I felt him looking at me.

I breathed in, deeply, and then moved toward him, with a forward lunge, and I kissed his mouth, hard, feeling the scratch of his mustache on my lips, and he returned my kiss, Laith, and our tongues pushed against one another, and I ran my hands over his buzzed hair and he wrapped his arms around my waist, and I reached down and unbuttoned his pants and felt his hardness, and it was a mirror of my own, and I felt tingles in my spine as his tongue wended its way into my eardrum, and then I fell to my knees, Laith, and I stayed there for a moment, my ear pressed against his thigh, his hairs tickling my face. I imagined the rush of blood inside his body, listening to the sea laughing around us, and I felt his smooth palms running through my hair, and the air was filled with cumulus clouds.

He surged forward toward me, lovely and gentle and veiny and smooth, and I took him in my mouth, as much of his beautiful hardness as I could. I wanted it all but I gagged, and he stroked my ear with his finger and told me to be slow, and I became slow, and I breathed in all of Salonica's air, scented with sweat, and I was empty and light, and everything felt strange but also safe, Laith, because he was a stranger, and a man, but he was also a Jewish man, and there was room for this, room for me to be with him like this, and to still be part of my family, part of my people, and I felt the breeze on my face as my tongue searched and my lips opened, and when he came, he grabbed a fistful of my hair and bitterness seeped between my molars, thickness filled my throat like undercooked pancakes in warm woolen winter, like better times that may or may not be yet to come, may have already passed. I swallowed and licked the edges of my teeth and then mucus blended into the clog of my throat as I started to cry, as I finally thought about you, Laith, and about Jacko, and how he had so few years to love his Rafi, and about your sister, and how I missed her so badly I thought my eyes might fall out, and about our ancestors, your grandmother and my grandfather, and about all that was lost and the little that was saved and all that was going to be lost again, soon.

I didn't know, Laith, I couldn't know, but maybe, somewhere inside me, as this strange-familiar man's fluids mixed with my own, I felt it. Or maybe not, Laith. Maybe it just seems now like I should have known. I held the smell of salt in my nostrils and I coughed and then I laughed and felt prideful and free and brave and I stood up and I was not so hard but I still kissed his mouth hard, drank his stubbled saliva thirstily, stroked the tendons of his unfamiliar nape, and then I was hard again and Rafi began to crouch down, but I pulled him back up, by his shoulders, needed him near me, and he took me in his hand, and his palm glided quickly and in the friction of the present and the past there was no future, and then I came, and I remembered that there was a future, and I felt afraid, Laith. We stayed up there for a few more moments, Rafi's arms wrapped around my torso, and I was shivering, and my face was wet and I wanted to say something, but I couldn't figure out what it was, so I kissed the sandpaper of his neck and prepared to become a warrior of Israel.

My grandfather had become a warrior of Israel. His family was in danger, but he had battle currents running through his veins now, new power swishing in his eardrums. That must have counted for something, right? Here's how I like to imagine that things happened, Laith:

I like to imagine that my grandfather stole a boat from the port master in Haifa and sailed to Salonica alone. That Jacko and their parents snuck out of their home in the blanket of night, hid in the White Tower, waiting. That my grandfather anchored the boat off the coast and swam to shore in the freezing water, pulling a raft behind him. That his older brother and parents climbed on, and they set sail for Palestine. That Jacko settled in Tel Aviv and found a new love, found that he could still love, and the two of them grew their hair long and tended a garden and hosted raucous parties to ward off the night. That Yuda got to grow old near his older brother.

But that's not true. Maybe I should just tell you the truth by now, Laith. You told me once that my stories made you tired. I don't know exactly what the truth is, Laith, but I can tell you what I do know: I know that there was no stolen boat, no raft, no swimming through freezing water, no garden, no new love, no parties to ward off the night.

I know that Jacko was turned into ashes in Auschwitz along with Saba Yehuda's parents and the rest of the Sadicario family, and forty-five thousand members of Saba Yehuda's Salonican family.

I know that sometime in the early 1950s, my grandfather read a book about Auschwitz that had been translated into Hebrew from Yiddish. In it, there was mention of the Sonderkommandos, the prisoners tasked with dragging the corpses from the "showers" and piling them into the ovens. I know that these crematoriums were diabolically efficient: three doors per crematorium, four bodies per door, hundreds of murdered Jews turned to ash per hour. I know that many of the Sonderkommandos were Salonicans, who were essentially mutes in the camp, their Espanyol sharing nothing but a few thin Hebrew threads with Yiddish.

I know that in the book there was mention of a revolt by the Sonderkommandos, in which they killed many Nazis and blew up one of their well-crafted crematoriums.

I know from Saba Yehuda that he read that one of the leaders of the revolt was a skeletal Sonderkommando, with a face that might once have been beautiful, a shaved head, and yellow eyes.

I know that when Saba Yehuda got married to my grandmother Varda they changed their family name to Shimshoni, after Shimshon, Samson, who pulled the pillars down. After Yuda's brother.

I know that they would definitely have cut Jacko's hair.

I know that it took Saba Yehuda and Savta Varda many years to have a child, with long desperate bouts of fertility treatment. I know that they were almost starved by their need to replenish the world with at least one more Jew.

I know that they finally succeeded.

I know that they named their daughter Raphaela.

My mom always told me that she was named after the angel of healing, Raphael.

But I know now that she was named after Yuda's brother's love.

———

Rafi and I walked down from the tower, and we hugged again, and I told Rafi I hoped to see him again, and that if he ever came to Israel, I'd like a rematch. "Chess," I clarified, too quickly, and he laughed and ran his finger along my jawline and told me to take care of myself, and I promised again that I would.

"Give me your phone?" he said.

I handed him my phone and watched as he typed in his number and above it, his name:

"Avraam (from Thessaloniki)."

I stared at my phone for a moment, and then I remembered that Rafi was killed. That Jacko was killed. I watched as Avraam blew me a kiss and then walked off into the grayness of the city of Salonica.

———

The next morning, I went to get breakfast in a small café. I didn't keep kosher generally, but I wanted to try then, out of some sort of sense of respect for what was, and maybe also with the echoes of the synagogue still reverberating in my stomach, the postsynagogue tastes dancing around the corners of my mouth. The only vegetarian option on the menu was a "Mediterranean sandwich."

When it arrived, it turned out to be olive paste on white bread, with mayonnaise and capers and two tomato slices and a sliver of lettuce. I hate capers, and the tomatoes looked soggy, so I took them off too, and then stared at the bread with the greenish paste and mayonnaise and lettuce and worried I'd break into tears right there, in the middle of this café, in the middle of Thessaloniki.

I wished I could have turned to you and Nimreen, sitting next to me. You could have just come as my friends, Laith. Even that would have been enough. Maybe, in some parallel universe, I could have told you two about the night with Rafi, whose name was Avraam, and you both could have listened, and laughed, and banished all the quivers from my stomach with the love that was in your eyes. You would have asked for an ashtray. Nimreen would have said something sarcastic to you about how you shouldn't smoke before ten a.m., and then smoked half your cigarette. Or maybe a quarter, and I'd have smoked the other quarter. You would have eaten the sandwich that I couldn't eat too, and Nimreen would have laughed at you, and you would have winked at me, capers in your teeth. Of course, I didn't invite either of you to come with me—the thought didn't even cross my mind—but I wish I had, Laith. I wish that I had.

FOURTEEN

WHEN I GOT BACK FROM SALONICA, I spent most of the rest of the summer with my other friends, my Jewish friends. Fridays included. We sat around, smoking our own joints, talking about the future. We stayed up late, checking each other out, full hard breasts, scraggly beards, new hairs, heavier softnesses. Some of us crawled off into the bushes together, emerging rosy-cheeked and shy-tongued, all stammer and loll. We were smug and gentle, enormous and generous. We wanted to snap off pieces of our new-adult selves and donate them to everyone else, so that they could feel some of the euphoric glory we felt. We were going to give of ourselves to our country soon. We walked all around the country. We went on hikes and watched as the wind blew little golden leaves into the air, as they caught the sun's glare and were perfect. We put sizzling coals on the hookah's foil and sat on upturned Goldstar beer crates, the hard plastic half buried in sand. We took buses to distant cities and towns, to Ashdod and Tel Hai and Dimona, just because. We talked about fate and meaning and novels. We restocked our supplies in the evenings: sunflower seeds and rolling papers. We did push-ups late at night, breath warm and beery in each others' ears.

Most of us started smoking cigarettes. We debated about the prime minister and the Situation. Some of us started reading the newspaper. We wrote journals and letters, scribbling our ideas down onto lined papers as best we might. We wrote our real sonnets, though, on ICQ and AIM. We made tea out of marijuana leaves snatched from Avichai's mom's garden. Some of us had sex. Some of us just blowjobs. Some gave fumbling cunnilingus. We drove just a little drunk. We played paintball and felt sticky as we shot our own friends and heard whispers of a less-perfect future, but then we felt better when we went out to pasta after, ate fusilli and tortellini and drank arak, those of us who could. We imagined what it would feel like, after. We promised we'd stay in touch. We touched urgently. We planned on getting an apartment together once we were postservice, starting a commune, composting and going to sleep at four a.m. and having naked dance parties and reading books about Buddhism and death. We loved death because it was so distant. We were ready to die because we were brave. We didn't want to die because we had so much more to give. We gave, Laith. We were good and decent kids. When we went in—and we all went in, every single one of us—there was some ego there, for sure, and some self-dreams of glory, some lustful imaginings of all the sex we'd get once olive-green, some puffed-up hopes that our parents and teachers would see how much bigger we'd got, some subterranean hummings of aggression, maybe, but mostly, it was generosity. We were ready to crack off pieces of ourselves and give, to something bigger and better than us, give as bravely and gently and savagely as we needed to. We were generous, Laith.

And where was I in all of this? I was trying to fall back in uncomplicated love with Rinat, short and wry and pretty and big-breasted and Jewish. We slept together four breathless times, but our most intimate moment came one morning when she buzzed my hair. Rinat smiled at me in the mirror, the electric razor humming in her hand, and asked if I was ready, and I smiled back and said that I was, and then she plunged the guarded blade forward and I was like Samson's inverse then, growing stronger as each curled lock fell limp onto the floor.

I was trying to run six days a week with Avichai on the beach, our calf muscles pulsing as our feet pressed hard into the wet sand. Rinat was a cluster of sparks, flickering bold and sensual. Avichai was chiseled stone, stoic, handsome, and tough. Through them, I almost managed to banish another part of me, Laith, the part that belonged to you and Nimreen. I was trying to move straight ahead, from my people's past into my people's future, my family's future. I was done zigzagging into the pasts and presents of other peoples, other families.

I was trying to forget Nimreen, and to forget you. I was trying to forget Nimreen's eyes, and the way Nimreen's laugh sounded, bursting from her chest in too-loud peels. I was trying to forget the glint of sun on her eyebrow, the taste of salt on her teeth. I was trying to forget the ways in which she was a mirror to my own national lusts and adolescent longings, the way in which I knew that the mirror was uneven. I was trying to forget your grandmother and your parents and your village and even your language, with its twenty-six synonyms for love. Habibi, I was trying to forget the word al-Kalf, and the word al-Jouah.

I was trying to forget the story Nimreen told me about how, when you were younger, the two of you watched the movie *E.T.* and you were so startled when E.T. came grumbling out of the bushes that you threw up. She patted your head and tried to clean up your vomit with tissues, even though you were both just six years old.

I was trying to forget the sidewalk color of Nimreen's irises. I was trying to forget your eyes, Laith.

I did make an effort, once, that summer, to build a bridge between my two worlds. Remember? Soon after I got back from Salonica, before my Paratroopers tryouts, I invited you and Nimreen to come with me and Avichai and Meron and Rinat and Maayan to the pasta restaurant in Haifa. It was awful, Laith.

You came bearing jokes like gifts, which I'd expected and banked upon, and Nimreen actually came, which surprised me. You were funny,

Laith, and managed to diffuse the tension quickly. I'd instructed my other friends, my Jewish friends, not to talk about politics, and they were game, even though they rolled their eyes at me. They were curious to meet the two of you, the mysterious twins, Yonatan's Arab friends. We all spoke in Hebrew to each other. It felt odd and somehow wrong, even, for me to address you and Nimreen in Hebrew, so I didn't speak to either of you directly. Small talk, mostly, everyone trying their best, you especially. Then Meron got excited, stood up, waved for someone to come over. It was his older brother, Tomer, off for the weekend but still in uniform. He came over, his gun swinging at his side, nearly brushing Nimreen's shoulder. Tomer said hi, looked conspicuously at Rinat's cleavage, looked up only when you and Nimreen gave him your names.

"Nimreen, huh?" Tomer said.

Nimreen didn't say anything. You stared intently at something on the wall, humming softly. I slumped in my chair. After a bit, Tomer left, went back to his friends, and my other friends chatted with each other breezily, and then Nimreen startled everyone except for you and me by standing up and asking for the bill, and you and Nimreen drove home without hugging me goodbye.

We didn't speak for a few weeks, Laith, until you called me, on a Tuesday evening, and asked to meet, one on one. I drove to Haifa with a dry mouth and heavy eyelids.

No more secrets.

"I'm joining the army, Laith," I said, not looking at you. We were sitting on a bench outside the university. No one was around except for the breeze and the lampposts. You were wearing a gray T-shirt and cutoff jean shorts.

"I know, Jonathan," you said.

Of course you knew. I turned to you. "Can we still—"

You cut me off: "It's like, I know *what* you're going to do, but I don't know who you'll be. I can't see you as a soldier, Jonathan."

"I'll still be me, Laith. No matter what clothes I'm wearing."

"I don't think it works like that."

You touched my cheek, and only when I saw the moisture gathered on your finger did I realize that I was crying.

"I wanted to say goodbye, before, J."

"Please don't make it like this," I said. "It's bad enough with Nimreen. Don't do this, habibi."

You didn't say anything, just chewed on the inside of your lip and looked out onto the sparkling lights of Haifa below us. You didn't light a cigarette then, which scared me. Your face was the farthest away it had ever been. You looked, Laith, just like your sister did a few days earlier, when she and I tried one last time. We sat at a hip café on Masada Street in Haifa, the only street I knew of where Hebrew and Arabic mixed easily, one of the only places in the world where maybe the two of us could belong.

"I'm sorry about the night at the restaurant," I said.

We sat opposite each other. Nimreen stared at me, silently, and then reached out to touch my head but withdrew her hand before it made contact.

"What the fuck happened to your hair?" she whispered.

I wanted to apologize again. I didn't say anything.

"You look like a skinhead," Nimreen said. "Or a cancer patient."

Nimreen must have seen me flinch, because her face softened. "I'm sorry. How is your grandfather?"

"He's okay," I said. "He's proud of me, proud that I'm going . . ."

Now it was Nimreen's turn to flinch.

The silence squirmed between us. Then Nimreen breathed deeply and reached her hand toward my head again. This time she brushed her palm over the prickles. "It feels nice at least. I'm glad you came, you idiot. I miss you."

"Me too," I said, guilt lining my throat, coating my voice. Because I missed her too, but I'd been drowning out my longing with Jewish sex, with Avraam in Salonica and Rinat in Pardes Ya'akov. Then I realized that maybe Nimreen had done the same, and I felt dizzy and bad. I tried to regain my balance and pulled a folded piece of paper out of my pocket. "I brought part of a poem, Nimreen."

"Look at you, Jonathan," Nimreen said, her eyes scanning mine, and I knew for a fact that she could read them and I wanted to look away, but I forced myself to stay as I was, looking at Nimreen's irises, and she took the paper from my hand. I watched as her eyes absorbed the words. Then she looked at me again, and I exhaled hard, realizing that I'd been holding my breath the whole time she read.

"Did you write this?"

"No." I laughed. "I wish. A different Jewish guy. I just copied it out of one of my mom's books. It's by Yehuda Amichai. It's called 'My Mother Baked the Whole World for Me.'"

"It's beautiful," Nimreen said.

"I thought . . . It reminded me of Darwish. I thought maybe we could translate it into Arabic."

Now the air was frozen around us. Haifa was frozen around us. The world was frozen around us. There was no world around us.

"I just thought it could be nice," I said.

Nimreen shook her head, looking down again. When she looked up, I saw that there were tears balanced on the rims of her eyelids.

"There's one line especially that made me think of you," I said. "Can we just translate that line?"

Nimreen stared at me, and I couldn't stand the silence anymore, Laith. So I started talking.

"Ahuvati mil'a et khaloni," I said, in the softest Hebrew I could manage, in this language of prophets, stones, black flames on white parchment, of a phoenix's resurrection. "B'tzimukei kokhavim."

My beloved filled my window with raisins of stars.

"Habibti mala'at shubbaki," Nimreen said, her eyes empty. "B'zabeeban nujuman."

Neither of us spoke for a few moments.

Then Nimreen said, "What the fuck are raisin stars?"

I laughed, and she laughed too, and it was the saddest laugh we'd ever shared, Laith.

"We probably won't see each other for a long time, huh?" Nimreen said.

I nodded, my eyes dry, and I felt stoic and rotten, like a crisp fruit with a mushy, spoiled core.

Maybe we could try to be together anyway, despite everything, I thought about saying but didn't. I wasn't that stupid, even then.

"Maybe we could send our kids to bilingual school," I said instead, "and they can learn Arabic and Espanyol."

Nimreen laughed, softly, and shook her head, and then I decided to try anyway, just to see if maybe, just maybe: "Nimreen, there were seven other villages."

"What?"

"There were seven other villages that had the same orders as Kufr Qanut," I said. Because I'd come prepared, not just with a poem but with a speech, Laith, as stupid as I feel admitting this now. "But we don't know about them in the same way because there weren't massacres there. Qalansawa and Jaljuliya and Tira and Kufr Bara . . . The commanders there refused their orders and made sure there were no massacres. One of the guys just shot into the air and another—"

"Jonathan."

"Another of the guys told his men they were allowed to shoot, but only when he gave the orders, and he never gave the—"

"Jonathan, stop it!" Nimreen's voice was taut, and when I looked at her face, I could see how angry she was. "No."

"No what, Nimreen?" I leaned backward, away from her anger.

"Don't, Jonathan. You can spin this a lot of ways, but don't try to say that you're joining the army 'for our sake.' To save us."

"That's not what I'm saying!"

"Then what are you saying?"

"I'm saying . . . What I meant to say is that I— It doesn't need to be like this, Nimreen. I need you to trust me that I'll still be me. That I won't do anything bad. You know me, Nimreen. I love you."

"That doesn't matter anymore, Jonathan," Nimreen said, and her voice then was resigned, not angry anymore, and I wanted her anger to return. "Of course I love you also. But it doesn't matter."

She touched my hand with her hand, and pulled her hand back to her purse, and pulled out a fifty-shekel bill, which was twice as much as our coffees cost, and she left it on the table and stood up and left.

I tried a different route, with you, Laith. I tried to tell you a story, about how my grandfather looked when I told him about the synagogue in Salonica, about the little puddles of light that splashed through his eyes. But you cut me off again, which wasn't like you. Or maybe it was.

"Stop. Your stories make me exhausted, Jonathan. You don't owe me any explanations. I'll see you around, inshallah."

I sat there on the bench, frozen, as you got up to leave, just like your sister had.

"Laith," I said, "don't go."

You hesitated before standing fully, and then you leaned over to me, quickly, and I flinched, just slightly, instinctively. You kissed me on the cheek, your stubbled face rubbing roughly against mine, your lips cooler than the hot August air, their slight moistness blending with my sweat, forming a little film of wetness that held your body to mine. I pressed my cheek into your lips. Then you stood up, straight. I thought you were going to walk away, but instead you bent down again, and you kissed my lips, hard. I leaned forward, trying to reach for you with my tongue, to pull you back toward me, but you stood up again, and this time you turned away.

"I miss you, J," you said, turning one last time back toward me. "I'll always miss you."

And then you were gone, Laith.

I didn't hear from either of you again until my draft date, in November, when you sent me those two text messages:

> [Laith!]: "He dreams of white lilies, an olive branch,
> her breasts in evening blossom."
> 09:16.

I was on the bus already, to the Tel HaShomer Draft Station, and my heart jumped when I saw your name on my phone, and then sank when I read the first message. I didn't understand it. Something about the words seemed vaguely familiar, like a nostalgic smell or some shadow taste from a dream, but they were so out of context, so lacking explanation. Only once I read the second text did I realize that these were segments of the Mahmoud Darwish poem that you'd promised to send me, sometime, back in Ahihud, in al-Birwa, before.

> [Laith!]: "Did you feel sad? I asked.
> Cutting me off, he said, Mahmoud, my friend,
> sadness is a white bird that does not come near
> a battlefield."
> 09:18.

V

White Lilies

FIFTEEN

ON JULY 25TH, 1859, THE JEWISH CHILDREN OF SALONICA learned a couple of nice songs and selected their white outfits in preparation for a visit by His Majesty, the Ottoman Sultan Abdul Medjid.

On July 25th, 1862, Abraham Lincoln's office issued an executive order for troops to be paraded about at ten a.m. and for thirteen guns to be fired at "the dawn of day," to commemorate the death of Martin Van Buren, who apparently found Lincoln uproariously funny.

On July 25th, 1938, forty-three Arab shoppers were killed by a bomb planted in a Haifa market by Jewish members of the Irgun. It was a Monday. Blood and pieces of flesh might have mixed with the juice and stalks and rinds of shattered fruits and vegetables.

On July 25th, 1957, Border Police first inspector Aryeh Menashes said that he disobeyed the "Allah yerhamu" orders in the village of Tira because he "could not kill women, children."

On July 25th, 1965, Bob Dylan went electric at Newport, which was highly upsetting for some, less so for others.

On July 25th, 2000, the Camp David peace summit ended. Everyone found the Maryland location to be charming, at least. Arafat's people noted that "jumping squirrels and other animals were a familiar sight, and with luck, you could even see a deer leaping from a bush to another."

On July 25th, 2006, two Israeli citizens were killed by Hezbollah rockets. One was an Arab and one was a Jew. Both their names began with the letter *D*.

I read about all these things on the Internet on July 26th. I was trying to find a pattern, a logic, something.

But there was only one July 25th that actually mattered: our July 25th, when history and the thick summer air pushed so heavily on my fingertip. I didn't mean to. Or maybe I did. My black angelic M-16 was burning my hands, Laith, and my yellow-green eyes were filled with saline and my tongue was deforming and my nostrils were sealing shut and the sounds were everywhere and there were people everywhere and I wanted them to move away, just so that I could breathe.

And then the cracking sound.

Eviad was right next to me.

Maybe it was Eviad, then, who shot into the crowd.

But it wasn't Eviad who shot. Sweet, sad Eviad always, always followed the rules. And I know the feeling of click and release, pointer finger sinking toward my body, tension snapping, heat and sound. Laith, it was me, Jonathan. I shot my tear gas canister directly into the crowd. I didn't mean to, I don't think. It wasn't something I thought to myself to do, something I thought I would do. It didn't feel like me. But of course, it was me: I was still me, Laith.

A crack from my lowered weapon.

A metal canister slicing through the swollen air.

A dull, fleshy thud.

The hiss of tear gas releasing into the sky.

The cluster of people scattered. Yelling swelled into the space around them, blending with the tear gas, blending with the dust. The shaggy drummers were still drumming, elsewhere, *kathump, ka-thump thump*. As the crowd thinned and the smoke billowed, I saw a thin figure with its hand raised toward its face stagger a few steps, wobble, and then crumple.

Then I heard it. I swear I did.

A scream. Your name.

"Laith!"

I saw another person, a girl, running in long strides toward where the thin figure had fallen to the earth, toward where the smoke was concentrated. I started running too, then, sprinting toward her, ignoring Eviad's shouts, which were soon joined by the Commander's.

"Soldier! Soldier! What the fuck are you doing? Get back here, now! This is an order! Everyone, hold fire. Soldier!"

But his voice was faded. I heard my own pulse pounding in my eardrums.

Ka-thump. Ka-thump.

My heavy gun was crashing down on my hip as I ran, my helmet banging on my head, but I didn't notice the pain, didn't notice the ragged spiked edges of my breath, the thorns mixing with oxygen in my throat, didn't notice the pins poke-stabbing at my soft eyeballs. Or noticed, but didn't mind. Couldn't mind. I was one of the fastest runners in the platoon, but even I usually ran awkwardly in all my gear. Now I flew. I heard Eviad's voice from not so far behind me, but it sounded like an echo in some distant lonely valley. "Yonatan, they'll hurt you! Yonatan, come back!"

A bead of sweat dripped into my eye, and the wet burning in my cornea brought my thoughts back into focus. Was I putting myself in danger? Would they hurt me? I was coughing so hard I could barely breathe. I didn't care, though. I needed to know what had happened. What the fuck had I done?

"Laith."

Was this possible? It wasn't. It was. It couldn't be, though. I kept running a few more paces until I had reached what remained of the crowd.

"I want to help! I want to help!" I yelled. The Arabic words tumbling out of my mouth seemed to catch the demonstrators off guard, and the crowd parted for me like a sea. No one laid a hand on me.

"I've come to hel—" I said, my voice catching in my throat. If everything had been moving quickly before, now it was as though time had slowed.

It felt now like mud was pouring into my windpipe, a sopping heavy slosh. I looked down at the body, splayed on the dusty ground.

I looked down at your body, Laith.

At your face, stubble lining your chin.

Your face looked swollen, odd, slack jowls, dusty strangeness, shrouded in smoke. Your lips, which I knew to dance around easy smiles, busy with the mischief of mocking the world for all its seriousnesses, were parted. I could still feel their soft-wet echo on my eyelids, from almost a year before. The right side of your face looked strange, but fine. Eye closed, cheek sagging ever so slightly backward, pulled by gravity toward the earth. It looked like you might just be resting. Taking a rest in the desert, in the middle of a demonstration, which was so like you, Laith! I almost laughed, but the left side of your face was

not fine.

In the place where your left eye usually was—the eye that you winked with, Laith, your winking eye—there was a flower of red. A bursting flower-fountain. No left eye left, just a flower, a pouring flower, a rushing red flower. Your left eye gone to sopping dark. Dripping down the side of your face, into the sand. Oh Laith, my softest love, my gentle friend. What happened to your eye?

Nimreen crouched next to you. She also looked strange: through the cloud of gas and dust, I could see that she was wearing a black hijab, wrapped tightly around her head. We all looked strange. Nimreen in a hijab. Jonathan in a helmet, holding an M-16 fixed with a grenade launcher. Laith with a flower instead of an eye. Only part of Nimreen's face was visible, rounded by the head covering's fabric. Dust and gas were all around us, but even through the haze, I could see that there was no glint on her eyebrow, that she had no ring above her eye anymore.

"Nimreen," I whispered, "it's me."

The look on her face was not one of recognition, Laith. It was one of horror. Her eyes were narrowed, and her lips were twisted in an expression I'd never seen on her face before. Then, on the ground, a movement. A quiver of your movement, Laith. A groan. Your right eye fluttered. Blinked open. Open! Everything snapped into sharp focus.

I kneeled down.

"Laith," I said, speaking quickly, "Laith, habibi, it's me, Jonathan, your friend, Jonathan. I'm going to help you. I'm going to get help. I'm so sorry."

Your eye fluttered again as you tried to focus on what you were seeing.

"Hatha ana, Jonathan," I said.

"Jonathan?"

I almost laughed out loud, almost burst into tears, real tears, not the forced ones pulled from my face by the gas. Your voice sounded so odd, Laith, but at least you'd spoken. The relief of hearing my name come out of your mouth didn't just fill my body, it became my body. A body made out of relief.

"Yes, Jonathan!" I said, and placed a hand on your shoulder. Your right eye was streaming translucent, almost like your left was still streaming dark red.

Then a voice from next to me, in Arabic. "Don't touch him."

I whipped my head around, and then withdrew my hand quickly, as if your body had grown suddenly scalding. I looked over at the misty, unfamiliar Nimreen.

"But I'm going to help . . ." I said.

Her eyes were streaming too. Her gaze was not identical to your gaze, Laith, was now twice your gaze, pouring from both her eyes rather than one. She looked so strange to me. It had been so long since I'd seen your sister, Laith, so long since I'd seen you.

———

Do you remember the walk we took in the Carmel forest, the three of us? The late-afternoon sun was dripping through the leaves, drenching the leaves, bathing us in its final offerings of warmth for the day. Nimreen wore a sky-blue tank top and had her hair tied in a complicated braid. Goose pimples had risen all over her arms, and she rubbed her hands up and down them. I offered her my flannel, and she shook her head sharply, conclusively, leaving no room for my dopey chivalry. You were wearing jean shorts and a long-sleeved shirt, and, like always, smoking as we walked. You had to stop a few times throughout the walk and put your hands on your knees, clearly winded, always grinning, though. Always winking. Nimreen and I teased you a lot. We loved you so much, Laith.

"Maybe everything could be okay here, despite everything," Nimreen said, looking upward. "You know?"

"How high are you, Nimreen?" I laughed. "You don't sound like yourself."

She punched me in the shoulder, hard, like usual, and laughed, and her laugh filled the whole forest and the whole of Haifa and the whole land and most of my heart.

"I'm just saying," she said, her face so shy, like it occasionally became, her eyelids fluttering like twin moths. I wanted to kiss both her eyelids, then and forever.

"Laith, you okay back there?" I called.

"Habibi, uskut," you said.

I did. I shut up and you caught up.

"What were you two talking about?"

"Nimreen here was just getting all optimistic. It was weird."

"Uskut, ya ahbal," Nimreen said, her eyes squinted in an exaggerated glare, a smile playing at the corners of her lips.

"Well, anything could happen. Earthquake, space invasion, peace," you said, and I laughed, mimicking the way I'd heard adults laugh: tired, cynical, thick-skinned.

"No, seriously," you said. "May peace be upon you, my friend."

You crumbled a leaf between your fingers and sprinkled it in my hair. I laughed again, now a real laugh, and tried to brush the detritus out of my curls.

"And upon you, Nunu." You moved toward your sister, but Nimreen swatted your hand away, also laughing.

Maybe, though, I thought. Maybe.

The three of us walked in silence on the dirt path toward home, one of you on either side of me. The sun was setting. The light was dying, as they say, as it was. I did the bravest thing I could think of doing. I took your right hand in my left hand, and Nimreen's left hand in my right one, threading my fingers through your knobby ones and through her thinner ones. Nimreen laughed, and then you laughed too, and then I laughed too. I held on to your hands for another moment, hard, and then let them go.

"Nimreen," I said, "Nimreen."

"Rooh min hoon," she said, her voice strange and foreign. I understood the Arabic just fine, though: "Get away from here."

I stared at her, as hard as I could, but I couldn't recognize her, couldn't get her to recognize me.

"Nimreen," I said again, my throat so close to closing that part of me just wished that it would. That my throat would close and I wouldn't have to stay in this world anymore: a world in which your eye, Laith, had become a flower, in which your sister couldn't even say my name. But then I swiveled around to look at the crowd gathered around us. They looked scary, Laith, like maybe they wanted to hurt me, to rip my limbs off my body. I wanted you to tell them I was there to help. I wanted you to protect me, Laith. I didn't want them to hurt me. The screen provided by the tear gas and dust and shock was fading. Nimreen, with her naked eyebrow, face wrapped in her hijab, began to yell in Arabic to get him out of here, pick him up, he's hurt, he's hurt, let's go. Around the edge of the crowd, I could see the Commander and Tal and Eviad and Gadi and maybe five other soldiers and Border Policemen running my way, coming to rescue me from amidst the Arabs. A Wolf and two jeeps bounced along the rocky earth behind them.

I stood up and pushed my way through the demonstrators, who parted without too much resistance. I ran back in the direction of Eviad and Tal and the others, intercepting them just as they arrived at the edge of the crowd. *Maybe they can help Laith*, I thought. Eviad grabbed me by the shoulders and Tal placed his hand on my back and he guided me toward the Wolf. The Commander and two of the Border Policemen kept their guns trained on the group.

"Yonatan, what the fuck is wrong with you?" Eviad said, his face gleaming with such softness.

"Yonatan, are you okay?" Tal said, his face pinched with such worry.

"Help him," I tried to say, but the words were drowned in a rush of masticated and digested birds—chickens and pigeons and doves—swarming up into my throat. I pushed Eviad and Tal aside and vomited brown rot onto the beige earth. I knelt down, and out of the corner of my eye, I saw an ambulance going as far as it could on the dirt road and then stopping. Three young medics jumped out, carrying a stretcher. Around them, some people were talking, others were running. Some were still shouting, others had fallen silent. One drum, somewhere, was still beating. Puffs of smoke, dissipating into the sky. The crack of another single tear gas canister being shot, a strange dark bird tumbling into the air and then downward. I lay flat on my back, next to the putrid pile of my vomit, next to the little beetles scouring the earth, next to the Wolf's tire, next to so many pairs of red-leather Paratrooper boots, and I stared upward, up into the barren blue sky.

Maybe, I thought, you were staring at the same sky, with the eye that had not turned into a flower. Maybe this was the last sky we'd ever look at together, Laith.

———

What a big sky.

VI

When I Lie Down and When I Rise Up

IV

SIXTEEN

THEN, ON THE AFTERNOON OF JULY 25TH, I went home. I was off for the weekend anyway. The Commander told me to leave early, to get some rest. To shake it off. I'd be okay, he said, thumping me on the shoulder. I'd be okay. He told me that he'd decided against disciplining me, even though he could have, for disobeying orders by running into the crowd, putting myself and others in danger.

"What if they'd taken your gun?" he said to me, his tone stern.

I felt momentarily grateful to him and then disgusted with myself for feeling grateful. I deserved to be punished. I nodded, was silent. I hadn't spoken a word since the demonstration ended. I wasn't able to. My tongue was cleaved to the bottom of my mouth. I would not speak. At least that, lest I forget you, oh Laith. I didn't speak to Tal or Eviad or Gadi. Eviad tried, for a few moments, telling me to snap out of it, that everything was fine now. Tal pulled him away, his eyes sympathetic, left me alone with my silence.

———

When I got home, my mom took one look at my face and started crying. She pulled me into a hug. At the sound of my mom's tears and the touch of another human, I felt a sob erupt from my own chest, accompanied by an ugly braying sound.

"Imma, what's wrong with Jonathan?" Zehava asked. I hadn't cried in front of my little sister for years, since I was a kid.

"Shh, sweetie, it's fine," my dad said, taking Zehava into the kitchen.

"Honey, are you okay? What happened?" My mom spoke in a quiet voice, in English. She told me that she'd gotten a call from my Commander, who told her that I had freaked out during my first mission, putting down a riot. That I had run into the middle of a crowd of rioters, for no reason.

For no reason.

He didn't know about you, Laith. My mom didn't either. No one knew about you.

I couldn't speak. I didn't know where to start.

"Jonathan, honey, please say something."

I began sobbing harder. My mom's face was a mask of fear. I didn't want to hurt her too.

"Sorry," I said, between sobs. "I'm—I'm sorry."

I moved away from my mom, away from the concerned gazes of my dad and sister, peeking out of the kitchen. I ran up the stairs, on all fours, like a dog, like I had when I was younger. I shut myself in my room and locked the door. I heard footsteps coming up the stairs after me.

"Jonathan." My dad's voice was low, overly calm. "Please open the door."

"I'm—" I tried to steady my breath. "I'm fine. I'm okay, Dad. I just need—I just need some time."

"Okay, well. I'll be out here if you need anything," my dad said, and I could hear his thin frame slumping downward outside my door.

"Dad, I'm fine. I'm not—I'm fine," I said. I wasn't going to hurt myself. I'd already hurt enough people for one day.

Right?

Right.

Right?

I took off my boots, placed them gently by the door. I took off my gun, tucked it carefully under my bed. Then I lay down. For a long time I didn't move at all. I tried to be as still as possible, breathing slowly, barely letting my chest rise, trying to sink into the mattress, to disappear, trying not to think of the awful thing that lurked below me (or maybe it was in me), trying to banish the thoughts and memories and images to another day, another time. I'd deal with it all later, Laith.

Laith.

Oh, fuck.

I stayed in my room all night. I didn't come down for Shabbat dinner, which was supposed to have been a birthday celebration for me. Happy nineteenth to Jonathan. The idea of celebrating anything, and celebrating me in particular, made my gut convulse. The delicious smells coming from the kitchen made me gag. I fell asleep around nine p.m. with all the lights still on, my phone next to my pillow.

I woke up on Saturday to a knock on my door. I rolled over and looked at the clock: 12:54 p.m. My room was filled with smells of dust and sweat and darkness. I checked my phone. No one had called, but the messages folder was open, and your name was at the top of my screen. I'd fallen asleep scrolling through your old text messages, again and again. You'd only sent two sections of the Darwish poem on my draft date, back in November. But over the course of the next few months, Friday after Friday, you'd texted me the entirety of "A Soldier Dreams of White Lilies," piece by piece. I'd saved each message.

> [Laith!]: "—And what did you see?
> —I saw what I did:
> a blood-red boxthorn.
> I blasted them in the sand . . . in their chests . . .
> in their bellies."
> 11:10

I was a soldier who dreamed of white lilies, sand everywhere. I pulled a flower from your body. Not from your breast or your belly, but from your face, Laith, from your beautiful eye. Your winking eye. I could feel it in my breast, though, the way your wink blossomed into a red flower, into white lilies. The desert and the smoke and the dust.

> [Laith!]: He collapsed like a tent on stones, embracing
> shattered planets.
> 11:47

The knocking on the door continued, shaking me from my swollen thoughts.

"Please go away," I said. "I'm fine. I just don't want to talk."

"Yonatan," said a voice that belonged to neither my mom nor my dad. "Zeh Saba. Tiftach et hadelet." Saba Yehuda's Espanyol-inflected Hebrew rolled smooth and authoritative through my thin wooden door, instructing me to open it.

I jumped out of bed, still dressed in my uniform.

"Just a minute, Saba," I said. I pulled off my uniform's pants and shirt and pulled on jeans and a button-up, wiped my nose with the back of my hand. I threw the sheet over the bed in a way that would make it look at least half made, shoved a pile of clothes under the bed with my foot, recoiling as I brushed the cool metal of the gun with my toes. I took a deep breath, rubbed my sleep- and tear-crusted eyes, sniffed deeply to check if the room smelled okay. It didn't, so I opened the window, let the hot summer air in, and then opened the door, panting.

Saba Yehuda stood there, his chest still broad even as his shoulders slumped with age, with the weight of his sickness, and with everything else. His posture was stiff. His white mustache sat elegantly on his upper lip. His eyes, his yellow-green eyes, stared unblinking into my own foggy yellow-green ones. I quickly averted my gaze. It wasn't that I didn't want to cry in front of Saba Yehuda; it was that I couldn't.

"Yonatan," said Saba Yehuda. "Sit."

I sat on the edge of my bed. Everything outside the room melted away, and for a moment, I was only a pair of ears, a heart, genetic threads of this powerful man, who happened to be my grandfather. I was ready for him to fix everything. Saba Yehuda pulled my swivelly desk chair out and sat down across from me. It was sweltering. The sun was pressing fiercely into the room.

"I don't know what happened," Saba Yehuda began, and I felt disappointment rush into my chest. I thought, I hoped, that somehow he would just know.

"I shot my—I shot someone," I said. My voice was a monotone. It was not mine. It was the voice of someone else. "I was not myself."

Saba Yehuda looked at me and nodded. His face showed no hint of surprise, or horror, or—worst of all—pity. Of course. Why would it?

Saba Yehuda was silent for another moment, and then he spoke.

"There are only two sides, Yonatan. Us and everyone else."

"But that's not—"

"If the person you shot had the chance to shoot you, would he not have done so?"

I felt tears rush up into my throat and swallowed them. He would not have, I didn't say.

"Each man has limited space in his heart, for sadness and for sorrow and for regret. Keep the space unoccupied, Yonatan. You'll need it, for your own people, for your own brothers."

"Not all of them are my enemy," I said.

"Of course they aren't. But neither are the Arabs your family. Think, for a moment, of your sister, of Zehava. If you had to kill many of them to save her life, you would. Even if some were innocent."

I thought of my sister, of little, frizzy-haired, round-faced Zehava, who got on my nerves far more often than not.

"I would kill myself to save her life," I said.

"That's not the question!" Saba Yehuda said, his voice suddenly angry.

I flinched and was silent and looked down at the floor. I did not want to risk his reading my eyes, for the stories buried there did not fit here, did not fit anywhere.

"Yonatan," Saba Yehuda said, his voice calmer again.

"It's not a fair question," I said, still looking at the ground. I sounded like a child.

"It is the only question," Saba Yehuda said. He rubbed a bony hand across his forehead and began to speak in a softer voice than before, softer than the voice I was used to hearing from my grandfather. "I was in the Palmach, you know."

I nodded, even though it was a statement and not a question. I knew. Oh, how I knew.

"By 1948 I was older than you are now, nearly thirty. I was a captain. Have you thought of becoming a captain?"

I nodded. I had.

"Good."

I nodded again, squirming inside my own skin, inside the silence that packed the room. I longed for sound, for words, for something to distract me from the shrieking inside my ears.

After another moment, Saba Yehuda continued, mercifully putting an end to the silence: "In the summer of that year, my company was sent into a village in the Galilee. We were given orders to neutralize the enemy there. When we arrived, it seemed that most of the enemy fighters had fled or had been killed or were off fighting elsewhere. I don't know. What I do know is that the people who remained, the teenaged boys, the women, the old men—they were angry. They had expected to win the war, believed that the Arab armies would sweep in and clear the Jews out for good. They thought that by then, we would be flailing in the sea, drifting corpses in the Mediterranean."

I shuddered at the image, the green-blue sea turned reddish. I realized with a start how little I knew about death. I shook my head.

"That wasn't what happened, of course. Their fighters were mostly volunteers from the surrounding Arab countries and local peasants who didn't know the first thing about war. They fought for honor, or to oust the Jews. On the other hand, we fought as though this was our last chance to survive as a people. And it was. Losing was not an option for us. We had nowhere to return to, nowhere to flee. This was our only home."

I nodded and looked at the floor again and thought about Thessaloniki. The only indication of the city's Jewish past was a small memorial statue at the edge of a parking lot—and the Jewish tombstones that had been used as building blocks inside churches and other buildings, or discarded across the city, whispers of Hebrew and Espanyol and genocide muffled by the modern Greek glow.

"Anyhow, the people in this village, they were angry. You could see it in their eyes. Some of the women spat on us. After conducting a search, we began to gather everyone into the center of the village. Then it happened. One of the Arabs was hiding in the doorway of one of the houses. As my men passed by, he leapt out and tried to ram a knife into the chest of one of my soldiers. He did not succeed. It is more difficult to stab a dull knife into another person's body than you would imagine."

I nodded and instinctively drew a hand up to my collarbone.

"Now, my men were well trained, and within seconds, the attacker was pulled off my soldier, onto the ground. He writhed and shouted for ten seconds or so, and then lifted one of his hands over his head. A crowd was beginning to gather around us. One of my soldiers—not the one who was stabbed, another one—he looked at me for a moment, asking. I looked away from him, toward the hills in the distance, responding. He shot the first bullet into the attacker. Another two soldiers shot the next. The crowd fell back. The village grew silent."

Silence in the village, silence in the room.

"It was the more merciful of the two paths, Yonatan. We needed to have them understand that we would not tolerate attacks against our forces. We had to then, like we have to today. They understood this then. No one else attacked us in that village, and no one else was killed there."

I was silent.

"Those were my responsibilities: my men, my people," Saba Yehuda said, clearing his throat again. "Your actions are not yours alone. They are all of ours, Yonatan. You are fighting for all of us. I am proud of you."

He stood up, with some effort. He shook my hand and walked out of the room.

After Saba Yehuda left, I decided to shower and then go downstairs. I didn't want to see anyone, but I wanted even less to be left alone with my thoughts, with the images flashing inside my head, of bodies and red, of flowers and dust and gaping holes. It was the worst during transitions. When I was absorbed in something, Laith, like brushing teeth, I was almost okay. It was when I went from brushing teeth to showering, that act of changing acts—it was then that all the pictures came rushing forward in my mind and it felt like my chest was going to crack and I wasn't completely sure if I wanted to live in a world where all the things I was imagining actually existed outside of my imagination. I turned the water as hot as it could go, and it hurt, and I prayed to the nothingness around me for the scalding wetness to peel layers of grime not only from my body but from my being.

After, I looked in the mirror for a moment. I stared at the reflection of my own eyes, nearly the same color as Saba Yehuda's, both of them intact and fragile, so soft that the tiniest sharpness could pierce them, ruin them. Let alone the force of a metal tear gas canister fired from an M-16's grenade launcher. I walked downstairs.

My parents both stood up when they saw me, like nervous peasants greeting a fickle king, and I smiled feebly. I was glad that neither of them forced me to speak and regretted that Zehava wasn't there. I imagined her rolling her eyes at me, telling me to "Stop being so mopey." I sat down on a big, soft red chair and curled my feet under me, and the three of us sat in silence for some long moments. Then my mom got up, saying it was time to make dinner. A few moments later, my dad went to help her, and I was left alone in the room with my thoughts: a transition, although I hadn't moved. I stood up, frantically, walked into the computer room, and logged on. My dad's homepage was set to the *Jerusalem Times*. I scrolled through it, barely reading, but finding a semicomfort simply in seeing the flood of words and pictures glowing on the screen. Then I stopped scrolling, the cursor hovering over one of the headlines, and clicked.

ARAB WOUNDED IN CLASHES WITH IDF;
CHARGED WITH INCITING A RIOT.

By Matityahu Kirschorn
Updated Friday, July 25th, 16:47

Jerusalem—An Arab rioter was injured during clashes with the IDF on Friday morning, July 25th, near Kerem El in the South Hebron Hills district. Clashes broke out between IDF soldiers and rioters, who threw rocks and other objects at the soldiers. Such clashes between Arab rioters and IDF forces are frequent in Judaea and Samaria. "There was a rain of stones," said "A.," a captain in the IDF. "We were afraid for our lives, but used restraint in our response, and used crowd dispersal methods according to protocol. I am very proud of how we responded with restraint." The IDF spokesperson, Shiri Rogel, said in a statement about the incident: "The rioter has been charged with stone throwing, and with inciting a riot. There are numerous eyewitnesses that attest that he not only threw stones at our forces, but was also among the instigators of the riot against our boys, who sought to calm disturbances outside an illegal Arab outpost near the community of Kerem El. The circumstances of his injury are being investigated, but there is strong indication that he was struck by a stone thrown by another rioter. We will begin legal proceedings against the suspect immediately upon his release from the hospital, where he is being treated by the best of our doctors."

I read the article a second time without breathing. I tried to tell myself that maybe this article was referring to a different event, to something else entirely. But nothing else had happened near Kerem El on Friday. I felt dizzy, and then I stood up.

For the first time since returning home, I didn't feel as though I was on the brink of tears. I left my house, through the front door. I heard my mom call from the kitchen, her voice frayed: "Jonathan, honey, where are you going?"

"Just a walk," I said. "Back soon."

I was astonished by how calm my voice sounded.

As I walked out into the afternoon sunlight, I pulled my phone from my pocket and squinted until my eyes focused. The skin of my arms was pulled into tight goose pimples, despite the heat. My breathing was shallow as I pressed the call button.

He picked up after a few rings.

"Alo? Who is this?" There were sounds of clinking bottles and laughter.

"Commander, this is Yonatan."

"Yonatan!" the Commander said, his voice filled with a warm tenderness that I had never heard before. "Soldier. How are you?"

"Fine," I said, listening to the sound of the Commander's heavy footsteps, the laughter fading into the background. "Thank you."

I was tempted to backtrack, to tell him never mind, to hang up. I forced myself to think of red flowers, of white lilies, soft skin, beautiful stubble, cracked earth. I took a deep breath. "No. Actually, not fine."

A door opened and then closed.

"I just read the news . . ."

The wind in my ear told me that he was now outside, somewhere, just like me. I realized that I had no idea where he lived. For all I knew, he could be five streets over or at the opposite end of the country.

"And . . . and the story is filled with lies. It isn't true. That wasn't what happened."

I heard the Commander inhale, then exhale sharply.

"Soldier, be careful. You've had a rough few days. I'm not sure your judgment is with you right now."

"I know what I'm saying!" My voice rose an octave. "Come on. 'Hit by a stone thrown by another rioter'? 'Charged with organizing a riot'? Laith wasn't organizing a riot."

"Who wasn't?"

"The Arab demonstrator."

"How did you know his name?"

"How can the army be pressing charges against him?"

"Soldier. There are things you don't understand. You're green. This was your first field mission. It's okay."

"It's not okay! He wasn't hit by a stone. He was . . . He was shot in the face."

"Soldier, you don't know that."

"I know it!"

"You don't."

"I do! I know it—I know it because I shot him."

"I didn't hear you say that. Listen to me, soldier. You don't know what happened to the rioter. Do you understand me?"

"What are you talking about? Did you not hear what I just told you?"

"Soldier."

"I do know what happened to him! I shot him. I shot him while he was protesting against our plans to destroy a whole fucking village in the West Bank, where we shouldn't even be in the first place, and now he's injured and might lose an eye, and then when he gets better—"

"Soldier, stop it, I'm—"

"When he gets better, and when they fix his eye, he is going to be charged with starting a riot? Which we of course have no way of knowing that he actually started or if he even threw stones at all, which I'm sure he didn't—"

"Soldier, stop!"

"Stop telling me to stop! Have we lost our fucking minds? This is insane! We can't—"

"Soldier, you could get in a lot—"

"Get in trouble? I don't care. Just don't punish him."

"Soldier, stop, please, I'm asking you once mo—"

"Just please fucking make them—"

"Yonatan!"

"—drop the char—"

"Yonatan, there aren't going to be any charges."

"Really? Are you . . . Thank you! Oh God. Thank you. Thank you, thank you, thank you. But how—"

"Yonatan, the rioter is dead."

"What?"

"Soldier, he's dead."

———

"Are you afraid of dying?" I directed the question at both of you, looking up from my book, *The Things They Carried*, by Tim O'Brien. The three of us were sitting around a wooden table in a quiet café, drinking hot chocolates and coffees and reading. We'd decided that this Friday, we'd read in silence, together, after Nimreen had said she was tired of talking, that everyone talked too much. It was late spring.

"Good morning, ya habibi." You laughed. "Where did that come from? What is that book about anyway?"

I shrugged.

"Okay. So, yeah, I'm afraid of dying, of course," you said, closing your book, *Infinite Jest*, by David Foster Wallace, which you'd been slogging through since before I met you. "But there are also worse things in the world than death."

"So much for silent reading time." Nimreen sighed and dog-eared her page in *The Beginning and the End*, by Naguib Mahfouz.

"Like what?" I said.

"Boredom, for example. Or, like, super severe loneliness. Anyway, though, it's too morbid to think like this. Why don't we talk about things that are *better* than death? Yeah? I'll start: So, hot chocolate, coffee, afternoons, weed, Flea's bass lines . . ."

"I'd die for my family," I said, ignoring you, "and for my friends. Not all of them, but a few."

"I'd add hedgehogs," you said, ignoring me. "And the sea. And seahorses! Did you know it's the male seahorses who get pregnant? Wild, right?"

"Do Laith and I make the cut?" Nimreen said, taking a sip of her coffee, her strange eyes flicking over my face.

I nodded. I had heard that thing about seahorses.

"Rain in the late spring," you said, pulling out a cigarette and holding it lengthwise between your thumb and pointer finger. "Mist. Fog in the early morning. Sleeping in, though, for sure. Sunsets. French fries.

Freedom fries! Drinking water when you're thirsty, or a really, really cold beer . . . Did I mention weed? No? So, weed."

"I'm willing to die for what I believe in," Nimreen said.

"Yeah, me too," I said quickly, puffing out my chest a bit.

"Come on, you two. You're ruining the game," you said, moving your head around to look at your sister and at me reproachfully. "'I'd die for what I believe in,' *bum bum bum bummm!* Sound the trumpets. Seriously. You two have both been brainwashed by everyone here's fetish for martyrdom."

"You have to have something worth dying for in order to have something worth living for," Nimreen said.

I nodded.

"How about killing?" you asked.

"Also," Nimreen said. I nodded again. We still hadn't kissed yet, Nimreen and I. I was paying attention only to her, was barely listening to you, Laith. What if I had been?

It probably wouldn't have made a difference.

"False," you said. "That's not true."

And then you sighed and lit your cigarette and took a deep drag and blew out a small beam of smoke and smiled. "I wouldn't kill anyone for hedgehogs or Nutella. Maybe for the chance to sleep in, though . . ."

Nimreen and I laughed. You laughed too.

We laughed and laughed.

We were always laughing when we were together.

SEVENTEEN

WHEN I ARRIVED BACK ON BASE, Tal, Eviad, and Gadi looked at me like I was made of glass.

"You okay, Yonatan?" Eviad said.

The way their hands touched my shoulders and my nape was tender and awful, so I pulled away and walked past them into our bunk.

"We'll see you at breakfast, Yonatan," Tal called out behind me.

I slumped down to sit on the edge of the bed and put my head between my hands. I squeezed as hard as I could, and listened to my own breathing. Every breath sounded like your name. *Laith Laith. Laith Laith. Laith Laith.*

I pulled out my phone and scrolled through my saved messages until I got to the second one you sent me on my draft date.

> [Laith!]: Did you feel sad? I asked.
> Cutting me off, he said, "Mahmoud, my friend,
> sadness is a white bird that does not come near a
> battlefield."
> 09:18

Before I knew what I was doing, before I could think too much, I clicked on the new message button, and typed in your name: "Laith!"

[Me]: Laith, I'm so sad.
08:11.

[Me]: Help me, Laith. I miss you. I'm so sorry.
08:12.

Then I stood up and placed my phone gently in my open palm like a small, fragile bird. In a single motion, I smashed it, face-first, against the wall. Plastic crunched against the concrete. I smashed it twice more and then let it fall to the ground. I climbed back into the bottom bunk and lay down, my gun cuddled next to me like a skinny metal doll, the grenade launcher nuzzled into my rib cage. I stared at the springs above me. I didn't move.

I wasn't sure how long I'd been lying there when I heard the door open. I glanced up, hopeful that maybe one of the guys had returned to help me, to pull me out of this, or at least to try, but it was not Tal or Gadi or Eviad. It was the Commander. He sat down on the bunk across from where I lay. I glanced over and saw that his gray eyes looked tired in the dim light of the room. Aside from his eyes, though, he still gave off an aura of agelessness, the same aura that had so impressed me when I'd first arrived on base. Now, though, as he sat in silence across from me, he struck me as more mechanical than godly. I was frightened.

"Soldier," he said, his tone gentle. "You okay?"

I didn't say anything and looked back up at the springs above me.

"Soldier, look at me."

I rolled my head toward the Commander. My eyeballs felt heavy in their sockets. I scanned his face and noticed a few hairs that he had failed to shave, sprouting by the base of his nose. If these hairs were there, if he wasn't infallible, then maybe he had lied to me before. Was that possible? These hairs gave me hope, gave me voice.

"We're doing not-good things," I said.

"What did you say?"

"I said, we're doing not . . . not-good things. I thought I could be good, but I couldn't. Did you lie to me earlier or didn't you? Is he dead or isn't he?"

"Soldier, get up. This is an order." The Commander's tone was back to being diamond hard, steel hard. There was no more softness, no more patience. "Get up now."

"No," I said, "and stop calling me soldier. I have a name. You know my name."

"Fuck," I heard the Commander say, under his breath, as he stood up. "This is too much for me."

I stared at his crotch. The barrel of his gun, slung from his shoulder, was pointing toward my head, the black chasm of its small mouth opening before me.

"Soldier, I'm telling you one last time. Stand up."

I didn't move. Couldn't move.

"Okay," the Commander said, breathing in through his nostrils. "Okay. I know it might be hard for you to believe, but what I'm going to do will be for your own good."

I thought for a moment that he was going to shoot me.

I hoped for a moment that he was going to shoot me.

But instead he just walked out of the room.

Sometime later, maybe a few minutes, maybe an hour, the door opened again. I looked up and saw two men I didn't recognize. When they stepped closer, I could see from their uniforms that they were military police.

"Soldier number 5410557?" one said. He was muscular and squat and had a thick neck and short black hair.

"My name is Yonatan."

"Get up," said the second military policeman. He was tall, thinner than the first one.

I got up and slung my gun over my shoulder. My last remaining friend.

"No," said the second policeman. "Leave your weapon."

He nodded to his colleague, who took my gun and walked out of the room.

"Can I bring my bag?" I asked.

"Yes," the policeman said. "Follow me."

His voice was toneless.

I became afraid again, and I wondered if I could still take it back. Say I was sorry. Fall in line. But then I thought of you, Laith. Even if the Commander had been lying, I'd seen the flowers rushing forward from your eye. I took a deep breath and walked after the policeman. I was glad that I wasn't in handcuffs. I didn't want to face the other guys looking like a convict. But no one was there when I left, anyway. Not Eviad, not Gadi, not the Commander. As I was about to climb into the back of the military police car, I heard a voice.

"Yonatan!"

I looked back and saw Tal running over.

The first policeman took a step forward and shook his meaty head significantly. Tal stopped running.

"Just—" Tal said, "just take care of yourself. Okay?"

I nodded.

"I know that what people are saying about you isn't the whole story, Yonatan—"

"What are they—" I started to ask, but the second policeman shoved me into the back of the car, not so hard, but hard enough for me to stumble a bit, and I hit my shin on the bottom lip of the vehicle.

The door slammed behind me, and through the window I could see the first policeman saying something to Tal and then walking around the car to the driver's seat. We drove off. I reached for my pocket where I usually kept my cell phone but then remembered my cell phone was lying on the floor at the feet of many bunk beds, disfigured by my own hand.

Where were they taking me? In my mind, I saw an image of my body being dumped on the side of some desert road, and I tried to grin at the image, to tell myself that it was absurd, but I couldn't. All the braveness I'd mustered in the bunk was flaking away. I needed to distract myself with something.

"What are your names?" I said.

"Be quiet," said the first policeman. The West Bank desert scenery flickered pretty and deadly outside the window of the police car, and I could almost hear the stones of this wicked land laughing.

"How does this work? Do I, like, get a lawyer?"

"Shut the fuck up. That's how this works."

I shut up, shut the fuck up.

Then, in the silence, I could almost hear a familiar voice:
"Everything is cool, my friend. I promise you, everything is cool."

Then I almost said your name out loud.

Then I gagged and almost vomited in the back of the police car.

Then I tried to focus on something else, something far away.

Mongolia.

I'd always imagined that there were beautiful, lush green woods off in some secluded part of Mongolia. Was that where the monks did the throat singing? Overtones. Lush Mongolian overtones in the woods.

"Everything is cool, my friend. I promise you, everything is cool."

After some amount of time, we arrived at some building, in some area. I followed as the policemen led me into a waiting room.

"You're not gonna run away, right?" the first policeman asked me.

I stared at him.

The second policeman shrugged and pulled out a pack of cigarettes, and the two left me alone in the waiting room.

"OoooEeeeOooh."

I started making a nasal humming sound, my lips pursed. I was trying to figure out how the Mongolian monks did their overtones. It didn't
sound right, but I kept trying.

"OoooEeeeOoooEeeeOoooh."

The door to one of the rooms swung open, and an angry-looking
man in a clean, well-ironed officer's uniform appeared. He wore all
sorts of pins and stripes on his chest and shoulders, indicating rank and
also, probably, the number of Arabs he'd neutralized and the number of
women he'd bedded.

"What the hell is that sound?"

I looked up at him, and then shrugged my shoulders and looked
around, as in, Huh, what sound? I don't see any sound.

The officer glared. "What are you doing here?"

I shrugged again. I had managed to not think about what I was
doing here for a few minutes now.

The officer stared at me for a moment longer.

"Ah, right. Okay. Come on in." He glanced down at a clipboard he
was holding. "5410557, right?"

I nodded and stood up and followed him inside the room. There, a
soldier standing at attention in the corner instructed me to stand a few
paces away from the officer. I stood, my hands clasped behind my back.

"So, why are you here?"

I didn't say anything.

The officer sighed and typed something into his computer. "It says
here: 'severe and continual refusal to comply with orders.' Is that right,
soldier?"

For a moment, something like relief flooded my chest. The Commander hadn't reported me for shooting at the crowd, just for refusing
his orders.

Of course.

I thought about Shai Dromi, the farmer in the south who shot the
four Bedouins: he'd gotten off, just like you said he would. And the

Israeli policemen who killed the Arab protestors in October 2000 had also gone uncharged. And I was above a farmer, above a policeman: I was a soldier who dreamed of white lilies, a soldier who made a minor mistake in the midst of a battle with my people's enemies, somewhere deep in the Territories, in the forgotten West Bank. But just as the relief started to settle in puddles around my rib cage, a wisp of memory slithered past the screen in my throat and up into my mouth.

"No!"

"What do you mean, 'No'?" The officer's tone was soft and had a mocking lilt to it.

"I mean, I'm not sure if I'm . . . if I should be here."

"I don't understand."

I took a deep breath. "I can't do this anymore. You made me not me."

"What did you just say?"

"We're supposed to be defending our people and our families, but instead we're just shooting tear gas at demonstrators in some stupid ugly village out in the middle of nowhere. I have the right to refuse unjust orders, according to, like, Israeli military code, right?"

"And what unjust orders precisely were you given, soldier? Were you told to loot some poor Arab village?"

I looked down at the floor.

"Were you told to shoot civilians?"

I was quiet.

"Were you?"

I flinched. His voice had gone from cool-calm to nearly ballistic. Would he hurt me? That seemed like it'd be against the rules. But what were the rules here, anyway?

"No," I said.

"So what exactly were these unjust orders you're talking about?"

Red flowers. White lilies.

"Why did you put me there?"

"Why did we put you there?" the officer mimicked my question, shaking his head. "Good God. So just to make sure I understand: what you're saying is that you know better than the State of Israel and the IDF what is necessary for security?"

I was silent. I thought about the swearing-in ceremony at the Western Wall, in which our families—Saba Yehuda, and my parents, and little Zehava—had come to watch us, the Wall sparkling with bright holiness, the crowd pulsing with almost-oneness, the flag of Israel fluttering in the wind. The Commander read the oath, asked each of us to swear to be "faithful to the State of Israel, and to its laws, to dedicate all my strength and even to sacrifice my life to defend the homeland and the freedom of Israel."

Two, three . . .

"I swear!" I had roared, along with the others.

"Speak!"

"I don't know!"

"You don't know what?" The officer's voice was calm again.

I wanted to say that I didn't know who I'd become, but I didn't say that. Instead I began to cry. I felt the soldier behind me recoil at the sound of my tears, but through the blur, I could see that the officer's face had softened.

"Listen," he said, "you seem like an okay kid. I'm going to give you a short sentence. Afterward, you'll pull yourself together, rejoin your unit. I'm sure you have it in you to be a good soldier. Right?"

"Right," I murmured. Maybe I could still be a good soldier.

Maybe everything would be fine, right? Maybe the Commander didn't know what he was talking about. Or maybe he was just making up stories because he was mad at me. To trick me. Or to test me! To see if I was a good soldier. Maybe everything was all mixed up! Maybe I'd get to see you and your sister again soon. Maybe everything could be okay after all.

"I'm just going to give you fourteen days in jail," said the officer. "You're lucky."

I stayed standing, waiting for something to happen. The officer looked at me.

"That's all. You can go, soldier."

When I walked back out into the hall, the two military policemen were waiting for me, as if they'd never been gone, except for the faint smell of smoke clinging to each of them. The first policeman took my arm and led me away.

"Where am I going?" I spoke, but my voice was barely louder than a whisper.

"To the Bahamas," the first policeman whispered back, loudly.

The second policeman laughed.

"You're going to Jail Seven. You'll have a great time there, I'm sure."

EIGHTEEN

IT WAS ALREADY PAST TWO A.M. by the time I was ushered into my cell, wearing the baggy surplus US Marines uniform I'd been given in the jail's processing room. Most of the bunk beds were already occupied by sleeping forms, but there was a fluorescent light on, so it was easy to navigate. I found an empty bed near the corner of the room and told myself that this felt sort of like Camp Samaria, only at summer camp we weren't locked in our cabins. It took me a while to fall asleep. The light poured down into my confused eyes. Eventually, exhaustion threaded its fingers through my eyelids, sewing them shut, and I drifted into a universe of strange dreams about water and light, damp animals and soft flesh.

A few hours later I was woken by the hoarse sound of screaming: "Ten minutes!" It was still dark out, with little bluish tones of approaching sunrise tinting the velvety sky, visible through the barred window at the edge of the cell. Maybe four thirty a.m.? Around me, guys began groaning and cursing. A few pulled themselves up and began making their beds intricately, preparing for the rounds.

Out in the dim light of the courtyard, everyone fell into formation. The Commander, a small woman, stood at the front and ordered us to stomp:

Foot out, foot back in.

Foot out, foot back in.

A series of boots pounding the ground in unison. The Commander stared angrily at the group and then zeroed in on a target.

"Oh no. Are you cold, soldier?" she cooed to one acne-faced prisoner, who'd stuffed his hands into his uniform's pants pockets. The soldier shrugged, and the Commander's voice turned to a magnified growl: "What are you, a little girl? Get your hands out of your pockets!"

"To the new soldiers here"—the Commander turned to face the rest of the prisoners—"I want to let you know something, right now. This is not some daycare for pussies. I don't care if you're cold. I don't care if you're tired. This is Jail Seven. You do what you're told. You stomp when I tell you to stomp. You keep your laces tied, your pants tucked into your boots. Otherwise, you *will* get extra days added on to your sentence, is that clear?"

"Yes, Commander," some of the guys mumbled.

"I said, is that clear?"

"Yes, Commander!"

The shout, in unison, echoed through the predawn, splayed across the quiet hills of Atlit on the other side of the barbed wire.

I shouted along with everyone else. As we broke from our formation, I found myself checking my laces and pants cuffs, just to make sure.

In line for breakfast, I overheard some of the other guys talking about the Commander.

One guy next to me, with big, droopy eyelids, said to whoever might be listening, "I'd like her to suck my dick."

Breakfast was white bread, hardboiled eggs, mealy tomatoes. The Commanders yelled at everyone not to speak, not to laugh. We ate in silence.

Then we returned to our cells.

In the afternoon, we were allowed to make a phone call.

I called my mom, who answered after one ring.

"Hey, Mom. It's—it's me," I said.

"Oh my God! Jonathan!"

"What's wrong, Mom?"

"'What's wrong, Mom?'" She let out a sound that was either a laugh or a sob.

"Mom, I'm fine."

As I said that, I remembered that I didn't feel fine, and I started to cry. We cried together, on opposite ends of the phone, and for a long time, we didn't say anything else.

"Two minutes is up, soldier!" one of the commanders said.

"I gotta go, Mom. I love you. I'll be okay. I'll be okay."

"I said your time is up, soldier!"

"Jonathan," my mom said, "your grandfather is going to come visit. He got special access. We'll come during regular visiting hours, okay? And you got some phone—"

The Commander walked over and hung up the call with his fingers. I wanted to strike him in the face. I didn't. Instead, I apologized.

"Sorry."

"Sorry what?"

"Sorry, Commander."

The rest of the day and the day that followed were mostly filled with smoke and random drills, shrieking commanders and silent meals. We took various outings to the jail's doctor or to the commissary, where I bought cigarettes, even though I didn't smoke. They made me feel steadier, somehow.

I spent most of my time listening to the conversations swirling around me. They were the only thing that helped me breathe. Most of the other guys were Mizrahi or Ethiopian or Russian, and were in for things like smoking pot in their base's bathroom, punching their commanders, or going AWOL. One of them, a diminutive Moroccan guy named Maor who had the bunk next to mine, seemed to be the spiritual leader of our cell. Every few hours he'd hold court. For the price of two cigarettes, he'd give advice or answer any question someone might have.

"The tall commander's a nashnash, a fag, right?" a heavyset guy whose name I didn't know asked, handing Maor his cigarettes.

"What difference does it make?" Maor replied. "Hu yizayen otcha. He'd fuck you up."

"Yeah, but he's gay, right?"

"Yeah," said Maor. "He wears makeup."

"How do you make a girl come?" asked a rail-thin Ethiopian guy named Or.

"So listen," Maor said, leaning toward Or. "When you go down on her . . ."

Or nodded and leaned even closer to Maor.

"You have to hum 'HaTikvah.'"

Some of the other guys cackled.

"Are you serious?" Or asked.

"No, dude. I'm fucking with you. There's not a single way to make a girl come. It's a mystical fucking thing. There's only one person who can tell you how to do it, when you're fucking a girl."

"You?" Or asked.

"No, bro. The girl you're fucking. You've gotta talk to her. Like, ask her what feels good and shit. That's it."

Maor handed him his two cigarettes back. Or shook his head. "Keep them."

"Who killed Rabin?" A square-shouldered Russian guy, Boris, asked Maor.

"The Shabak," Maor said, lighting both his newly acquired cigarettes at once. "For sure. Yigal Amir supposedly shot him twice, but there were three holes in his shirt. So."

"Why did the Shabak kill him?" Boris asked.

Maor held out his hand, waiting. Boris shrugged. He was out of cigarettes. The question would have to wait.

"Whoever killed Rabin," chimed in Elad, another guy in our cell, "I'm glad they did it. That son of a bitch traitor was the worst prime minister in history. He wanted to destroy the State of Israel." Elad's face was pockmarked. He was muscular and wore a white kippah.

"If he'd done it, if he'd made peace, bro," Maor said, dragging deeply from his cigarettes, "most of the soldiers who have died since then wouldn't have died."

Elad had already been in the army for two years. He shot back: "Let me tell you something, Maor. Between Arabs and Jews, there will never be peace. They hate us."

"Oh yeah?" Maor said. "Don't we have peace with Germany? They hated Jews there too, a little, no?"

"That's different," Elad said. "It's far away. Plus there are still tons of anti-Semites there."

"I was just there right before enlisting, bro. I told everyone I was from Israel and no one cared," Maor said. "Actually it helped with the girls. You can't even imagine how much German pussy I got. They ich liebe dich the Juden now, my man."

Other times, Maor would spontaneously distribute his thoughts throughout the cell, and everyone would listen:

"Fuck the army, am I right?" he said one afternoon, looking up from his crossword puzzle to speak to whoever was listening, twin cigarettes dangling from his mouth. "What has the army ever given any of us?"

"I don't know, man," said Solomon, another Ethiopian guy, with round cheeks and long eyelashes, who had arrived when I did. "But as soon as I finish up here, I'm going back into my unit."

"Why?" Maor said.

"Because I want a job. I want to be a firefighter, and if not a firefighter, a security guard, or something like that."

"Not me," said Maor. "When I finish my sentence, I'm out of this whole mess."

"What are you going to do for work?" Solomon asked.

"I'll work at my dad's shop, in Jerusalem."

Solomon was silent for a moment, thoughts rushing over his pudgy face, and then he spoke, in a soft voice: "My dad doesn't have a shop."

I liked listening to these conversations. As long as they were going on, I could almost not remember.

On my second day in jail, I missed my phone call because I was visiting with Saba Yehuda. On the third day, I called my mom again. We talked for a bit about nothing, both of us straining to sound calm. Then my mom said:

"Jonathan, your friends called. They really want to talk to you. They're worried about you."

"Which friends? From the army? Tal?"

"Tal called once. But mostly it's the twins," she said, and suddenly her voice was light, almost joyful. "They've called three or four times!"

"What? Who did?"

"Nimreen and Laith . . ."

"Nimreen and—and Laith?"

"WHAT DOES YOUR NAME MEAN, ANYWAY, LAITH?" I asked, putting my hand on your shoulder to steady myself as I walked along a raised beam, somewhere along the coast of Akko.

"Me?" you said. "Ferocious lion."

Nimreen laughed. "More like a lion cub."

"So, 'ferocious lion cub'?" I said.

You crinkled your nose, bared your teeth, made your fingers into claws.

LAITH.

You'd think I would have felt relief so powerful that it could blow open the walls of the whole jail and burst open the gut of this land and then shatter the whole planet itself. And maybe I did feel a little of that.

But it also fucked me up. I thought about looking at you, at your eye, at the blossoming redness there in the desert. I asked my mom four times in a row if she was sure, and then asked a few more times, until I heard fear creeping into her voice, and then I stopped asking. Then the time for my phone call was up. I couldn't breathe right. I walked through the rest of the day in a trance, moving from formation, where I stomped when I was told to stomp, to the dining hall, where I did not eat, to the bathroom, where I avoided the mirror, to my bunk, where I lay on my side and stared at the wall. No one noticed. Why would they? I imagined hearing your voice. I imagined calling you. I wasn't sure if I could believe my mom. I didn't know what the truth was. The next afternoon, I didn't try calling you. I called my mom again, instead, and asked her to go online.

"Why?" she said.

"Can you just google, like, 'Arab rioter killed in clashes with IDF'?"

"What?"

"Please, Mom."

"Okay . . ."

I heard the clackety patter of a keyboard on the other end of the phone.

"What do you see?"

"There are a few articles about last Friday, near Kerem . . . Oh. Oh my God, Jonathan. You don't—"

"Mom, not now. My phone call is about to end. Does it say what his name was?"

I heard her crying on the other end of the phone. I felt angry. This wasn't her turn to weep.

"Mom, stop it. What's his name?"

"Oh, Jonathan . . ."

"Time's up, soldier!" The Commander's voice punctured the air behind me.

"Mom, please!"

"It doesn't say. No name is listed."

"What about the other articles?"

"Soldier! Did you hear me?"

I waited for a moment and listened to the clicking of my mom's mouse, her uneven breath. I squared my back against the Commander, whose footsteps I heard approaching.

Then my mom's voice came through the receiver, barely a whisper.

"It says . . . It says Ali. Ali Sha . . . I don't know how to say this name. Jonath—"

Click.

The Commander stood next to me, smirking.

"Did you not hear what I said?"

I stared at his face.

> [Laith!]: "Her anguished voice gave birth to a new hope
> in his flesh that doves might flock through the Ministry of
> War."
>
> Maybe those little birds will flock there after all, J.
> 19:47.

But they won't, Laith. There is no hope left in my flesh.

I didn't call you, Laith.
I couldn't.

You are intact, I think.

But I am still a murderer.

Laith, I'm sorry!
Tell Nimreen I'm so sorry.

In the poem, Darwish asks: "Will we meet again?"

The soldier, whose name might have been Yossi, answers: "In a city far away."

Outside the poem, I stared into the face of the Commander and then brushed past him, not speaking, and walked back to my cage.

"I want out."

"Of jail?" Maor yawned. "That's weird. Why in the world would you want out of this palace?"

"No . . . out out."

"Oh ho. Paratrooper wants to fly away."

I nodded.

"Just hop over the barbed wire and run for the hills," Maor said, grinning.

I couldn't smile in return, and his face grew serious. "You gotta show them you mean business."

"How do I do that?" I looked around the cell, at the bunk beds filled with young men, some of them trying to sleep, others staring vacantly at the fluorescent lights buzzing on the ceiling.

"You could punch a commander," Maor said.

My nostrils flared at the thought, but then I imagined blood oozing from a punctured eyeball.

"I can't. Is there any other way?"

"Sure. You could just act crazy. Like start running around and talking about purple monsters or some shit."

"Really?"

"Yeah, but don't take it too far. Maybe no purple monsters. This one guy, a few months ago, they took him straight out of jail and into a mental hospital. Much worse, bro."

"So what do I do?"

"You could just shut up. Like, stop talking, stop responding, stop moving. They'll probably take you down to solitary, but you'll be fine. And from there, you'll have an easier time getting out."

"Are you sure?"

"Sure?" Maor shrugged. "Who can be sure about anything?"

I blinked.

"Okay, Paratrooper? Let's meet up some time for a beer, as civilians, not in this shit hole."

I reached into my pocket and handed Maor my entire pack of cigarettes.

"What is this?" Maor said, holding it with two fingers as if gripping a rat by its tail, or a dirty dishrag by its corner.

"Just take it," I said. "I don't need it."

"My price is my price."

"Okay," I said, taking back my pack and pulling two cigarettes from it.

"Nah." Maor clucked his tongue. "Keep them. Good luck, Yonatan."

I returned to my bunk, lay there staring at the springs above me, and remembered everything. I just stared and stared and stared.

Ali, I thought to myself.
White lilies, I dreamt to myself.

Oh, Laith.

NINETEEN

FOUR STRONG HANDS WRAPPED AROUND MY LIMBS. They grabbed me and dragged me out of the bed. My back scraped painfully against the metal side of the bunk, and I winced but did not speak. I had nothing left to say. I had just stared at Maor when he patted my shoulder before leaving me alone in the cell. The commanders had noticed quickly that someone was missing during the count, but no one had ratted on me. The commanders' shouts were loud and furious. Were they faking it, or were they really as mad as they sounded?

"Who is not here? Where is he?"

I opened my eyes and recognized one of the two commanders, the tall pretty one, who Maor said "wore makeup." The second—circular face, soft cheeks—looked like a little cherub in military jailer's uniform. He had a few hairs sprouting from his chin, for which he must have gotten a special beard permit.

The other prisoners stared as I was carried off. Then someone began to clap, and others joined in, and soon the group was hooting and whooping and whistling, and everything was sound and surge. Another commander marched in, screaming, face red, veins bulging from her thin neck.

"Shut up! Stop it! Now!"

But there was nothing they could do to silence everyone.

I was taken to a set of stairs I'd never noticed before, toward the far end of the compound, and the sound of the group faded into a faint, singular, undifferentiated hum.

"All right. Walk," the first commander growled. "Game's over."

I didn't want to be dragged down the staircase. I stood up and walked down the stairs on my own, my legs wobbly.

"What's wrong with you?" said the second commander.

I didn't reply. I was fasting from speech. I was also not sure how I'd reply even if I were speaking. At the bottom of the stairs, I was shoved into a cell, lightly. In it: a single metal bunk bed with no mattress on it, a video camera in the top left corner of the room. There were flowers sprouting all over the ground, white and red and beautiful. There weren't flowers sprouting all over the ground. It was—it is—completely empty in here, just concrete and metal and air. And the human form known as soldier number 5410557.

"If you need to shit, just bang on the door," said the first commander. "This soldier will be here to make sure you don't do anything to yourself."

I noticed a fat, bored-looking guard sitting in the hallway. He tipped his US Marines hat and gave me a lugubrious grin, his eyes bulging from his face, as if he was trying to tell me something.

"Belt and shoelaces?" said the second commander.

I blinked.

"Give me your belt and shoelaces, soldier."

He sighed. He sounded sad. I didn't want to make him sad, to make anyone else sad.

I unthreaded my shoelaces first and then took off my belt. My pants, which were too big, almost sagged off my narrow hips, and my hands rushed instinctively to grab their edges. The second commander snickered. Now I wanted to hurt him.

I didn't want to hurt him.

I did. I imagined ramming both my fists into his sternum and feeling the snap-crack of bone, little shards breaking off inside his chest.

I didn't. I kept my hands wrapped tightly around the fabric of my sagging pants.

The commanders both shook their heads and then closed the door to my cell.

Down the hall, I could hear someone shrieking and slamming against a metal door.

And now I am truly alone, Laith.

After a while, I do a set of push-ups but grow tired quickly. I stop after nineteen. I usually do forty. I haven't eaten or drunk anything yet today.

I notice that there are some etchings on the wall, mostly just names and soccer teams.

"Liad was here."
"Beitar Yerushalayim forever."
"Omer 2006."
"I was here."

I was here too.

I am here.

I look over the etchings, three times, and then lose interest. There is no sound in here except for the murmur of a distant fan, the buzz of the fluorescent light in my cell, and the crash of the prisoner down the hall, banging into the door now and then. It makes me feel nervous, Laith, and dizzy and scared. The sound, its unevenness, like a sort of Chinese water torture.

Drip. Crash.

Drip drip.

Drip.

Drip.

Drip.

Crash.

Shriek.

Drip.

Drip drip drip drip crash shriek.

Drip.

Drip.

"Aaaaaggh!"

I wonder how much time has passed. There is no clock in the cell. No sunlight, either. I think about asking the guard in the hall, but I don't know whose side he is on, really, even though he is a prisoner too. If I start talking again, and the guard reports me, they might let me out and send me back, Laith. I don't ask him anything.

Some time passes.

But not enough time.

My breath doesn't feel exactly right. It feels like there is a balled-up pair of socks stuffed in the bottom of my throat.

Breathe, Jonathan. Breathe.

But it's not that easy. To breathe. I let out a whimper, and the sound, small and clogged and pitiful, pulls some lever inside me. I start weeping, and it comes rushing out in a flush of rancid wetness, like sweat from a rotten fruit. I sit down in the corner of the room and pull my knees to my chest. It feels almost good. It feels, at least, like something.

"The fuck is wrong with you?" A voice says.

I look up and see the guard peering through the bars, a grimace hanging from his face, two enormous brown eyes blinking.

I snuffle and say nothing.

The guard shakes his head slowly and turns away.

I want him to come back.

"Come back," I whisper.

The guard does not come back.

My tears don't either. I am left with ragged breath and a scraping feeling inside my face, like some ugly black bird's talons, trying to gouge out my eyes from within.

"Stop!" I say, in English. I need to hear the sound of a voice, even if it's my own. I look around me and am astonished. Walls on each side. Not even a hint of sky or sunlight. This is where I've come to. This is where I am. I am here. I try to smile but I can't reach. It's been a long week, Laith. It's Friday, our day. I am alone in a cage in the basement of IDF Military Jail 7, somewhere in Israel. Somewhere, on the outside, you are still alive, I believe, dancing and whirling on the plains of Palestine. Somewhere, Nimreen's laughter might be piercing through clusters of air, inflating some other young man's body with a wild joy.

Somewhere else, some other young man's body, missing one eye, is buried in the earth.

Ali.

I lie down on the cold floor.

It's almost Shabbat.

Peace be upon you
Angels of peace.

I try to sing in the melody of Salonica, but I don't know it well enough.

I don't know it at all.

The door opens.

"Lunch, soldier," a voice grunts.

I open my eyes, and the paint chips on the ceiling of my cell come into focus. I look slowly to the front of my cell, where the door is already closing. There is a tray with two slices of white bread, a greenish liquid, a slab of gray meat.

The only utensil is a plastic spoon. I stare at the food, not comprehending. My chest spasms as I sit up, cross-legged. I poke at the green mush. I want to scream. I don't. I shove the tray back toward the door, where it hits with a soft thud. The greenish liquid wobbles, and a bit of it splashes against the door and then drips down onto the bare floor. I am so hungry. I lie back down.

I close my eyes and sink into the reddish darkness behind my eyelids.

It covers me like a blanket, a warmth over my shivering. Then my eyes adjust to the darkness, and I see figures moving around me. I try to stand, but I feel a hand pressing down on my shoulder. I turn my head to the left and see a beautiful young man, a boy, about my age, his face covered in shadow, long hair falling around his head, pressed flat to the ground. His eyes are yellow-green, glinting in the dimness.

"Don't move. Not yet. They're everywhere," he whispers. His face is serious, but his eyes are dancing, two orbs of light, two forest-tinted suns.

"Who is?" I whisper back.

A faint smile creeps onto his lips. "You look like him."

"Like who?" I ask.

"Like Yuda."

Jacko smiles again. Around us, footsteps crashing down, heavy boots. Below us, the sound of swishing wetness. Above us, an enormous sky. Now the room has no ceiling, and I look up and see that the sky is littered with stars, so many that the sky is more gleaming white than silken black. It's filled with color also, distant planets catching fire in the night.

"It's beautiful here," I say.

"Perhaps," Jacko murmurs. "I can't see beauty anymore."

I look to where he is looking and see, slumped against the wall, a handsome young man. Where his left eye should have been there is just emptiness and a gentle trickle of red.

"Who did this to him?" I ask.

"The Italians, perhaps. Or the Greeks. The Germans. The Border Police. The Arabs. The Jews. The Paratroopers. Someone this time. Someone else last time. Someone else next time. It doesn't matter. Did you know a boy named Laith? Or a boy named Ali?"

I look back toward Jacko and see that his hair has begun to fall out, and his face is losing its shape, the flesh thinning.

"Jacko," I say.

"Tell Yuda to be good," Jacko says, and a small smile flickers over his cracked lips.

There is a crash of metal, a faint splashing sound.

"Do you, uh, want some water?" the guard asks. I look up. He is holding a cup.

I nod and push myself up to a crouching position, then grab the bunk in order to stand. I take the cup and drink the water greedily, the dusty tunnel of my throat opening to allow the rush of wet inward.

"Do you need to, like, pee or anything?"

I stare at the guard. He has dark bags under his eyes and thick shoulders. He looks like a kindly dwarf.

"Come on," says the guard, and I follow him out of the cell and down the hallway.

"So, are you, like, really this bad, or are you just playing it up?" the guard asks.

I don't answer, can't answer.

The bathroom stinks of congealed piss. I step into one of the open stalls and release a stream of dark, rust-colored urine into the toilet bowl. I can feel the guard hovering behind me. I pull up my sagging US Marines pants and wash my hands in the grimy sink. I glance upward to the mirror, only there is no mirror, just a slab of white wall. I feel, in an instant, an urge to smash my face into the wall. I don't, though, and instead I just turn off the faucet.

I follow the guard back to my cell. He locks the door behind me.

I pace around like an animal trapped in a small box. I feel like I have to decide something, but I'm not sure what it is I have to decide. I stare up at the fluorescent brightness. I try to take a deep breath, but it is as if my lungs don't have space for that much oxygen. I lie back down on the floor.

I can hear the prisoner from down the hall banging on his door, shrieking softly.

I shut my eyes.

At some point, a thin black mattress is thrown into the cell. A voice accompanies it, disembodied: "Sleep, soldier."

My name is Jonathan, I think.

I lie still, Laith, and wait for the ground to open.

DO YOU REMEMBER HOW BEAUTIFUL THE SUN WAS? How the light was dying, and I did the bravest thing I've ever done? The residue of THC was on our lips and the wind was in our hair and some forgotten joke about the truth was tumbling through the sky. I took your right hand in my left hand, threaded my fingers through your fingers, and I took Nimreen's left hand in my right one. Do you remember how she laughed, and then you laughed too, and then I laughed too?

How hard I held on to your hands, as hard as I possibly could?

How I let go?

ACKNOWLEDGMENTS

Gratitude beyond gratitude.

First, again, always: to Kayla Rothman-Zecher, my love, my best friend. Thanks, Kay, for bearing witness to my life, for inviting me to bear witness to yours. And for telling me to write a book—which ultimately became this book—on that afternoon as we walked between the redwoods. And to Jesse Rothman, my brother. Thank you for persevering through the darkness of injury and uncertainty and fear and recovery. I am so goddamned proud of you, Jess. And thank you for your unflagging solidarity, generosity, and love. Kayla and Jesse were the two earliest readers of this book; they accompanied it through virtually all its various stages, propping it up when it slumped and guiding it when it soared.

The third reader of the first draft was my agent, Julia Kardon. In Julia's first editorial letter, she wrote that the draft had many beautiful moments, but "needs some serious work." In other words, as she later told me: I needed to rewrite the whole thing. The parts of me then that were daunted and disappointed to read that letter were the parts of me that were wrong. Thank you, Julia, for gently but firmly pushing me to do more, and better; for believing that the sparks you noticed in the first draft could, with enough tending, catch fire; for your brilliant suggestions, your patience, and your faith.

To the brave and discerning readers who waded through subsequent early drafts of this book, and whose ideas pulse throughout these pages: to Amani Rohana—alf shukran bkefish, habibti, 'anjad. To Andrew Forsthoefel—for climbing this mountain with me, my brother (agrimark be damned). To Arthur Asseraf—what a gift from this strange world of ours to encounter in Tahannaout, of all places, such a kindred spirit. To Avner Gvaryahu—met aleikha, man, mamash. To Bianca Giaever, from oak rails to yak molars. To Jacob Udell—for your unwavering, unparalleled friendship.

To my friends and mentors who read later drafts and sections, and whose thoughts, support, wisdom, and generosity sharpened, shaped, chiseled, and uplifted this book: to Ayelet Waldman, to Angie Hsu, to Eimear McBride, to Geraldine Brooks, to Kirstin Allio, to Madeleine Thien, to Michael Chabon, to Noa Yammer. Thank you all, one thousand times over.

To my editor, Daniella Wexler, who was the first person to read the draft that grew out of the rich soil of contributions from all of the aforementioned readers—and who *got it*, so deeply, right away. Thank you, Daniella, for your sharp insights, graceful edits, and profound commitment to this book. And to Albert Tang and Ella Laytham of the Atria art department for the cover design. To Peg Haller for the thorough, smart copyediting. To Judith Curr, Lisa Keim, Stephanie Mendoza, Amy Trombat, and the rest of the team at Atria Books and Simon & Schuster. To everyone at Mary Evans, Inc.

To my family: my parents, Jay Rothman and Randi Land Rothman; my sister, Liana Rothman; my sister-in-custom, Chloe Zelkha; my parents-in-law, Susan Elster and Steve Zecher; my siblings-in-law,

Chana Kranzler, Yannai Kranzler, Ari Zecher, and Aurora Zecher; and my niece and nephews, Netta, Tidhar, and Noam Lev Kranzler. I love you all so much.

To Silly Department, even though there is a 75 percent chance she will never read this book (given that she is a dog). I am overwhelmingly grateful to the living being that was physically present for the vast majority of this writing process, snuggled near my desk as I spent morning after morning typing, and loping by my side as I ran through the wooded trails of the Jerusalem forest, where I revised much of this book in my head (and occasionally out loud, generating confused looks from Silly).

To the MacDowell Colony, where I was deeply fortunate to spend almost a month in the Phi Beta Studio as I worked on the final round of edits for this book (and where I began, already, to dive into the next one). To the staff, the board, and my companions there: Thank you.

To my YS boys: Abeo Miller, Andy (Fuzz) Sontag, (Old) Carey Dixon, Kumar Jensen, Nick (P.) Eastman, who were unequivocally the least-surprised segment of the population of my life when I told them I was writing a novel. Love you guys.

To the many teachers and friends whose work and words impacted this book in countless, boundless ways: Ala Hlehel, Amira Hass, Aurelia Blake, Daniel May, Daniel Roth and Karen Isaacs, David Shulman, Elizabeth Lutz, Febe Armanios, Hagit Ofran, Hamutal Blanc, Huda Fakhreddine, Jacqueline Woodson and Juliet Widoff, John Day, Josh Weiner, Matan Mazursky, Mutasim Ali, Natan Devir, Olivia Grugan, Quinn Mecham, Robert Schine, Ron Ben Ami, Susan Schwartz, Shai Hadad, Uri Agnon, Usama Soltan, and Yehuda Shaul.

To Rihan and Maryam Titi and their family, who taught me the meaning of generosity, and to Jamal Assadi and Martha Moody, for helping facilitate those life-changing months living in al-Bineh and Deir al-Assad (where Mahmoud Darwish and his family first lived after al-Birwa was destroyed in 1948).

To the folks in Military Jail 6: to Igor, for your bravery. To Natti, for the beatboxing battles. To Raz, for laughter amidst the dimness. To Sahar Vardi, for guiding me through that maze, and to Rawan Eghbariah, Emily Schaeffer Omer-Man, Michael Sfard, Ishai Menuchin, and Johanna Wagman, and to everyone else who lent their support, love, and solidarity during those weeks, and during the periods before and after.

And to the hundreds and hundreds of other decent, brave, gentle, weird, creative, wild, pious, sacrilegious, harsh, silly, sweet, generous, and expansive human beings I've encountered throughout my days and years in this breathless, broken land.

In memory of my dear friends and family members who passed away during the period in which this book took form: Baha Nababta, a truly brave and good man; Eli Zelkha, a person of such enormous kindness, humor, and generosity; Jack Elster, whose gentle spirit shines on in the eyes of my beloved; Philip Rothman, my grandfather, who told me, during our final afternoon together, that he still had a book in him, and that he believed it was time for me to start writing mine; and Esther Rothman, my grandmother, whose joyous celebration of virtually all of my creative endeavors was a source of light and strength throughout most of my life. I wish I could have given her a copy of this book. I know how deeply proud she would have been, and how deeply proud she was.

May their memories continue to be a blessing.

ADDITIONAL NOTES

This book is a work of fiction. With that, some of the sections—particularly those that follow the stories of Jonathan's grandfather Yuda, and of Laith and Nimreen's grandmother Selsabeel—draw from the historical wellsprings of the twentieth century.

The story of Kufr Qanut—which is a made-up name, like those of most of the villages and towns in this book (Pardes Ya'akov, Beit al-Asal, Suswan, Ein Tzvi, etc.), and which means, loosely, "despairing village" in Arabic—is based in large part on the events that took place in the village of Kufr Qassem in the fall of 1956. I am grateful to Fahima Issa, a survivor of the massacre in Kufr Qassem, who welcomed me into her home and shared her story; to Naim Issa, also of Kufr Qassem, who recounted the village and family histories he had gathered over past decades; to Latif Dori, an Iraqi-Israeli Jewish peace activist who was among the first to expose the details of the massacre to the Israeli and international public in 1956, and who shared his memories and knowledge with Yuval Orr and me some fifty-eight years later; to Ibrahim Sarsour, Dalia Karpel, Ruvik Rosenthal, Jamila Titi, Seraj Assi, and Dr. Mustafa Kabha for their teachings about these histories, either in person or on the page.

Like the other cities mentioned in this book (Haifa, Jerusalem, Akko/Akka, etc.) Salonica/Thessaloniki is a real city. The Bos del Pueblo neighborhood is fictional, and its name is wholly dissimilar to the actual names of neighborhoods in Salonica in the 1930s, and is taken instead from a saying in Judeoespañol, "Bos del pueblo, bos del syelo" ("the people's voice is the voice of heaven"). The events described there are based on those that took place in and around the Campbell neighborhood in the summer of 1931. In the context of my learning about some of Salonica's histories, I am first and foremost grateful to Iosif Vaena. Iosif's encyclopedic knowledge about Jewish history in Salonica over the centuries, coupled with his generosity of time and spirit, deepened and enriched my understanding of this city's past (and present). I am additionally grateful to professors and historians Devin Naar, K. E. Flemming, Mark Mazower, and Yitzchak Kerem for their research and scholarship; to Albertos Azaria; to Yad V'Shem; to the Jewish Museum of Thessaloniki; to the Jewish Virtual Library; to the Glosbe online dictionary; and to the nineteenth century memoir about Jewish Salonica written by Sa'adi Besalel a-Levi.

I am immensely grateful to the poet Mahmoud Darwish, who passed away in 2008. I can think of no single poem that has had a more profound impact on my life than "A Soldier Dreams of White Lilies." (See: "Why I Refuse," published on the Leftern Wall, fall 2012.) And in this context, I am grateful, again, to Professor Huda Fakhreddine, in whose Modern Arabic Poetry senior seminar at Middlebury College I first encountered Darwish's poetry in Arabic, and first attempted to translate some of his works. Snippets of three of Darwish's poems are woven throughout this book, in transliteration and in translation: "Identity Card," "The Earth Is Closing on Us," and "A Soldier Dreams of White Lilies." I translated the segments from "Identity Card" in loose, dialogical form, with reference to a number of other translations. The transliterated Arabic sections were used here with generous permission from the Mahmoud Darwish Foundation in Ramallah. The translation of the lines from "The Earth Is Closing on Us" was done with reference to Abdullah al-Udhari's translation in the collection *Victims of a Map: A Bilingual Anthology of Arabic Poetry*, published by Saqi Books, and used here with generous permission from Saqi Books. The sections of "A Soldier Dreams of White Lilies" that appear in this book were drawn from a marvelous translation of Darwish's poem by Carolyn Forché and Munir Akash, published by UC Press in the collection *Unfortunately, It Was Paradise*, and used here with generous permission from UC Press. This poem's title was originally translated in this collection as "A Soldier Dreams of White Tulips"; the translation in this book of the Arabic word "zanabiq" as "lilies" was done with permission from UC Press. The detail about Darwish's friend Yossi was gleaned from Adam Shatz's 2002 *Journal of Palestine Studies* interview with Darwish.

In Professor Fakhreddine's course, I first noted the threads of connection between Darwish's poems and the Israeli poet Yehuda Amichai's; in Shatz's interview, Darwish said of Amichai: "We compete over who is more in love with this country, who writes about it more beautifully. . . . When I read him, I read myself." Part of one of Amichai's poems, "My Mother Baked the Whole World for Me," which I first translated into Arabic with Professor Fakhreddine, is included in the latter section of this book. I am grateful to the poet Yehuda Amichai, who passed away in 2000, and to his Estate.

Finally, I am grateful to the research and publications by the organizations Adalah, Breaking the Silence, Mada al-Carmel, and Zochrot, and to so many other people and organizations whose writings, work, scholarship, and knowledge has seeped into my consciousness and my fingertips over the years. These notes are far from comprehensive; in the likely event that I have forgotten to acknowledge any individuals or groups whose work influenced this writing: please know that my gratitude is to you too.

I am fortunate, thankful, and humbled to have learned from and been in conversation with so many brilliant minds, decent hearts, and firesome souls.

ABOUT THE AUTHOR

Moriel Rothman-Zecher, an Israeli-American novelist and poet, is the recipient of a 2017 MacDowell Colony Fellowship in Literature. His writing has been published in the *New York Times*, the *Paris Review*'s "The Daily," *Haaretz*, *ZYZZYVA*, and elsewhere. He lives in Yellow Springs, Ohio, with his wife, Kayla, and their daughter, Nahar. Read more at TheLefternWall.com and follow him on Twitter @Moriel_RZ.

W

SADNESS
IS A WHITE BIRD

MORIEL
ROTHMAN-ZECHER

This reading group guide for Sadness Is a White Bird *includes discussion questions and ideas for enhancing your book club. The suggested questions are intended to help your reading group find new and interesting angles and topics for your discussion. We hope that these ideas will enrich your conversation and increase your enjoyment of the book.*

QUESTIONS AND TOPICS FOR DISCUSSION

1. Given that Jonathan shares an intense bond with both Laith and Nimreen, why do you think he addresses the novel to Laith? How does this second-person perspective contribute to the experience of the novel?

2. Throughout the story, Jonathan keeps referring to the twenty-six Arabic synonyms for love that he learned about from Laith and Nimreen that night on the beach. Why are these so important to him? What do you think the novel is trying to communicate about the connection between language and culture?

3. The title of the novel comes from a poem by Mahmoud Darwish called "A Soldier Dreams of White Lilies." Why do you think the author chose this title? What is the significance of the poem to the story the author is trying to tell?

4. What did you think of the author's decision to make Jonathan's sexuality fluid? How did that aspect of his character affect the story?

5. Does it make a difference to the story that Jonathan knows Arabic? How does the author's inclusion of Arabic and Hebrew phrases affect your reading experience?

6. Consider the conflict that transpires when, on page 97, the three friends hitchhike a ride back to Haifa with a pair of Jewish siblings before Shabbat. Can you identify a turning point when the car ride goes awry? Do you feel the blame lies entirely with the driver and his sister?

7. On page 128, Nimreen takes Jonathan to meet her grandmother Selsabeel Ziad, and there he learns about her past, beginning with her marriage in 1956. How does reading her story influence your perspective on the conflict? How does her account compare with Saba Yehuda's perspective?

8. Why does Jonathan embark on a pilgrimage to Salonica, Greece, in chapter twelve? What is he hoping to discover there, and what does he end up with?

9. What did you make of Jonathan's insubordination in chapter eighteen, following the riot at the climax of the story? He knew there was no way he'd go unpunished, so what do you think was going through his head?

10. Near the end of the novel, on page 261, Jacko, Saba Yehuda's late brother, appears to Jonathan as he is languishing in his cell. What exactly is going on in that scene, and why do you think the author chose to end the book with it?

ENHANCE YOUR BOOK CLUB

1. Read the author's *Paris Review* essay about writing, friendship, and leaving Jerusalem: "Writing Fiction in the Shadow of Jerusalem," https://www.theparisreview.org/blog/2018/01/18/writing-fiction -shadow-jerusalem/.

2 Watch *5 Broken Cameras* (2011) or *The Lemon Tree* (2008), critically acclaimed movies that humanize and explore different aspects of the Israeli-Palestinian conflict.

3. Read about the Palestinian poet Mahmoud Darwish and explore some of his poems at https://www.poetryfoundation.org/poets /mahmoud-darwish. Read about Israeli poet Yehuda Amichai and explore some of his poems at https://www.poetryfoundation.org /poets/yehuda-amichai. Compare the two poets and their works.

4. Learn about grassroots organizations like Breaking the Silence and Adalah that are working to promote human rights in Israel-Palestine. Visit http://www.breakingthesilence.org.il and https:// www.adalah.org/en for more information.